THE GHOST
OF HALLOWEEN PAST

Annie's Book Stop LLC
676 Post Road #7
Wells, Maine 04090
(207)646-3821
anniesbookstop@netscape.net
www.anniesbookstopwells.com

HAUNTING DANIELLE

HAUNTING DANIELLE - BOOK 5

THE GHOST
OF HALLOWEEN PAST

BOBBI HOLMES

The Ghost of Halloween Past
(Haunting Danielle Series – Book 5)
A Novel
By Bobbi Holmes
Cover Design: Elizabeth Mackey

Copyright © 2015 Bobbi Holmes
Robeth Publishing, LLC
All Rights Reserved.
robeth.net

ROBETH
PUBLISHING, LLC

ISBN 978-1-949977-04-2

To the 'original' Walt, my dad, Walt Johnson.
I like to think when loved ones leave us,
they are somewhere around the corner—waiting, watching.

ONE

The shouting woke him. Max opened his eyes. Someone was in the house. Reluctant to leave his hiding place under the bed, he remained still, listening: male voices. It sounded like two men arguing—loudly. *Who are they, and why are they in the house?*

A single gunshot silenced the men. Max flinched. All was quiet. He lifted his head and glanced around. From the corner of his eye, he spied a cockroach scurrying across the dusty wood floor. There were too many cockroaches in this house; it was difficult to keep up with them all. Then he heard it again: more shouting. But this time it was a different voice. *Is that Harvey yelling?*

Inching out from his place beneath the bed, Max peeked under the hem of the tattered and soiled bedspread. Aside from the double bed, the only furniture in the bedroom was a vintage oak dresser, its varnish worn and faded, layered in dust. The cracked mirror, attached to the dresser by just one bolt, hung lopsided, on the verge of falling to the floor. Dim lighting came from the bulb of the small lamp sitting atop the dresser. It flickered, periodically going out.

The shouting continued. It sounded as if it was coming from downstairs. *Who is Harvey yelling at?* There was only one way to find out; Max needed to investigate.

He made his way out from under the bed. Creeping into the dark hallway, keeping low to the floor, he headed toward the staircase. Peering through the railing, he could see Harvey's silhouette standing below in the darkened entry hall. There was a man with him. A man Max did not recognize. The overhead light flickered on for just a moment. It provided just enough light for Max to notice the body lying on the floor—facedown—at Harvey's feet.

"Answer me! I asked you a question!" Harvey shouted.

The man standing next to Harvey stood mute, incapable of speech, staring down at the motionless body.

"I asked who are you?" Harvey demanded.

"Bart Haston. I'm Bart Haston," the man finally managed to stammer. "This is all a mistake."

"Where's the gun?" Harvey glanced around the room. There was no gun in sight.

"I don't know." Bart shook his head.

Max expected the man to start crying.

"I heard the gunshot. And look…" Harvey pointed to the dead man's back. "This is obviously where the bullet went in. So there has to be a gun. What did you do with it?"

"I didn't do anything with it, I promise. I don't know what happened. But I didn't shoot anyone!" Bart insisted.

Harvey knelt by the body and started to roll it over.

Bart reached out, trying to stop him. "Wait! Should you do that?"

"Do what?" He looked up and scowled. "I don't think I'm going to hurt him any more than he already is."

"Shouldn't we call the police or something?"

"Police? Are you sure you want to do that?"

"I don't know. What should I do?" Restless, Bart combed his fingers through his hair. He started to pace back and forth in front of Harvey, who continued to kneel by the body.

Shaking his head in disgust, Harvey roughly turned the corpse over. He paused a moment and stared at the dead man's face. He then looked up at Bart.

Bart stopped pacing and looked down. "What do we do?"

"I'll take care of the body, but you need to get out of here."

"I have to leave? But where should I go?" Bart asked.

"I don't care where you go. You just can't stay here. Go. Get out of here, and I'll get rid of this. Just don't come back. I mean it!"

Max watched as the man who called himself Bart Haston ran from the house, fleeing into the dark night, while Harvey dragged the body from the entry toward the door leading to the basement.

From his hiding place, Max could no longer see Harvey, but he could hear the squeaky hinges of the basement door as it opened, and then he heard the thumping sound of the body as it roughly made its way down the wooden stairs.

Wanting a closer look at the dead man, Max crept stealthily down the stairs. He paused when he reached the first-floor landing, thinking better of the idea. What if Harvey locked him in the room again? While Max had no aversion to small dark places, he didn't want to be trapped without access to food or water. He wouldn't have survived this long without exercising some degree of caution. Harvey was unpredictable: ally one moment, nemesis the next. Before Max could make up his mind on how to proceed, Harvey returned from the basement, slamming the door shut behind him.

I guess that settles that, Max thought, preparing to slink back upstairs.

"There you are," Harvey said when he spied Max by the stairs. "You could have helped me, you know."

Sitting down on a step, Max silently watched.

Harvey sat next to him. "What am I thinking of? When have you ever been of any help?"

Max closed his eyes for a moment, waiting for him to go off on the same old tangent. Harvey had been searching since the day they had met, and he continued to search. Sometimes he blamed Max for not finding it. Yet Max could tell he had other things on his mind right now, namely a corpse in the basement.

"The body is going to start smelling. But I imagine that's going to bother you more than me." He smiled at Max. "That old trunk down there was going to waste. The body fit inside nicely, but it took a little convincing." Harvey laughed. "Folded him up like a pretzel. Of course, once rigor sets in...well, I wouldn't want to be the one to have to unwrap that package."

Max looked away and stared across the room.

"Don't look so smug. It's not like I shot the guy, and I've seen how you deal with some of the dead bodies you drag in here. At least I didn't dismember the guy like you did the last one."

Max looked back to Harvey with lazy eyes. He blinked several times and yawned.

"I suppose it was best you stayed upstairs during the commotion. You might have gotten yourself shot. And then, what good would that do me?"

Max stood up and started to go back up the stairs.

"Hey, where are you going?" Harvey stood up and watched Max make his slow way up to the second floor.

"Fine, go hide under the bed. All you do is sleep anyway!" Harvey called out.

When Max reached the second-floor landing, he paused and silently looked down at Harvey, who had turned his back to him and started walking back to the door leading to the basement. Even the threat of being locked in a room hadn't completely dampened Max's curiosity. He wanted to get a closer look at the dead guy.

HARVEY STOOD OVER THE TRUNK, its lid open. The overhead light flickered on.

"I bet you had no idea you'd be spending the night in a trunk in the basement of this old boarded-up house," Harvey said aloud. "How did you manage to get yourself shot? Is someone going to be looking for you?"

Hands on hips, he glanced around the basement, trying to decide what to do next.

"I can't really leave you down here. It isn't just the smell, but he could come back looking for you, and then I might never get rid of him. And frankly, I don't need anyone else hanging around here. I have less than two weeks to find it, and I can't do it if I have to deal with him.

He scratched his head and considered his options. "Maybe I should leave you for those meddlesome kids to find." He laughed at the idea and then slammed the trunk's lid shut.

Max stood in the shadows by the open basement door and silently watched. Maybe Harvey would be gone after Halloween, but Max hadn't planned to go anywhere. Yet now he might have to. How could he stay? It was one thing putting up with the teenagers who threw rocks at the windows on Halloween night or made dares to see who was brave enough to sneak into the house, and once inside they would run wild down the dark corridors while Max hid in one of his many hiding places. But he couldn't stay if the police showed up, asking questions and poking through every room—every nook and hidey-hole. If they found him, which they might, they would take him, as they had before, and lock him up.

Not wanting Harvey to notice he had been spying on him, Max hurried back up the stairs from the basement, treading lightly. When he reached the entry, he noticed the front door was ajar. Seizing his opportunity, Max slipped out of the house and into the dark night.

Keeping in the shadows, he started down the street, searching for a new hiding place. If he didn't find one by sunrise, he would have to go back. Maybe he could convince Harvey to move the dead body somewhere else—in the ocean perhaps, it was only a few blocks away. Although, he doubted that would be possible.

Making his way down the street, he noticed it was trash night. *When was the last time I had something to eat?* Finding food suddenly became his number one priority. It proved to be his lucky night. In the first trash can, he found a partially eaten chicken breast sitting atop the garbage. Looking around nervously, afraid something might jump out at him from the darkness, he looked back in the can and snatched the piece of chicken. Certain there was some monster in the night, prepared to pounce and steal his prize, Max ran down the street with the piece of chicken, looking for a safe place to savor his meal.

He found temporary shelter amongst the shrubbery between two houses. Ravenous, he used his teeth to rip every last bite of meat from its bone. When he finished, he left the evidence of his meal under the bush and continued on his hunt.

Max had been wandering for over an hour when he came to a three-storied house, if one included the attic. Its dormer windows faced west. A row of homes separated it from the beach and Pacific Ocean. He approached the house and discovered someone had failed to shut the front gate. Glancing around, making sure no one was watching, Max slipped through the gate and made his way to one of the windows in the front of the house.

The window was open, yet it had a screen, preventing him from getting inside. However, it did make it possible for him to hear whoever was just inside the window. By the voices, he surmised it was at least two women. Careful not to make any sound, Max peeked in the window. He had been right—there were two women.

"Are you going to be up much longer?" one of the women asked. She stood by the door leading to the hallway. Or at least, Max assumed it led to the hallway.

"Not much longer. But I'd like to finish this book. I only have a couple more chapters," said the woman who lounged on the sofa with a book in her hands.

"Well, I'm going to head up to bed. After moving all my stuff back upstairs, I'm exhausted."

"Night, Lily."

"Night, Dani. See you in the morning."

The woman called Lily left the room. Max focused his attention on the remaining woman—*Dani? Was that what her friend had called her?*

Max sat quietly in the darkness, watching the woman. She continued to read, periodically turning the pages of the book. The room was well lit; he could clearly see her face.

I like the way she looks, Max thought. *Yes, I like it very much.*

TWO

Yawning, Lily stumbled out of bed and rubbed sleep from her eyes. She glanced at the alarm clock sitting on her nightstand. It was almost 8:30 a.m. *I've gotten lazy*, she thought. If she were still working, she would already be at school, facing a roomful of rambunctious second graders. She missed her second graders. Grabbing her flannel robe from the chair, she slipped it on over her pajama bottoms and T-shirt.

In the bathroom, she looked in the mirror and brushed her teeth. With her free hand, she ruffled her short red curls. Lily no longer hated her hair. For one thing, it had grown out some since Stoddard had ordered it cropped short like a boy's. Now, it almost reached her shoulders. Ian insisted the short hairdo accentuated her green eyes and looked sexy. *Maybe he was telling the truth*, she thought, *or perhaps he's just being kind because he loves me.*

When she finished in the bathroom, Lily stepped back into the hallway. Until yesterday, she had been using the downstairs bedroom. But she had recently ended her IV treatments and was walking better now, so she decided to move back up to her old room to free up the only downstairs bedroom just in case any of Danielle's future guests requested a room on the ground floor.

Lily noticed Danielle's bedroom door was open. She peeked inside on her way down the hall. The room was empty. Heading down the staircase a moment later, she smelled coffee brewing.

7

Taking a deep breath, she smiled and picked up her pace, hurrying down to the first-floor landing.

Before going to the kitchen, Lily went outside to grab the morning newspaper off the front porch. Danielle never seemed to remember to bring it in. Lily walked into the kitchen, reading the headlines. She looked up only long enough to find her way to the coffee pot and pour herself a cup while skimming through the front-page article.

"Morning, Lily. Something interesting in the paper?" Danielle asked from the kitchen table, where she was eating her breakfast of toast and scrambled eggs. Unlike Lily, Danielle was already dressed for the day, in black slacks and a lavender sweater.

Lily glanced up from the article. "You aren't going to believe this."

"What is it?" Danielle asked before taking a bite of toast.

"Christiansen and Haston have disappeared." Lily tossed the newspaper on the kitchen table.

Danielle immediately snatched up the paper and looked at it. "What do you mean disappeared?"

"Apparently, they skipped bail, both of them. They were supposed to appear at court on Wednesday, and neither of them showed up. They've vanished. Poof. Into thin air." Lily took a seat at the table.

Shaking her head, Danielle said, "I thought it was stupid letting them out on bail. After all, Haston pretty much confessed to everything, what's the point? Just sentence the guy."

"I guess it doesn't work that way." Lily shrugged. "Especially when his attorney was claiming he only made his confession under duress."

"Yeah, right." Danielle rolled her eyes.

"I imagine they'll find them. Where are they going to go?"

"Out of the country? I would assume they have some money stashed away. But kind of odd they both disappeared at the same time. I can't imagine they took off together. After all, Christiansen was pretty pissed at Haston." Danielle tossed the newspaper back on the table.

Lily was just about to take a sip of coffee when the newspaper floated up from the table, hanging in midair. Setting her mug down, she looked up at the newspaper and watched as the pages seemingly turned on their own volition.

"Good morning, Walt," Lily finally said.

"Tell Lily I said good morning." Holding the newspaper in his hands, Walt continued to read the article as he took a seat at the table.

"Walt says good morning," Danielle said and then mumbled under her breath, "Why do I always feel like a translator?"

Lily laughed at the comment and then glanced up at the kitchen window. Abruptly, she snatched the newspaper from Walt and unceremoniously slammed it on the table. She held her hand on the paper so Walt couldn't pick it up again.

"What was that for?" Walt grumbled. He didn't expect an answer; after all, Lily could neither see nor hear him.

"Ian's here," Lily whispered.

The kitchen door opened and Ian stuck his head inside and said, "Knock, knock."

"Come on in, Ian," Danielle greeted him. "Coffee's on, help yourself."

Lily lifted her hand off the paper and smiled at Ian. "Morning."

Sadie raced into the house, charging straight for Walt. When she reached him, she sat down and then turned to Ian and started barking.

Lily and Danielle glanced at the golden retriever and then to Ian. It was then they realized Ian was cradling something in his arms. Whatever it was—it wiggled.

"What do you have there?" Lily stood up and walked toward Ian.

"I found this little guy under Danielle's car. I was afraid she might not see him and run over the poor thing." Ian held up a squirming calico kitten for them to see.

"Aww!" Lily and Danielle chorused.

"A cat? Where did it come from?" Walt asked.

Sadie continued to stare at the kitten. No longer barking, she let out a low growl.

"Sadie, shame on you," Walt scolded. The dog immediately stopped growling and looked up at Walt, cocking her head.

"It's only a baby," Walt told Sadie. "A defenseless kitten. I can't believe you'd growl!"

Disgruntled, Sadie flopped on the floor, her chin propped on her paws as she continue to stare at the interloper.

"Oh, she's adorable," Lily gushed, taking the wiggling bundle from Ian.

"A she?" Danielle asked. "I thought Ian said it was a he?"

"It's a calico, has to be a female." Lily lifted the squirming kitten into the air for a moment and peeked. "Yep, pretty sure it's a girl kitty." Once again cradling the kitten in her arms, Lily sat back down at the table.

"I confess, I didn't look." Ian walked to the coffee pot. "But, Lily's right, calicos tend to be females. However, I remember reading that's not always the case."

"Well, it is for this one." Lily continued to stroke the kitten.

Ian poured himself a cup of coffee and walked to the table. Lily was about to nudge the empty chair in his direction when he took it anyway, sparing Walt the annoyance of having Ian sit in or—more accurately—through his lap.

"I wonder where she came from," Danielle asked.

"The way she's purring in my arms and making herself at home, I don't think she's a feral," Lily noted.

Danielle leaned toward Lily, wiggled her fingers over the kitten's head for a moment, and then leaned back in her chair. "I've never noticed any cats in the neighborhood."

"She belongs to the new neighbor," Walt announced.

Danielle looked at Walt.

"The one who just moved in two doors down," Walt explained.

Danielle frowned at Walt, silently asking, *How do you know?*

Taking a guess at Danielle's unvoiced question, he said, "Because she told me, of course. Her name is Bella, by the way. She snuck out to explore her new neighborhood and ended up in your yard; when it started drizzling, she sought refuge under your car. She was quite relieved to be rescued by Ian, but she would like to go home now." Walt glanced over at Sadie. "I think Sadie would like her to go home now too."

"Really? She said all that?" Danielle murmured under her breath.

"Who said what?" Ian frowned.

"There Dani goes again, talking to herself." Lily smirked, looking to what appeared to be an empty seat—where she assumed Walt sat.

Walt gave Danielle a nod and explained, "Really. She's quite the chatty cat. But Sadie isn't thrilled to share her turf with someone of the feline persuasion."

"I've considered getting a cat," Danielle said, raising her voice above a murmur.

Sadie's head jerked up; she looked at Danielle.

"A cat? Really? I sort of saw you as a dog person," Lily said, still cuddling the kitten.

"I had a cat when I was a little girl."

"Well, this little girl looks like she could use a home," Lily said.

"Now that I think about it, I'm pretty sure I know where she came from," Danielle said.

Lily looked up. "Where?"

Danielle flashed Walt a smile. "We have a new neighbor, two doors down. I bet this little girl belongs there."

"If she doesn't, can we keep her?" Lily asked.

Sadie let out a grunt, stood up, and started walking in a circle before flopping back down, her back to the kitten. Resting her chin on her front paws, she closed her eyes.

"Ian, did you see the morning newspaper yet?" Lily asked.

"I don't get the paper, remember. I steal Danielle's." He snatched the newspaper from the table and opened it to the front page. "What the—"

"Exactly," Danielle said before Ian could finish his sentence. "Dani seems to think they may have made it out of the country already."

"It's possible they've already slipped over the border into Canada. It's the most logical place for them to go, closer than Mexico," Ian suggested. "After all, if they make it to Canada and are later captured, Canada would probably require the death penalty be taken off the table before they can be extradited."

"I still don't understand why they let the guys out on bail." Lily shook her head in disgust.

"Bail was set high, which they were both able to make," Ian said. "For some reason the judge must not have felt they were a flight risk or a danger to society."

"I guess the judge didn't take into account Christiansen had me at gunpoint," Danielle grumbled.

"I imagine about now the judge—not to mention the DA— doesn't see this as their finest hour." Ian continued to look over the article.

Lily glanced at the newspaper in Ian's hand. "So neither of you feel we need to be concerned about this?"

"Obviously, I'm not thrilled. The man did try to kill me. But I'd think his first priority would be to put miles between himself and this place."

"I have to agree with Danielle on that." Ian tossed the paper back onto the table. "Of course, it wouldn't be a bad idea to start exercising a bit more caution around here. Such as keeping the doors locked." Ian looked over at the kitchen door he had recently entered.

"You have a point." Danielle glanced over at Walt. She had learned from past experience that having a resident ghost didn't always protect her from unwanted intruders.

Walt frowned. "What are you looking at me like that for?"

The kitten stopped purring and began meowing. Now standing up on Lily's lap, she looked around for a way to jump down.

"I think someone is ready to go home," Danielle said.

"Either that or she's looking for a litter box." Ian snickered.

Danielle stood up. "Here, let me take her."

"What are you going to do with her?" Lily handed the kitten to Danielle.

"I'm going to see if she belongs to our new neighbor," Danielle explained as she took the kitten and headed to the back door.

THREE

Millie Samson tugged the front of her terrycloth robe closed and tightened its belt before opening the front door. She had no desire to expose her nightgown to the neighborhood. She had called the police ten minutes earlier, yet assumed she had time to get dressed. She was wrong.

When she opened the front door, she found Sergeant Joe Morelli standing on the porch. Opening the door wider, she stepped outside and pointed across the street to the old boarded-up house three doors down.

"It's started already, Joe. And Halloween isn't for another week. I've put up with it since I moved to this neighborhood because I figured it was just one night out of the year, but each year it starts earlier and earlier. This is ridiculous." Yellow plastic rollers, held in place by Millie's blue-gray hair, bobbed erratically as she punctuated her point, waving her hand in the direction of the offending property.

Joe glanced over to the Presley house. "What happened this time?"

"Someone's been in there. I noticed a light coming from inside. And since that house doesn't have the electricity turned on, I have to assume someone was in there with a flashlight. It kept going off and on."

"You mean like they were walking around the room?"

13

"No, like they were standing in one place, turning a flashlight off and on. Probably some kids thinking they were playing Morse code."

"Which window?"

"The only window in the house that isn't boarded up. And about that, isn't there anything the city can do? It's terrible for the neighborhood. Each year some kids break another window and the property owners respond by boarding up the window instead of making repairs."

"I suppose they don't want to keep buying new windows for kids to break."

"And isn't that *your* job? To keep hooligans from destroying personal property."

"Yes," Joe said with a sigh, looking back to the Presley house. "Each year around Halloween we try to patrol this neighborhood more frequently. Especially right before Halloween. When was it you saw the light?"

"Last night." Millie wrapped her arms around herself, clutching her robe tightly to her body.

"Why didn't you call last night? I'm sure whoever broke in is gone by now."

"I would have, but I was on the way to the museum. We had a docent meeting last night. I noticed it when I drove by the house. You wouldn't have wanted me to use my cellphone while I was driving, would you? That's dangerous."

"Maybe when you got to the museum?" Joe suggested.

"I'm afraid I forgot about it. Didn't remember until I got up this morning. Called right away so I wouldn't forget again."

"Well, we do appreciate you for calling. I'll go have a look and see if anything's been disturbed. But I'm sure it was just some of the local teenagers getting into the Halloween spirit."

"Halloween spirit? Breaking and entering?"

Joe smiled sheepishly. "You're right, of course, breaking and entering is never the right thing to do. But I'm afraid Halloween tends to bring out the pranksters who love to fuel that old story about Presley House being haunted."

"So what are you going to do about it?"

"Like I said, I'll go check it out, see if anything has been disturbed. When I get back to the station I'll have a talk with the chief about starting those extra patrols sooner than normal."

FIVE MINUTES LATER, Sergeant Morelli pulled his squad car up to Presley House and parked. After making a call to the station to let them know he would be checking out the property, he got out of his vehicle and looked across and up the street to the Samson house. Millie remained standing on her porch, watching him. When their eyes met, Millie waved. Joe smiled and returned the wave and then turned back to Presley House and made his way to its front gate.

Pausing at the gate, Joe stood on the sidewalk and looked up at the weathered Victorian house. It was really a shame, he thought, that the owners of the property had virtually abandoned the house. From what he knew, Frederickport Vacation Properties was responsible for maintaining the property, yet it didn't appear they did much aside from boarding up broken windows each Halloween. From what he could tell, there was just one window left to be broken.

Even without the boarded-up windows, it was obvious the house was vacant. Weeds had overtaken the yard and several dying trees begged to be removed. He had to agree with Millie, the city really needed to do something about the property.

Joe opened the front gate and started up the walk. He was about six feet from the house when he noticed the front door was ajar. Normally, he wouldn't be overly concerned about the open door of the vacant house, considering the time of year and the house's history. But there were two escaped fugitives to consider; although he doubted they were still in the area. He also couldn't imagine they would leave the front door open—should they be hiding out in the vacant house.

Joe then remembered another old house he had investigated during the past summer—Marlow House. That was before he had met Danielle Boatman. She and Lily had gone to Astoria for the morning and Danielle had hired Joe's brother-in-law to clean up the grounds. His brother-in-law had discovered the front door wide open and had called Joe to check out the house.

Someone had definitely been inside—and he suspected it was kids, considering the broken window in the library and the croquet set someone had tossed around in the attic. At one time, Danielle claimed Adam Nichols and Bill Jones had been responsible for the break-in, yet he suspected she had since changed her mind, considering she and Adam seemed rather chummy these days.

Shaking away the memories, Joe looked back up to Presley House. It was probably kids, like with Marlow House, but there was no reason to take any unnecessary chances. Returning to his vehicle, he called for backup.

OFFICER BRIAN HENDERSON arrived at the scene fifteen minutes later. He pulled behind Joe's vehicle and parked. Slamming his car door shut as he got out, he walked to Joe. "I thought you didn't believe in ghosts."

Joe, who was leaning against the hood of his car, stood up straight and said, "It's not the ghost I'm concerned about."

"You seriously think Christiansen and Haston might be here?"

"Not really, but I didn't think it would be smart to just barge in."

"Okay, let's check it out," Brian said as he removed the gun from his holster.

"IT LOOKS as if we're about to have company," Harvey told Max.

Max looked up from the bed. Harvey stood at the bedroom window, peering through the tattered lace curtains. It was the only window in the house that had not been broken.

"A couple of cops. You better make yourself scarce. If they catch you, you know what will happen," Harvey said.

Max quickly got off the bed and retreated to one of his favorite hiding places.

"I wonder if I should tell them about the body in the basement," Harvey asked the now empty room. "Or maybe I'll wait and see if they find it on their own." Harvey laughed and then decided to make himself scarce.

Downstairs, the front door inched open. Gun in hand, Joe cautiously entered and glanced around. All was quiet. There was enough sunlight coming in through the edges of the boarded-up windows to see without using a flashlight. Yet he had one with him just in case he needed it.

He nodded to Brian, who entered right behind him. They had both been in Presley House on previous Halloweens—under similar circumstances—so they knew their way around the property. Of course, on previous visits there hadn't been fugitives on the loose. Joe went to the left and Brian to the right.

The two officers quickly and efficiently checked the first floor. They found no one—nor any evidence someone had recently been in the house. Together they made their way upstairs and checked out the second floor.

Harvey silently watched the officers move from room to room, looking for intruders. He smiled from his hiding place, confident they would never know he was there—unless he felt the urge to make his presence known.

Joe entered the bedroom Max had been in just moments earlier. Glancing around the room, he peeked under the bed and then looked in the closet. Just as he turned from the closet to the door leading to the hallway, a light flickered on. With a jerk, he turned toward the light source. It was an old lamp sitting atop the dingy oak dresser. Its lampshade had long since been removed, exposing the lightbulb, which now flickered off and on.

Joe walked to the lamp and wiggled the bulb; it was loose. After tightening it, he turned off the lamp.

"I didn't find anything that seems out of place," Brian said from the doorway. "Except for a couple broken beer bottles I found on the floor in one of the bedrooms. I'm pretty sure they weren't there the last time we were here. But by the looks of them they've been here for a while." He then noticed Joe fidgeting with the lamp. "Did you find something?"

"Maybe the source of the light Millie claimed to have seen. This lamp was on, but the bulb was loose, so it kept flickering on and off."

"The electricity is on?" Brian frowned. "I thought it was turned off."

"That's what Millie thought too, but apparently someone had it turned back on. I wonder why."

"I suppose it would have to be the owners of the property. Do you think they're planning to come back?" Brian asked.

"If so, that will make Millie and the rest of the neighbors happy. This place looks as if it's ready to fall down, which is a shame."

"Let's wrap this up and get out of here. Whoever it was is obviously gone now."

"There's still the basement," Joe reminded him.

"Damn. I forgot the house has a basement."

From his hiding place, Max watched as the two officers made their way downstairs, heading for the basement. When they were no longer in sight, Max closed his eyes and wondered if he would be forced to leave Presley House. If so, he knew where he would go. Something about that house with the two women fascinated him. If he was careful, they might not even know he had moved in. After all, it was an old house, and old houses typically had ample hiding places.

BY THE TIME Brian and Joe reached the door to the basement, they were convinced the house was empty. Checking out the basement was simply a formality. When Joe opened the door leading to the stairwell, the rusty hinges betrayed the silence. Yet other than the squeaky hinges, all was quiet. Brian agreed to wait upstairs while Joe checked out the basement.

There was no sunlight to illuminate the confined space. Joe turned on his flashlight, holding it far from his body. Letting the beam lead the way, he slowly moved down the wooden stairs. They creaked with each step.

Once in the basement, he moved the flashlight's beam across the room; it zigzagged along the four walls and back again. The dark space was virtually empty save for a trunk and some debris scattered about.

"All's clear down here!" Joe called to Brian. In the next moment, Joe heard Brian's footsteps clomping down the stairs. Brian paused a moment, let out a little curse and then continued on his way.

"I found the light switch, but it doesn't work," Brian said when he reached Joe.

"The lightbulb is probably out," Joe suggested.

"So no ghosts or boogeymen down here?" Brian asked with a laugh.

"No. But it smells pretty raunchy. What is that smell?"

Brian took a whiff and wrinkled his nose. "Smells like piss to me."

"Probably rats," Joe suggested.

"Let's get out of here before I ruin my appetite. I haven't had breakfast yet."

FOUR

Danielle sat on the front stoop of her new neighbor's house, holding the squirming kitten in her arms. She was reluctant to let Bella go, afraid she might take off and get lost again. She had to believe Walt knew what he was talking about, and Bella—assuming that really was the kitten's name—belonged to the new neighbor.

She had rung the doorbell several times and could hear music playing from inside the house. But so far, no one was answering the door, and she had already been waiting for more than twenty minutes.

A few minutes later, she looked down at the kitten, who was no longer squirming but now curled up on her lap, purring. "This is silly; they're never going to answer the door. Should we just go back to my house and try later? Whoever is in there obviously can't hear over that music."

Just as Danielle scooped up the kitten and got to her feet, the front door flew open and a young woman stepped onto the porch, shouting, "Bella!"

By the woman's startled expression, it was obvious she hadn't expected to find a stranger at her door. For several moments, the two women just stared at each other. Danielle guessed her new neighbor was younger than she was, in her mid-twenties or younger. She wore her blue-black hair pulled into two ponytails; they fell at least six inches past her shoulders. Her severe bangs, cut in a straight line across her forehead, covered her eyebrows and gave her an almost childlike look. She stood several inches taller than Danielle and wore a black, floor-length dress. Its jersey fabric hugged her petite frame. Danielle thought the girl looked like a combination of Goth and hippy, if there was such a thing.

Bella broke the silence when she meowed. The woman's gaze darted to the noisy kitten now squirming in Danielle's arms. "You have my Bella!"

Before Danielle could respond, the woman lunged forward and snatched her pet. The startled kitten extended her claws as she was pulled from Danielle's arms, leaving behind several scratch marks.

Danielle glanced down at her right wrist and watch the fresh marks turn from pink to angry red. Looking back up into her neighbor's gray-blue eyes, she said in a dull voice, "I found her in my yard and thought she might be yours. You didn't answer your door. I rang the bell."

Embarrassment replaced outrage. The woman glanced down at the now injured wrist. "You live around here?"

No, I like to wander in random neighborhoods and steal people's cats.

"Yes, down the street." Danielle rubbed her wrist; it was beginning to sting.

"Oh dear…" The woman stared at the red marks. "I'm sorry. She scratched you."

A more accurate description, you scratched me with your cat.

"Yes, two doors down, at Marlow House," Danielle said instead.

"Don't tell me, you own Marlow House?" the woman practically squeaked.

"Yes."

"I'm sorry. I'm afraid this move has been a little overwhelming. And when I couldn't find Bella this morning, I…well…I' m sorry I overreacted, and you got scratched."

"Well, just glad I could bring her home. Have a nice day." Danielle started to turn from the woman.

"Wait, please," the woman called out.

Danielle stopped and turned to face her new neighbor.

"I haven't thanked you for bringing Bella home. And we really need to do something about that nasty scratch. Come inside."

"It's okay," Danielle said as she rubbed her wrist again. "I'll take care of it when I get home."

"No, please, come inside. I have just what you need to take care of that so it doesn't get infected. Unfortunately, cat claws can be dirty nasty things when it comes to infections."

When Danielle didn't answer immediately, the woman added, "I'd love to give you a cup of coffee and cinnamon roll for bringing Bella back. They're fresh from the local bakery." The woman smiled sweetly while Bella tried to escape her arms.

"Cinnamon rolls?" Danielle perked up. "From the local bakery? With the pecans on top?"

"Yes, and decadent butter cream frosting." The woman smiled.

"Well...I suppose I need to be neighborly." Danielle grinned, unable to turn down a cinnamon roll from the local bakery. They were even better than homemade.

"My name is Heather Donovan," the woman said as she held out one hand to Danielle while holding a squirming kitten in the other hand.

"Nice to meet you, Heather. My name is Danielle Boatman."

"Oh, I know!" Heather gushed. "I mean, I know that must be who you are if you own Marlow House."

"You've heard about me?" Danielle said with unease. *I wonder what she's heard—that I've been arrested several times for murder?*

"Oh yes! I read all about you finding the Missing Thorndike! How exciting! I'd love to find something like that in the walls of my house!"

"Yes, it was exciting, but it's currently sitting in the bank vault, and the buyer I had for it changed his mind. Unfortunately, when you find something like that, Uncle Sam expects a percentage. That means coming up with the taxes before you find a buyer. And it's not really something I can wear out." Danielle failed to mention that with her recent inheritance from her cousin, Cheryl, taxes on the valuable heirloom necklace were no longer a concern for her. It was one reason she hadn't been actively seeking a new buyer.

"I suppose." Heather sighed. "I guess it's true what they say, you really can't get something for nothing."

"Pretty much." Danielle shrugged and followed her into the house. Once inside, Heather tossed the kitten to the floor and shut the front door. Bella scampered off, disappearing down the hallway. The music was even louder inside.

"Excuse me, let me turn that off," Heather shouted over the music and then rushed off in the direction Bella had gone, leaving Danielle alone.

Standing in the entry, Danielle closed her eyes and took a deep breath. It smelled like...*What is that scent? Apple, no, lemon...rose?*

"Geranium rose," Heather said when she walked back into the entry hall a moment later. She had turned the music off.

Danielle opened her eyes and looked at her host. "What?"

"You were trying to place that scent, right? It's geranium rose."

"Is it a candle?" Danielle asked.

"No, essential oil. I have it in my diffuser. It's used to bless homes, and this being my new home and all. Plus, it breaks hexes, and one can never be too careful."

"Hexes?" Danielle tried not to giggle.

"Yes. Geranium rose is also good if you have diarrhea," Heather said seriously.

"Diarrhea?" This time Danielle was unable to stifle her giggles.

"Diarrhea is nothing to laugh at and neither is a hex. Trust me, that's nothing to fool with." Heather turned from Danielle and said, "Let's go into the kitchen. I have my oils in there."

"Oils?" Danielle followed Heather.

"For your scratch, of course."

When Danielle walked into the kitchen, she glanced around. Heather was in the process of unpacking. Moving boxes littered the floor and counter space. A heap of carelessly stacked empty boxes sat in the corner.

Like all the homes in Danielle's neighborhood, Heather's was at least sixty years old, and considering its pink and gray kitchen counter tile and speckled floor tile, Danielle suspected this section of the house had never been remodeled.

"Do you live here alone?" Danielle glanced around the room.

"Yes. Well, no, not if you consider Bella." Heather opened one of the overhead cabinets, revealing rows and rows of neatly ordered tiny glass bottles. Danielle recognized them—essential oils. She had several friends back in California who used essential oils, and one who sold them, but she had never really used them before.

Danielle watched as Heather sorted through the vials until she found what she was looking for. "Here it is!" She picked up the bottle and turned to Danielle.

"What is it?" Danielle watched Heather unscrew the bottle's black lid.

"It's my own blend...mostly melaleuca." Heather paused a

moment and glanced down at Danielle's wrist. She pointed to the sink and said, "You should probably wash that first."

"Yeah, you're right." Danielle felt a little foolish for not doing that immediately.

A few minutes later, Danielle stood quietly in the kitchen while Heather carefully applied her oil blend to the scratch.

"So the stuff really works?" Danielle asked.

"Yes. Healers have been using oils for centuries. It's all very natural."

Danielle looked at her wrist. *What the heck, might as well give it a try.*

After Heather finished applying the oil, she returned the small glass vial to the cabinet and then turned back to Danielle. "You ready for that coffee and cinnamon roll now?" she asked cheerfully.

Ten minutes later, Danielle and Heather sat at the kitchen table, each with a cup of coffee and cinnamon roll.

"Where did you move from?" Danielle asked after taking a sip of coffee.

"Southern California. I've always loved the Oregon coast. So different from Southern California beaches. I've wanted to move up here for a few years but never was able to until now." Heather tore off a piece of cinnamon roll and popped it in her mouth.

"I love it up here—but I'll be honest, until my great-aunt left me the property, I never considered moving to Oregon, much less running a bed and breakfast."

"I've read all about your story, how you inherited Marlow House and found the Missing Thorndike. In some ways, your story was the catalyst to get me to move—that and my own inheritance."

Danielle arched her brows. "How so?"

"My mother recently passed away, left me a little money. The only reason I ever stayed in Riverside—that's where I grew up—was so I could be close to her. It was pretty rough on her when my father died; she needed me."

"I'm sorry about your mother."

Heather shrugged. "Thanks. Me too. But it was for the best, I suppose; she was pretty sick. Anyway, with my inheritance it made it easier for me to try something new—leave my familiar surroundings. I happened to read about your story when I was trying to decide what to do next, and it seemed to be a sign."

"A sign?" Danielle frowned.

"Yes. You were in Frederickport. A sign."

Danielle didn't understand what that was supposed to mean. Instead of asking her to explain, she asked, "Do you have any brothers and sisters?"

"No. It's just me now."

"So what do you plan to do here? Do you have a job yet?"

"I'm a writer."

"Writer?" Danielle asked curiously.

"Yes. I'll be working from home. Perfect, really."

Another writer in the neighborhood! We have Ian Bartley, aka Jon Altar, and now Heather…I wonder if she has a pen name too.

"So what have you written?" Danielle asked.

"Written? Oh, I haven't written anything yet."

In response, Danielle silently sipped her coffee.

"But I know what I'm going to write about."

"What's that?" Danielle asked.

"About real haunted houses," Heather explained. "That's why I moved to Frederickport."

FIVE

Wearing gray polyester slacks, a blue silk shirt, and an orange tie, Adam Nichols kicked off his leather loafers, leaving them under his desk. He leaned back in his office chair and surfed through a few of his favorite raunchy websites. Smiling at the images, he shifted in his chair and glanced up to the open door. While it was none of his employees' business what websites he visited, he didn't intend to give them gossip fodder.

He glanced back to the screen and about jumped out of his seat a moment later when he heard his receptionist, Leslie, call out from the doorway, "Sergeant Morelli is here to see you."

Hastily clicking on the X in the upper-left-hand corner of his monitor screen, Adam closed the webpage he was viewing and sat up straighter in his chair while his feet searched for the missing shoes under his desk. Joe Morelli, dressed in his police uniform, stood behind Leslie outside the doorway in the hall.

"Hi, Joe," Adam said, waving him in. Leslie moved to one side, giving Joe room to enter Adam's office.

"Sorry to interrupt you like this," Joe said as he walked through the doorway, flashing Leslie a smile as he made his way around her. Once he entered the office, Leslie closed the door, leaving him alone with Adam.

"No problem, I was just going through my email. What can I do for you?" Adam leaned forward, his shoes now back on his feet. He rested his elbows on the desk.

Joe fidgeted with the baseball cap in his hand, its Frederickport Police Department insignia barely visible to Adam. "I wanted to talk to you about the Presley house."

Adam pointed to one of the two empty chairs facing his desk. "Please, sit down."

Joe took a seat. "I thought you should know someone broke into the house. They left the front door open, but it doesn't look like they did any damage."

"The Presley house is no longer my problem. I don't manage the property anymore." Adam leaned back in his leather office chair.

"You don't? Do you know who does?"

"I doubt anyone. I managed the property for about seven years, but about six months ago, the owners decided to stop paying me, and when they wouldn't return my calls, I stopped taking care of the property. As far as I know, they haven't hired any of the other firms in town."

"Do you have a contact number for the owners?"

"I did. But the last time I called it, it was disconnected. Crazy, really. Renting out the house might have solved their problem."

"Problem?" Joe frowned.

"I assume the reason they stopped paying me is because they ran into money problems. Which, of course, might have been solved had they listened to me."

"How is that?" Joe asked.

"They never had much luck renting out the house due to those crazy stories about a Halloween ghost. When I took over the property, I convinced them to set it up as a vacation rental. Got the house about ready—you know, furniture, linens—when at the last minute they decided not to rent it. It's been sitting there deteriorating ever since. I wouldn't be surprised if they're about to lose the house for back taxes."

"That's odd. If they can't pay their taxes or property manage-ment, why are they paying to have electricity to the property?" Joe asked. "No one's ever there."

"They aren't. That's one reason I knew they were in trouble. They always kept the utilities hooked up to the house. Paid a minimum fee each month. But about seven months ago, when Bill went to check on the property, he noticed the electricity was off. I called the electric company and they told me the power had been turned off for nonpayment."

"I assume the property owners paid their own utility bills; it didn't go through you?"

"They always handled that. After they decided not to put it in the rental program, they pretty much hired us just to keep an eye on the place, make repairs when needed, especially considering all the haunted house nonsense that would go on each year. Of course, I can't really complain about that. When I was a teenager, I remember breaking into that house."

"I guess the statute of limitations has expired on that, and I can't arrest you for breaking and entering," Joe teased.

"Pretty much." Adam grinned. "Anyway, this was about the time I was trying to contact them for their late payments to us. I wrote them off about a month later."

"Their finances must have turned around."

"What do you mean?" Adam asked.

"They have the power back on."

Adam shook his head. "That's impossible."

"No, it's back on. I was there this morning and turned on a light in one of the bedrooms. It worked."

"That's impossible because the electric company pulled the meter," Adam insisted.

"They must have put it back in. Which, of course, means the electric company must have the property owners' current contact information, so I suppose I should be talking to them instead of you."

"Bill was in the neighborhood just last week and I asked him to stop by the house to see if they ever put the meter back in. They hadn't."

Joe stood up and shrugged. "They must have just done it."

"I guess..." Adam muttered.

"I'd still like any information you have on the property owners," Joe said.

"Sure, no problem." Adam stood up and walked to his file cabinet. After thumbing through one drawer, he found what he was looking for. He pulled a slip of paper from a file, made a photocopy of the document, and then handed the copy to Joe.

Joe took the piece of paper and looked at it briefly before folding it in two and slipping it in his shirt pocket. "Well, thanks for the information."

After Joe left the office, Adam sat back down at his desk and picked up his phone. He called Bill Jones, his handyman.

"I have a favor to ask you," Adam said when he got Bill on the phone.

"What do you need?" Bill asked.

"Run by the Presley house, see if they ever put the meter back in and if the electricity is back on."

"I don't have a key to get into the house to see if the power's on."

"Okay. Just see if they put the meter back in. That should be enough."

"Why? Are we taking on that property again? I think there's only one window left to be boarded up."

"No. But I'm curious to see what's going on over there. I'll explain it after you check on the property."

Twenty minutes later, Bill called Adam back.

"Nope, the electric meter is still gone," Bill told him.

"Are you sure?" Adam asked.

"Of course I'm sure. What kind of question is that?" Bill sounded insulted.

"It's just that Joe Morelli was over here earlier and insisted the electricity was on in the house. Said he turned on a lamp in one of the rooms."

"What's Morelli doing, hiding out in abandoned houses and boozing it up when he's supposed to be working?" Bill laughed.

"Hardly. He seemed pretty sober to me. Although, I'm starting to wonder what he's been smoking, if he's so certain there was electricity on in the house."

"Water's off too," Bill told him.

"Are you sure?"

"After I saw the electric meter was still gone, I figured I'd check to see if the place had any water. If you'll remember, Presley House still had water when we stopped looking after it. But it's off now. I guess you and the electric company weren't the only ones who got tired of not getting paid."

BRIAN HENDERSON STOPPED at the doorway to Joe's office and looked in. Joe sat alone at his desk, looking blankly at the telephone in his hand.

"You okay?" Brian asked after watching Joe for a few moments.

Joe looked up at Brian, shook his head, and then hung up the phone. "It's the damnedest thing," Joe muttered.

Brian walked in the office and sat down at Joe's desk. "What's the problem?"

"Remember when that lamp went on over at Presley House? The one in the upstairs bedroom, with the loose lightbulb?"

"I remember you telling me about it. Why?"

"I just got off the phone with the electric company, and they insist there isn't a meter over there. There's no electricity."

"They must have made a mistake. It wouldn't be the first time."

"On the way back over here this morning, after we locked up the house, I stopped over at Frederickport Vacation Properties and had a talk with Adam Nichols. I found out they don't take care of the property anymore. He's the one who insisted there wasn't a meter over there, and the electric company just confirmed it."

"If you saw the lamp work, then they're obviously wrong. I wouldn't get all worked up about it. So who's taking care of the property now?"

"I have no idea. I suspect no one. The contact information Adam had for the property is out of date. I get a 'no longer in service' message when I called the number. It was the same number the electric company had for the property."

"I'm sure it'll be easy enough to track them down using the tax records. Whoever they are, I wish they'd do something about the property. It gets more run-down looking every year."

"But this thing about the electricity…"

Brian stood up abruptly. "Come on, let's go to lunch. I'll buy you a burger."

"Eat now? Didn't you just have breakfast?"

"That was two hours ago, at least. Come on, it's almost noon. We can swing by Presley House first and you can see the electric meter for yourself."

Joe stood up. "I suppose they could have made a mistake."

"Either that or the place really is haunted." Brian laughed.

BRIAN WASN'T LAUGHING twenty minutes later when he stood with Joe outside Presley House and looked at the spot where the electric meter was supposed to be.

"Well, I'll be damned…" Brian muttered, scratching his head.

Joe stared at the meter-less spot. "This doesn't make any sense."

"Are you sure you saw the lamp light go on? Maybe it was a reflection from the sunlight on the bulb."

"No. I'm certain. That lightbulb was on! It went off, but when I screwed the bulb tighter, it went on again. Right before you came into the room I turned the lamp off."

The two men stood silently for a few moments. Finally, Brian spoke up. "There can only be one explanation."

"Please don't say the place is haunted again," Joe said.

"No. I was going to say—batteries. The light is probably battery operated."

"It was an old lamp. Didn't look like it had batteries to me."

"Did the lamp have a cord?" Brian asked.

Joe shrugged. "I think so. I really don't remember seeing one—or not seeing one."

"Then let's go inside and have another look."

"We locked the door when we left this morning," Joe reminded him.

"So we'll break in. I'll pick the lock."

"Break in?" Joe asked.

"Hey, it's all in the line of duty. You tried to contact the owners of the property—no one seems to know where they are. We'll be in and out of here before you know it, and you'll feel a lot better figuring out your lamp mystery."

"I DON'T FEEL ANY BETTER," Joe said ten minutes later. He stood with Brian in the upstairs bedroom of Presley House, staring at the antiquated lamp sitting on the dresser. There was no doubt—the lamp did not use batteries.

"Maybe it's the lightbulb," Brian suggested.

"How so?" Joe asked.

"You know, one of those trick bulbs that magicians use." Brian unscrewed the bulb and inspected it. He gently shook it. "No. This is a regular bulb all right. And it's bad. Hear that rattle." He shook the bulb again.

Bewildered, Joe frowned. "I don't understand."

Brian screwed the bulb back into the lamp's socket. "Just means you *thought* you saw the light go on. It obviously didn't."

Before Joe could respond, the lightbulb lit up.

"Oh yeah, explain that," Joe said in a low voice, his gaze riveted on the brightly lit bulb.

SIX

M ax had been sleeping in his favorite hiding place when the
cops had barged into the room, waking him. Thankfully,
neither of the men bothered to look under the bed. Their attention
was focused solely on the lamp sitting on the dresser.

He had to give the cops credit. Neither one went running and
screaming out of the bedroom and down the stairs. Harvey would
have liked that. Instead, the one called Brian calmly pulled the lamp
cord from the wall, picked up the lamp, and took it with him as the
two men left the room. The cops didn't even flinch when the bulb
remained lit as they carried it downstairs.

Max knew Harvey was not happy the cops had taken the lamp.
Yet he didn't think he had a reason to be mad; after all, it was
Harvey's own fault. If he hadn't been up to his old tricks, the cops
would never have come back. As it was, there was still the matter of
the dead body in the basement. If the cops started making a habit
of twice-daily visits, they were bound to eventually find the dead
guy once he started smelling. Max needed to get out of here.

He waited until the police car drove away to make his exit.
Harvey didn't notice Max slipping from the bedroom. He was too
busy standing at the upstairs window, ranting at the cops as they
drove away with the lamp. There were other ones in the house, yet
none had lightbulbs. Not that they hadn't at one time, but over the
years, Harvey managed to break each one, or to be more accurate,

each one had exploded, leaving behind the twisty end of the bulb plugged into its lamp's socket. A few of the house's light fixtures still had unbroken lightbulbs. Harvey would have to make do with those.

"Just where do you think you're going?" Harvey demanded.

Max froze. He had only made it halfway down the staircase. He turned to face Harvey, who stood on the second-floor landing, staring down at him.

"I don't want you leaving again," Harvey told him.

Wide-eyed, Max stared up at Harvey, who shook his head in disapproval.

"Don't stand there giving me that innocent look. I know you snuck out last night. You have no business roaming around town by yourself. It's dangerous out there. Don't forget what happened when that cop picked you up the last time. You'd be dead by now if you hadn't managed to escape. I'll keep you safe. Anyway, you need to stay here and help me look for it. I only have a week left. I have to find it this time!"

Riveted to his place on the stairs, Max silently considered his options. He could try to make a run for it, but the chances of him getting out of the house before Harvey intervened were nonexistent. He had learned long ago he was no match for Harvey. Reluctantly, Max made his way back up the stairs.

Harvey smiled. "That's better. I knew I could count on you, ol' reliable Max. You're the only one who has never let me down."

Max experienced a twinge of guilt over Harvey's praise. It was true; Harvey really had no one else to help him. Yet it wasn't enough guilt to stop Max from escaping when the next opportunity arose. Which, of course, would have to be when Harvey was occupied elsewhere.

Max understood that once someone found the dead guy in the basement, the cops would be all over this place, searching from top to bottom for any clues on the killer. Max suspected that was what Harvey wanted.

When Max reached the top of the staircase, Harvey turned and started walking down the hallway. He expected Max to follow him, which he did.

"I thought we could go through the attic again. I keep thinking that has to be where they put it. Don't you think so?" Harvey looked back to Max, expecting an answer.

Max silently followed, thinking they'd had this same conversation a hundred times already. They were just going through the motions. Halloween would come and go—as it always did—without Harvey finding that which he so desperately sought. Harvey would leave, only to return again next year to start his search all over again. The only difference with next year, Max would not be here to assist Harvey on his quest. He would either be locked up someplace —captured because of the attention brought to the house by the body in the basement—or living elsewhere. Max preferred the latter.

When they reached the attic, Harvey told Max to climb up into the rafters and have a look around. Max silently did as he was told, without reminding Harvey they had both been through the rafters countless times before. That would only upset Harvey, which Max had long since learned was not advisable.

Last year, Max had foolishly balked when Harvey had announced they needed to search through the closets on the second floor. It was something they had done just the day before. At the time of Harvey's suggestion, Max was at the top of the ladder in the basement, peeking into a vent. Weary from poking through every inch in the dusty old house and wanting to get off the ladder and take a nap, Max had foolishly reminded Harvey that they had just been through the closets.

While Max had wanted to get down off the ladder, he hadn't expected it to happen so abruptly. Within a moment after mentioning the recent search, Harvey angrily hurled him from the ladder onto the hard concrete floor. By the time Max had managed to get back to his feet, he found himself locked in the basement, where he stayed for two days—without food or water. Later, Harvey apologized, regretting his impulsive behavior—and the fact Max limped for several weeks. It was the irrational side of Harvey that so terrified Max.

Clinging to a rafter, Max looked down. Harvey was no longer watching him, but indulging in his own exploration along the floorboards. From Max's vantage point up high, Harvey looked not much different from those teenage boys who came every year to play Halloween tricks on their friends at the old abandoned house.

His tangled mop of brown hair looked as if it hadn't seen a comb in years. He wore faded denim jeans—several sizes too large —with a makeshift belt made of rope to keep the pants from falling down, and a white button-down shirt, it's ragged collar stained in blood. The blood didn't belong to the body downstairs. Max wondered if the boy ever owned a pair of shoes. His feet were bare. There was something a little endearing about Harvey—in spite of the fact he occasionally inspired moments of sheer terror.

A part of Max sincerely wanted to help Harvey, yet he had long since realized it was a hopeless cause. It wasn't in the house. They would have found it by now. They were simply going through the motions, and Max was doing whatever he needed to keep Harvey from going off the deep end again—at least until Max found a new place to live.

Max knew where he wanted to go. He wanted to see *her* again. Closing his eyes, forgetting for a moment that Harvey was below, Max's mind wandered to another pretty young thing.

She was a beautiful girl, with hair as dark as his was—if one did not count the bit of white around Max's ears. Their first meeting included stolen kisses and false promises. They called her Victoria and she told him he could live with her—but it would have to be their secret—no one could know. To prove his love, Max had killed for her. In looking back, that seemed to be what ultimately had ended their relationship.

She had led him on. Each night they had met under the large tree in her backyard, where she would hold him and promise to love him forever. But then the day after he proved his love, she turned him away and told him to never come back.

He didn't understand. Had it all been lies? Unable to stay away, Max returned to her house, and when she refused to come outside, he pounded on the door, demanding to see her. When the door opened, it wasn't his Victoria but an angry-looking man. The man wasn't alone; he had friends with him and they were all shouting ugly words at Max. He could see Victoria in the kitchen. She was crying, but she made no effort to come to his defense. Max instinctively knew he was in danger, so he turned from the door and tried to get away, but the man and his friends were on him before he got off the porch.

The next thing Max knew, the man had turned him over to the police, and he was locked up. Had he not managed to escape, he would be dead now. While on the run, Max had come across the abandoned old house and it had become his refuge. But now it was too risky to stay, especially with Harvey's reckless behavior. If captured again, he was certain to face a death sentence.

Max crawled along the rafters for over an hour before Harvey wandered off, forgetting about the attic—forgetting about Max. When Max was certain Harvey wasn't coming back, he climbed down from the rafters and made his way downstairs, careful to stay out of Harvey's way.

The moment Max slipped outside he felt a mixture of freedom and fear. When the outside world wasn't trying to invade Presley House, it was a safe harbor, a shelter. It seemed as if he'd spent most of his life there. Yet even without threats from the outside, it could be a lonely place. He then thought about the woman—the woman with the braided hair. *Was she the answer?*

Max wanted to go back to her house, learn what he could about her, decide on his best plan of attack. There was still a lot of daylight left, and he didn't want to just show up at her house in the middle of the afternoon. He had tried that tactic with Victoria, and the results proved disastrous. This time he would need to be crafty and cunning. He decided to head down to the beach, lie low, and kill a little time before the sun went down.

By the time he reached the beach, he was ready for a nap. Climbing around in the rafters earlier had been exhausting. Walking along the boardwalk, he glanced down the beach and was pleased to see only a few people milling around. Looking for a quiet stretch of sand to call his own, Max picked up his pace. Then he saw it, a quiet area where he could take a nap without anyone disturbing him. Looking around nervously, making sure no one was watching him, he darted from the boardwalk onto the beach, racing some three hundred feet to his ultimate destination.

Lying down on the sand, he closed his eyes. It was chilly out, yet the sun warmed him, and he quickly fell asleep. Max hadn't been asleep for more than thirty minutes when a brutal kick to his side sent him sprawling across the sand. Momentarily stunned, he looked up into the angry face of a man carrying a piece of driftwood.

"Get out of here!" the man shouted, raising the driftwood over his head. "You don't belong here!"

Max didn't have to be told twice. Scrambling to his feet, he barely escaped a second blow. Racing toward the boardwalk, he didn't look back. He ran until he could no longer run. Finally coming to a stop, now more exhausted than before, Max looked back. The man was gone. It hadn't always been this way for Max. Once he had a home, someone to love.

SEVEN

Danielle peeked into the doorway of the downstairs bedroom. She found Lily wiping down the furniture with a rag. "Whatcha doing?" She stepped into the room.

Lily looked up at Danielle and stopped dusting. "Getting rid of my cooties so this room will be ready for a guest."

"You can let Joanne do that. It's her job." Danielle leaned casually against the doorjamb and watched as Lily resumed her dusting.

"I know, but I'm not helpless. Plus, I need to do something around here to earn my keep."

"I'm just grateful you're here and doing so well."

Lily tossed the rag to the dresser and turned to face Danielle. "Me too. And I'm so darn grateful I don't have to be hooked up to that IV anymore!" Lily glanced down to her arm where her PICC line had been. She then looked at her tattoo.

"What are you thinking?" Danielle asked.

Lily looked from her tattooed arm to Danielle while rubbing her hand gently over the colorful dragon. "I got another compliment on the tattoo the other day."

Danielle studied Lily's expression. "Does that help?"

Lily shrugged. "Not really. I don't think I ever told you this, but last year I considered getting a tattoo. Because of work, I was going to go with something I could easily cover up with clothes. Maybe a cute little something on my hip or back."

"Why didn't you do it?"

"Figured if I was going to ink something permanently on my skin, I wanted it to mean something. But I just couldn't get worked up over the butterflies and flowers I looked at."

Danielle nodded to Lily's tattoo. "Unfortunately, that one is kinda hard to conceal without long sleeves."

"That's not what bothers me," Lily explained. "It's the artwork. It's not me. Not something I would have ever chosen. It was forced on me by that idiot."

"Are you still thinking of having it removed?"

"You know what they told me. Because of the colors, they won't be able to remove it completely. And they're afraid the original tattoo will leave scars simply because of how it was initially done."

"And it's painful," Danielle added with a sigh.

"Yeah." Lily looked back down at her unwanted tattoo. "More painful than actually getting one, which is why I'm seriously thinking of having it covered up."

"Really?"

"Think about it, Dani. If I get it removed, my arm will never look like it did before. If I decide to wear a sleeveless dress, my arm will look weird...scarred. People might ask questions, questions I won't want to keep answering."

"Yeah, makes it hard to move past all this."

"We have friends with full sleeves—guys think they look hot in sleeveless dresses. Well, maybe not all guys. But you know what I mean."

"Are you going to cover this one completely?"

"Yes and no. I'm thinking more along the lines of adding to it, changing the picture. In some ways, it's a connection to Isabella, and while I never met her, I feel a connection to her because of all that happened. She chose this tattoo for herself. I just want to transform it to fit me."

"Have you talked to Ian about it?"

"Yeah. He said whatever I do, he'll support me. If I could work with a tattoo artist to create something out of this that reflects me— my journey—well, maybe that will be a victory of sorts. Do you understand what I'm saying?"

Danielle considered Lily's words for a moment. Finally, she smiled. "Yeah, I do."

"And one plus," Lily added with a giggle. "Last year, had I

gotten the tat, I would have gotten such crap from my folks, especially Mom. She hates tattoos."

Danielle laughed. "And this way, your mom would be supportive?"

"Yep." Lily grinned. "Knowing Mom, she'll tell me how beautiful the new tattoo is just to make me feel better."

Danielle laughed and then asked, "By the way, where's Ian?"

"He went to pick up the stuff for the party. He's so funny. Insisted on doing all the food. I'm glad we're having it here and not going out like we originally planned. It would be hard to visit at a restaurant."

"So what have you decided…on the other thing. What are you going to tell your mom?"

For the last few weeks, Lily's mother had been calling her, asking her to come home when she finished the six weeks of IV treatments. Lily glanced out the window. "I don't want to go back there."

"Ian's not there." Danielle smiled.

"That's part of it…and I like it here. I thought maybe…" Lily looked back to Danielle. "Maybe now that I'm back to the living, I could see what it would take to get an Oregon teacher's credential. Look into the schools here…not for this year, of course, but see about next fall. Maybe I could sub for now."

"You hate subbing. How many times have you told me that?" Danielle reminded her.

"I know. To be honest, if a local school called me tomorrow and offered me my own class…I'm not up to it yet. I just hope I'll be up to it next fall."

"You know you're more than welcome to keep staying here. I love having you."

"But I want to start paying rent," Lily insisted.

"That really isn't necessary," Danielle said.

"Come on, Dani, if the tables were turned, wouldn't you feel funny about staying with me rent-free?"

Danielle let out a sigh, "Yeah, I suppose you're right. But instead of rent, maybe we can just work out something where you help me run Marlow House. Heck, you do a lot around here already. Let me hire you. The job comes with room, board and a salary."

Lily laughed at her offer. "You crack me up, Dani! Your solution to end my freeloading days is to put me on a salary?"

"Don't think that just because you happen to be my best friend, I'll let you be a slacker. I can be a demanding boss!"

Lily considered Danielle's offer for a moment. "Okay, but I don't want a salary. Let me do more around here in exchange for the room."

"You're still going to need some spending money."

"Maybe not." Lily smiled. "I was going to tell you tonight at our No-More-Damn-IV Celebration Dinner—my attorney called. It looks like there will be a settlement before the end of the year. Maybe sooner."

"Oh! I'm so happy for you, Lily!" Danielle gave Lily a quick hug and then pulled away. "Are you okay with the settlement amount?"

"Well…considering it is in the millions, uhh, yeah…" Lily smiled.

"Wow. That's a turnaround."

"I suspect part of it had to do with pressure Will Wayne put on the trust," Lily told her.

"And to think I once wondered if Will was in some way involved in Stoddard's murder."

"Hey, I just realized—you don't have the kitten." Lily glanced around, as if she expected the kitten to suddenly appear.

"Walt was right, the kitten—whose name is Bella, by the way, something else Walt told me—belongs to our new neighbor." Danielle glanced around. "I wonder where Walt is."

Lily glanced up to the ceiling. "The last time I checked, he was in the attic, rolling the ball around for Sadie. At least I assume that's why the ball was flying around the attic on its own. So tell me about the new neighbor."

"She seems nice enough. A little offbeat. I assume she's not married because she's living alone. I don't know if she's renting or buying. Claims to be a writer. Not that she has ever written anything before. Actually, she made it perfectly clear she hadn't. But she intends to."

Lily laughed and said, "According to Ian, when someone asks him what he does for a living, and he says writer, they often respond with something like, *I plan to write a book someday*, or *if I had time, I would write a book*, or my favorite, *I have a story you should write*."

"Is it your favorite because that's what you said to Ian?"

Lily frowned. "What are you talking about?"

"Did you forget you're the one who convinced Ian to do a story on Emma Jackson? *Ian, I have a story you should write!*" Danielle laughed.

"Well...I suppose you're right, but I didn't say it quite like that. And you have to admit, Emma does have a fascinating story."

"I know, I'm just teasing you."

"So did this new neighbor mention what she intends to write about?" Lily asked.

"That's what I found peculiar: haunted houses."

"Any specific haunted house?" Walt asked when he appeared the next moment.

Danielle looked at Walt. "She didn't say."

Lily frowned at Danielle and then smiled. "Ahh, Walt must be here now. Hi, Walt."

The next moment Sadie came bounding into the room, her tail wagging.

Danielle leaned down and petted Sadie, who was now sitting by her side. "Walt wondered if she intended to write about any specific haunted house."

"I wondered the same thing," Lily said.

"She didn't say. But if she intends to write about a local haunted house, the only one I can think of is Presley House. At least that's the only house in Frederickport that has a reputation of being haunted."

EIGHT

"So what am I supposed to be looking at?" Chief MacDonald asked. Brian Henderson had just plunked an old lamp on his office desk. Brian and Joe Morelli stood over him, looking down at the lamp as if the two officers expected it to jump up and start dancing around.

"We brought this back from Presley House," Brian explained.

The chief looked up at Brian. "Didn't you go over there this morning?"

Brian nodded. "Yes, but we went back again."

"I don't understand. Why did you go back? What's with the lamp?"

"You aren't going to believe this, Chief," Joe said.

"I know I don't believe it, and I saw it!" Brian added.

"Maybe it would help if you two would start at the beginning." MacDonald pointed to the two empty chairs facing his desk. "Sit down. I don't need you two hovering over me."

Joe and Brian each sat down. After taking a deep breath, Joe started to explain. Periodically Brian would interject a comment. When they were done, the chief just sat there a moment, quietly looking from the lamp to his two officers.

"It isn't lit now," MacDonald finally said.

"Like I told you, the bulb went out the minute we stepped outside Presley House. Never went back on again."

MacDonald let out a sigh and leaned forward. He inspected the lamp and removed the bulb, giving it a gentle shake. "This bulb is out."

"I know." Brian nodded. "I took it out, just like you did, and put it back in. And then it went on."

"And you're saying after you shook it and heard it rattling around, it turned on?" MacDonald asked incredulously. "Without any electricity?"

"I know it sounds crazy, but that's exactly what happened," Joe insisted. "We both saw it."

"I know a little about electricity—enough to know it takes electricity to run a lamp like this." The chief leaned back in his chair and studied his men.

"I think we need to have this lamp checked out," Brian said.

"Checked out?" the chief asked.

"It has to be rigged someway. Someone's screwing with us," Brian insisted.

"Or maybe...Presley House really is haunted." MacDonald smiled.

"That isn't funny," Joe snapped.

MacDonald laughed. "Well, maybe not, but you start telling people you saw this old lamp light up—without being plugged in— you're going to make a lot of people laugh. I'm sure they'll think it's hilarious."

"So what do you want us to do?" Brian asked.

The chief didn't answer immediately. Instead, he silently studied the lamp. Finally, he said, "I tell you what...I know someone. I'll have him discreetly look at the lamp. Let's figure out first if there is something different about it. Who knows, maybe it was used in a magic act or something. But even then, we don't want this to get out. I'm afraid everyone will find it far too amusing to learn a trick lamp freaked out a couple of our officers. And if it isn't some sort of trick lamp, well, that's an entirely different issue. Considering all that has gone on in the department over the last four months, we really don't need any more bad press, especially with Christiansen and Haston on the loose."

"Any word on them?" Joe asked.

"Aside from finding Haston's car parked at the Frederickport Beach parking lot this afternoon, no," the chief said.

"Are you saying you found his car here, in town? Why is this the first we've heard about it?" Brian asked.

"Probably because you two have been out stealing lamps from abandoned houses."

"Does this mean you think they're hiding out in Frederickport?" Joe asked.

"According to the guy who reported seeing the car, it was sitting there since Wednesday. Never moved. My guess, he and Christiansen are long gone."

"Wednesday, when he should have been at court in Astoria. Haston doesn't live here, so why did he come to Frederickport, and where did he go?" Brian asked.

"I would love to know the answers to those questions too. But since Christiansen is also missing, and he does live in Frederickport, I have to assume they met up here and took off. Although, I still find it hard to believe they took off together, considering Haston rolled over on Christiansen," MacDonald said.

"I take it Christiansen's car is still missing?" Brian asked.

"Yes, which is why the general consensus is that the two took off together and are already in Canada."

"You don't sound like you believe that, Chief," Joe said.

"I don't think they stuck around here, but take off together? That doesn't feel right. But since Haston's car is still here, Christiansen and his car are missing, and there haven't been any reports of a stolen vehicle, I have to assume they took off together."

"Or Haston is still in town. Hiding out somewhere," Joe suggested.

"Yeah, I thought about that. I had some of the guys check out Stoddard's rental properties in Frederickport, see if he's lying low in one of them. I even had them check out Stoddard's estate, but nothing. Of course, there are plenty of other vacant houses in town. But why? Why stick around?"

"Was there anything wrong with Haston's car? Maybe it broke down," Joe suggested. "Maybe he wanted to talk to Christiansen before they showed up at court, so he stopped at Frederickport first, but then his car broke down."

"No, it was in perfect working order, half a tank of gas. I can only see one reason for him coming to Frederickport—to see Christiansen. Which would mean Haston knew Christiansen never intended to show up at court but was waiting for Haston, which means I'm running in circles and maybe those two worked out their differences and decided to team up and head to Canada together."

———————

"WE SHOULDN'T STAY HERE. Someone is going to find us!" Bart Haston said for the tenth time. Agitated, he paced the living room floor of the Gusarov Estate.

Chuck Christiansen looked up from his seat on the couch and stared at Bart. *He's like a bad penny; he keeps coming back.* "I told you they already checked this place. We're safe here. And if you want to go, there's the door!"

"I don't want to be alone. Please don't make me leave!"

"I don't care if you stay, just *shut up*! You've been blabbering nonstop since—hell, I don't know for how long. I just don't want to listen to it anymore!"

Bart took a seat across from the couch. "I'm just afraid." He looked down at his hands; they fidgeted nervously on his lap. "I never wanted to go to prison."

"Then I guess you should have thought about that before you opened your mouth!" Chuck snapped.

"I just thought..."

Chuck glared at Bart. "You thought what?"

"That if I came clean, told the truth, things would work out."

"Work out for who? You? Did you think throwing me under the bus was going to buy you the magic get-out-of-jail card?"

"I don't know..." Bart shook his head, confused. "I've never done anything like this before. I never even had so much as a parking ticket."

"Apparently the courts don't take into account your driving record when charged with murder."

Bart looked around the room nervously. "Do you think he's here?"

"Do I think who's here?" Chuck frowned.

"Stoddard. This is where Darlene did it. He died...just over there." Bart pointed toward the entry. "At least that's what I heard."

"Well, do you see him?" Chuck snapped.

"You know what I mean. His spirit. They say when someone is murdered, their spirit lingers. Do you think this place could be haunted?"

"Don't be an idiot."

They were quiet for a few minutes. Finally, Bart asked, "So what do we do now?"

Chuck stood up. "I don't know about you, but I'm going upstairs. I'd appreciate it if you don't come with me. I want to be alone."

"We're just going to stay here, indefinitely?" Bart asked with a frown.

"Like I told you, there's the door." Chuck pointed to the entry. "I really don't know what I'm going to do or where I'm going to go. I didn't expect to have problems with the car. I should be in Canada now. Obviously, things don't always work out like we plan. I mean, look, here I am with you."

"I wish you'd stop being mad at me. It doesn't make it very pleasant, since we are sort of stuck here together."

"And whose fault is that?" Chuck asked.

Bart looked up at Chuck. "That's one thing you can't blame me for."

Chuck silently stared at Bart for a few moments, studying him. Finally, he sighed. "I suppose you're right. That's one thing I can't blame on you. That one's totally my own fault."

Without saying another word, Chuck walked from the room and made his way up the stairs.

Bart slumped back in the chair and glanced around the room. Sunlight flooded in from the overhead windows, making it unnecessary to turn on the lights. However, it would be dark in a couple hours.

He looked over to where he believed Stoddard had died. He sat up straight in the chair and stared at the spot, concentrating.

"Stoddard? Are you here?"

There was no answer.

"If your spirit is here...I'm sorry for my part in your murder. But you need to understand. I didn't want to go to prison. I was afraid you were going to tell them how we helped you cover up Isabella's death—how I knew that was Lily Miller upstairs instead of Isabella. You shouldn't have asked us to do that. It was wrong. We were wrong."

There was still no answer.

Bart slumped back in the chair again and closed his eyes. Then he saw it: the body on the floor of Presley House. His eyes flew open.

BART STOOD in the basement of Presley House, looking into the open trunk. Instinctively he knew this was where he would find it—the body he had abandoned, left for someone else to take care of.

The basement door was already open when he arrived. Light filtered in from upstairs, lending some visibility to the dark space. The sun would be setting soon. When that happened, it would be impossible to see in the basement.

"I told you not to come back!" Harvey shouted from the doorway, startling Bart, who was lost in his own private thoughts.

"Are you just going to leave him here?" Bart asked.

"What do you care? I told you I would take care of it, and I did. Now leave. I don't want you here!"

"This isn't right. People need to know...there is family to consider...his mother will wonder what happened..."

"If it makes you feel any better, I don't intend to leave him there forever. He'll be found soon. No later than Halloween."

"Halloween? What does Halloween have to do with it?"

"Don't you know anything about this house? According to local legend, this place is haunted." Harvey laughed. "So every Halloween tough-guy teenagers show up to prove how brave they are by breaking in and poking through the house. This year they'll get a special surprise." Harvey laughed again.

"Don't you think that's kind of gruesome? Won't those kids be traumatized?"

"Gruesome? Are you serious? You're the one responsible for the dead guy, not me."

"It's just that..." Bart looked in the trunk. "The body's all scrunched up in there. How did you get it to fit in the trunk?"

"It wasn't easy. I imagine it will be rather *gruesome* getting him out of there." Harvey laughed wildly. He then stopped laughing and looked at Bart. "So what's the deal? You want to take him with you now?"

"No." Bart shook his head.

"Then get out of here, and don't come back!"

NINE

The man with the dog had left the gate wide open, making it easier for Max to slip into the side yard. While Max wasn't especially afraid of dogs—and this one looked rather harmless, in spite of its size—they tended to be nosey creatures, prone to barking. Fortunately, the man had taken the dog inside with him, along with what appeared to be a significant amount of groceries.

The sun had set just minutes earlier, and the interior of the house was brightly lit. From his hiding place in the bushes, Max could see inside.

The afternoon hadn't gone as he had hoped. Instead of napping on the beach, he spent most of the time avoiding people. Aside from the obvious dangers associated with sleeping out of doors, it was too damp and cold this time of year to spend the entire night outside. He needed to make this work because he didn't want to return to Harvey. He wanted to spend the night here, inside this house.

He could see the man in the kitchen, moving around, doing something—cooking perhaps or putting the groceries away. Looking up to the windows on the second floor, he spied the girl with the short red hair. Yet he wasn't interested in her. Max wanted to see the other one—the one with the long dark hair. Glancing back to the kitchen window, he noticed the man was no longer in that room. The kitchen was empty. Max wondered if the door was unlocked.

So focused on watching the house, he failed to notice a woman approaching from the sidewalk, entering through the open gate he had come through just minutes earlier. Moving farther back into the shelter of the bushes, he watched as she went to the kitchen door and knocked. While waiting for someone to answer, she turned her back to the door and looked Max's way. With the limited light, he doubted she would be able to see him, even if he wasn't hiding amongst the foliage. She carried something. Max wasn't sure what it was until he heard it—*meow*. The woman carried a cat. Max loathed cats.

The dog had initially worried him. But then Max remembered he had noticed the same dog in the window of the house across the street during his previous visit. Minutes earlier, the man had pulled up to the side drive—in the same car that had been parked across the street on the previous night—and parked by the kitchen door. He had let the dog outside to do what dogs did—pee on trees—before letting him back inside the house while bringing in the groceries. Fortunately, the clueless dog failed to pick up on the stranger lurking in the yard.

Max was fairly certain both the man and dog lived across the street. Although, this coming and going whenever he felt like it—and bringing along his dog—needed to stop. Max would see to it. The man and his dog could complicate matters.

SADIE CHARGED DOWN THE STAIRS, the pads of her paws barely touching the landing as she headed for the doorway leading to the kitchen. En route, she almost tripped Ian, who had just stepped out from the bathroom.

"Whoa, girl!" Ian called out as he quickly regained his footing.

Following Sadie into the kitchen, he found her at the door leading to the side yard, barking. Through the window, Ian could see what had caught Sadie's attention.

"Sit!" Ian snapped before answering the door.

Reluctantly, Sadie sat down, barely able to contain herself.

"What's all the ruckus about?" Walt asked when he appeared a moment later.

Sadie looked up at him, her body still wiggling.

"Hello," Ian greeted when he opened the door. He assumed the woman standing on the stoop was the neighbor Heather Donovan —Danielle had already told him about her. She held the kitten he had rescued earlier, along with a small paper sack.

"Oh…hello." She seemed surprised to find Ian answering the door. "I was looking for Danielle Boatman. I'm sorry. I saw the light on, and I cut across the side yard. I hope that's okay."

"You must be the new neighbor. I met your kitten earlier," Ian greeted her. "I'm Ian Bartley. I live across the street. Come on in." He glanced down at Sadie, pointed across the room and said, "Go lie down!"

Reluctantly, Sadie moved to the far wall as she looked over her shoulder at the unwanted guest.

"She's our neighbor," Walt said as he leaned against the wall next to Sadie. "You might as well get used to her. I'm sure you two will become grand friends." Bella and Sadie lifted their heads and looked at Walt.

Walt glanced from Sadie to Bella, who let out a little hiss in Sadie's direction. "Hmmm, maybe not," Walt mumbled as he summoned a cigar.

Now standing in the kitchen, Heather kept a tight hold on Bella, who seemed determined to jump down. "I heard you lived in the neighborhood. You write under the pen name Jon Altar, don't you?"

"Guilty as charged," Ian said as he shut the door.

"I'm Heather Donovan and very honored to meet you. I've watched all your specials and read everything you've written about Eva Thorndike. So fascinating and to think you found the Missing Thorndike!"

"Thank you." Ian smiled. "I'm glad you enjoyed my work. But I didn't find the necklace, Danielle did."

"I'm a writer too."

"That's nice," Ian said politely.

"Of course, I'm not famous like you!"

"Let me get Danielle." Just as Ian turned from Heather, he found Danielle standing at the doorway.

"I wondered what Sadie was barking at." Danielle walked into the kitchen. "Hello, Heather."

Heather hadn't noticed before, but considering what was sitting on the kitchen counter and table, someone was in the middle of preparing food—and by the looks of it, food for a party.

"Oh, I'm sorry. I didn't realize you were entertaining." Heather handed Danielle a sack. "I just wanted to bring you this."

"What's this?" Danielle asked, accepting the bag. She opened it and pulled out a small vial of oil.

"For your scratch. I meant to send it back with you. I'd hate for you to get infected."

Danielle glanced at her wrist. The scratch was barely visible. "Looks like your oil already did the trick." She returned the bottle to the sack and started to hand it back to Heather.

"No, you keep it," Heather insisted. "I have more."

"Thanks." Danielle smiled and set the bag on the counter.

"Well, I'll be going. Looks like you're about to have company."

"Please stay," Lily said from the doorway. They all looked to Lily, who had just entered the kitchen. "By that little ball of fur in your arms, I take it you're the new neighbor."

"Yes…and you are?" Heather asked as she watched Lily walk to Ian's side.

"I'm Lily. We're having a little celebration tonight, and you're more than welcome to join us. It'll be a way for you to meet some people. I understand you're new to town."

Ian wrapped his arm around Lily's shoulders, pulling her closer.

"That's sweet of you to ask, but I really didn't mean to crash your party."

"Nah, the more the merrier." Lily looked up into Ian's face. "Right?"

Ian smiled down at Lily. "Sure." He dropped a quick kiss on her nose.

Heather glanced down at the kitten. "I appreciate the offer, but I have Bella with me."

"That's okay," Danielle said. "She's welcome."

"I also have something in the oven at home," Heather said quickly. "I only intended to drop this off and get right back."

"Well, we wouldn't want you to burn the neighborhood down." Danielle smiled.

"SO THAT'S THE NEW NEIGHBOR," Lily said after Heather left.

"Yes. I wonder if she really had something in the oven at home. She didn't seem that anxious to leave before you came in," Danielle said as she glanced out the window. It was dark outside, yet she could see Heather's silhouette as she made her way toward the sidewalk.

"It probably had something to do with how she was checking out Ian." Lily snickered.

"What are you talking about?" Ian asked as he went back to preparing the food for dinner.

"The look of disappointment on her face when you put your arm around me." Lily sat down at the table and started removing items from a grocery sack.

"What look?" Ian frowned.

"I noticed it too," Danielle said. She began sorting through grocery bags, looking for items that needed to go in the refrigerator.

"You're both crazy," Ian scoffed.

"I saw it too," Walt said, flicking an ash from his cigar. It disappeared before it hit the floor. "Of course, you can't hear me, so what I saw doesn't count."

Danielle silently flashed a smile at Walt and then continued putting the groceries away.

"Of course, she is a little young for you," Lily said with a grin.

"You're both crazy." Ian shook his head.

"No, Lily is right. I was standing at the doorway when she was fan girl-ing all over you."

"Fan girl-ing? Is that a new word?" Walt asked.

Danielle shrugged and then looked back at Ian.

"I think you two are just imagining things. The girl was just being friendly. And Lily is right; she is way too young for me."

"Does that make me old?" Lily asked with a frown.

Ian laughed. "Just means you're old enough for me."

"Didn't I tell you she was a writer?" Danielle asked.

"I think you mentioned something about her wanting to be a writer." Ian wadded up a piece of paper towel and tossed it in the trash. "I think you two should leave me alone so I can get this finished before everyone arrives."

"You trying to get rid of us?" Lily asked.

"Yes." Ian glanced at the wall clock. "Everyone is going to be here in less than thirty minutes."

"I can help," Danielle offered.

"I would think Ian could use your help," Walt told her. "If he wants to throw a party for Lily and doesn't want you to prepare the food, he should have hired someone like Joanne to do it for him. Do men actually do this sort of thing these days?"

"No. Remember this is my thing. You two go, get out of my way!" Ian said playfully, pointing to the door.

When Ian turned his back to Danielle, she spit her tongue out at Walt and wrinkled her nose.

"And also in my day, a young woman who behaved in such a manner would find her backside severely paddled," Walt said with mock seriousness.

Danielle managed to contain her giggles as she prepared to leave the kitchen and get out of Ian's way. Just as Lily stood up, Sadie picked up her head and let out a bark. The next moment, she jumped up and raced across the room to the back door, barking ferociously.

"What is it, Sadie?" Ian looked out the window.

"Is someone here already?" Danielle asked. She and Lily walked to Ian's side and peered out the window into the darkness.

No longer barking, Sadie stood by the door, growling.

"Something's out there," Walt said.

Danielle turned to face Walt.

"She told me there is something out there—something that doesn't belong out there."

Danielle turned back to the window.

"I'll go check," Ian said, reaching for the door.

Danielle grabbed his wrist, stopping him from opening the door. "No. Don't just go out there. Remember, there are two fugitives loose."

"Those guys are long gone, Danielle," Ian said, reaching for the doorknob again.

"No, please," Danielle said, glancing briefly to Walt and back to Ian.

"Dani, you're freaking me out," Lily said as she looked to where she believed Walt was standing. *What is Walt telling her?* Lily wondered.

"I'm sorry, but I don't think it's wise, going out there when it's dark, with Sadie growling like that, and two fugitives are on the loose."

"Danielle, this is the last place those two are going to show up.

Trust me, they're probably over the Canadian border by now."
Ignoring Danielle's concerns, Ian opened the back door. Sadie raced
outside, barking ferociously, while Ian followed her.

MAX CLOSED his eyes and leaned against the block wall. *That was
a close call. Something will have to be done about that dog—and that man.*

TEN

Max chose to watch the house from a safe distance across the street. Of course, he would need to take off before the man and the dog left because they would be coming his way. He watched as the cars started to arrive. It was dark out; the only light came from the houses nearby, the cars arriving, and the streetlights.

The first car brought a man and a woman. By the woman's slouch and the way the man had to help her make her way up to the house, Max assumed she must be much older than her companion. It was impossible to see their faces from where he hid.

The second car brought another man and woman. Max assumed they were a couple, close to the same age. They held hands as they walked up to the house. Other cars started arriving, and Max found it impossible to keep them all straight.

He glanced to the second floor of the house. The curtains were open in one of the windows. He almost looked back down to the street and the arriving cars, but then she walked into the room. It was her, the one with the dark hair. She had it pulled back into a braid. He rather liked braids. Victoria had worn braids. But she had betrayed him.

Max closed his eyes for a moment. He was so sleepy; he simply wanted to nap. But he couldn't sleep now; he needed to stay alert. His life counted on it. He thought back to his early life when he was loved and had a place he could call home. But then everything changed.

After he had lost his home, he drifted for a while until he met a woman who claimed to love him. She did everything to make him happy, but she didn't understand. It simply did not work that way. Max had to be the one to choose. He found it wasn't easy to replace his first love. So one day, when this woman who loved him went off to work, he took off, never to see her again.

Unfortunately, when Max got around to making a choice, he made the wrong one. Victoria made him believe she wanted him, but it had been a lie. She almost got him killed. This one would be different. He wasn't going to timidly wait around to win her affections. While watching her guests arriving, he made a decision. Instead of slipping into her house, hiding, and studying her, as he initially considered doing, he would take the assertive approach. Max was simply getting too old to play it safe and wait.

"I'M SURPRISED you didn't invite Joe. Or did you?" MacDonald asked Danielle as he sipped his wine. They stood together in the library while other partygoers filtered through the room and lower level of Marlow House, chatting and visiting.

"Lily made the guest list; it's her party," Danielle explained. "She asked me if I wanted to invite him. While Joe and I are on good terms now, I really didn't want to send him the wrong message. I hope his feelings aren't hurt that he wasn't invited."

"I never said a thing to him about tonight. Didn't figure it was my place." MacDonald glanced across the room and smiled at a pretty blonde who was visiting with Marie Nichols.

Danielle looked over to the blonde. "Glad to finally meet Carol Ann. She's lovely."

"The boys adore her." MacDonald took another sip of wine.

Danielle raised her brows. "And you?"

"Yeah, me too." MacDonald blushed.

"How did you ever get so lucky with someone like Carol Ann Peterson?" Adam Nichols asked as he walked up to Danielle and the police chief. Beer in hand, Adam glanced over to his grandmother and the blonde—the subject of his admiration.

"Because he's a nice guy," Danielle said with a grin.

Adam glanced back over to Carol Ann and took a swig of beer. "She's hot."

"She's also a very nice lady," the chief began, unable to mask his annoyance.

"Yeah, yeah, whatever. Don't worry, I'm not stupid enough to try to get between the police chief and his woman."

"Why do I suddenly feel like chopped liver?" Danielle asked.

Adam looked Danielle up and down and smiled. "Hey, you're hot too. But since you're off-limits, considering my grandmother would have us standing in front of a preacher if I showed any interest, I'd rather think of you as my average-looking pal who has a penchant for getting herself arrested...whom I have to occasionally bail out."

"Umm, gee...thanks...I think." Danielle rolled her eyes.

"And, Chief"—Adam turned his full attention to MacDonald —"maybe spending all this time with your good-looking girlfriend isn't so good for the Frederickport Police Department."

"And why is that, Nichols?" MacDonald asked.

"Joe Morelli stopped in my office earlier today. Asked me about Presley House, wanted to know why they had the electricity turned on since they can't afford to pay for property management." Adam began to laugh.

Danielle looked at Adam with a frown. "Why is that so funny?"

"Because," Adam said while trying to control his laughter, "he insisted the lights were on at Presley House—but the house doesn't even have an electric meter!"

"He probably saw someone in there with a flashlight," Danielle suggested.

"It's just the same old thing. Around Halloween each year, local teenagers love to prank that place," the chief said.

"Like I told Joe, I can't really come down too hard on the teenagers, considering when I was in high school my friends and I broke into the old house a few times," Adam confessed.

McDonald raised his brows. "And you used to property manage Presley House?"

"Hey, I was just a dumb kid back then." Adam shrugged. "Although, I don't recall mentioning my teenage antics to the property owners when they interviewed me for the job."

"I understand you aren't managing it anymore," MacDonald said.

"No. When owners stop paying, I stop managing."

Their conversation ended when Marie called to Adam, waving him over to her.

When Danielle and MacDonald were alone again, MacDonald said, "Danielle, I need to talk to you alone about something. It has to do with what Adam just mentioned."

"About Presley House?" she asked.

"Yes. I was hoping we could go alone somewhere and discuss it —preferably somewhere where Walt is."

"Walt? Are you saying you have something you want to ask Walt?"

"In a way."

Danielle glanced around the room, looking to see who would notice their departure. "I know he's in the attic with Sadie. We can go up there. But you'll probably want to say something to Carol Ann first. I don't want her to get the wrong idea."

"I'll go tell Carol Ann where I'm going, and then I need to run out to my car and get something I left in the trunk. How about I meet you in the attic?"

DANIELLE SAT in the attic with Walt and Sadie, waiting for the police chief. She could hear the sounds of the party drifting up from downstairs.

"So how is Lily's party going?" Walt asked.

"You should come down and see for yourself. I don't know why you're hiding up here with Sadie."

Walt shrugged. "I will, later. Just thought I'd give Sadie a little attention first. I didn't want Ian to think she was in the way and take her back across the street. She doesn't like to stay at the house alone."

"She doesn't?" Danielle looked down at Sadie, who was curled up where Walt stood, her body blending with his legs.

"I'm afraid it's my fault," Walt said with a sigh, looking apologetically at Sadie.

"Your fault? How?"

"The dognappers," Walt explained. "That episode was quite traumatic for her."

"Did she tell you that?"

"I assume you aren't talking to yourself," Chief MacDonald said from the doorway. He walked into the attic, carrying a small box.

"No, Walt's here." Danielle glanced from Walt to MacDonald.

"Good. Maybe he can help me figure this out."

"I will confess, I find it fascinating how he seems to accept my presence without actually seeing me," Walt murmured as he watched the police chief open the small box.

"What's that?" Danielle asked as MacDonald pulled a lightbulb from the box.

"Remember how Adam mentioned Joe claimed to see a light on over at Presley House?"

"Yeah, so?"

"This is what Joe…and Brian…claimed to have seen lit up. They took it from Presley House to show me. It was screwed into a lamp, which they also took. But I didn't think I should haul the lamp over here. Figured the bulb would do."

"I don't get it." Danielle frowned.

"According to both Joe and Brian, they witnessed the lamp turn on in Presley House. As Adam said, there's no electricity at the house. In fact, the electric company pulled the electric meter months ago."

"Okay…" Danielle still didn't understand where this was going.

MacDonald shook the bulb. Danielle could hear the broken bits rattling around. "As you can hear, this bulb is no longer good. Even if it was screwed into a lamp with electricity, it still wouldn't work. Brian claims he shook it and heard the same thing. Yet when he screwed it back into the lamp, the light went on. The light stayed on after they carried the lamp from the house. It went off when they went outside. It hasn't gone back on again."

"Okay…so what are you asking?"

"For years, there have been stories about Presley House being haunted. I never gave it any serious thought, after all, a haunted house? Who believes such things?"

Danielle chuckled and looked at Walt. "Who, indeed?"

"But now, after …well, you know…" MacDonald looked to where he assumed Walt stood. "I'm wondering if there is a spirit who hangs out at Presley House, causing problems each Halloween."

"So what do you want from us?"

MacDonald held the bulb up with one hand. "I'm wondering if

it's possible for a spirit to make a lightbulb—one like this, that isn't plugged into electricity and is broken—to light up. Is that something a spirit can do?"

Danielle looked at the spirit in the room. "Walt, is it possible?"

Waving his hand, Walt summoned a lit cigar. He took a puff and then exhaled. "You have to understand, harnessing energy is not the same for every spirit. You know that, Danielle. Some of us are confined to specific areas while others are free to roam. Not every spirit can move objects—Angela can't. And those who can are normally confined to limited areas."

"What is he saying?" MacDonald asked.

"He's rambling a bit," Danielle said impatiently. "Can you cut to the chase, Walt? Is it possible? You think a spirit could make this broken bulb glow?"

Walt looked at the object MacDonald held and gave a shrug. Staring at it, he took a puff off his cigar. In the next moment, the lightbulb lit up.

MacDonald stared at the bulb. It shone brightly.

"Well," Danielle said with a smile, "I guess you have your answer. Looks like Presley House may really be haunted."

"Looks like it," MacDonald said in a dull voice. "But now what do I do?"

"Do you have to do anything?" Danielle asked.

"Not sure...but..." MacDonald continued to hold the lit bulb. He looked at it with unease. "You think you can have him turn it off now?"

ELEVEN

The one with the red hair had left the front door wide open while she made her way to the sidewalk with the departing houseguests. It was so dark outside no one even noticed Max lurking in the bushes by the front door. Thankfully, the dog was nowhere in sight, but he was somewhere in the house, and that troubled Max.

Once inside, he ducked into a bedroom on the first floor; its door was ajar. Seeking refuge under the bed—his favorite hiding place—he waited for the man to come for his dog. Max's plan wouldn't work if the dog were still lurking around in the house. With the bedroom door still partially open, he could hear the comings and goings on the first floor.

It seemed as if he had been under the bed for hours—yet it hadn't even been an hour—when he heard the man call, "Sadie!" A few moments later, the scratching clickity-clack sound of a dog running down wooden stairs and hitting the hardwood floor was heard from under the bed. Max peeked out nervously. The dog raced by the door.

Worthless animal, Max thought. *There's an intruder in the house and the mutt doesn't even have a clue.*

The next moment he heard the dark-haired one call out, "Goodnight, Ian, thanks again. It turned out great. Night, Lily."

"Night. I'll be back in the morning to help clean up!" the man called back from the front doorway.

"Night, Dani, I'll be up in a minute," the redheaded woman then shouted.

Max heard the one called Dani walking up the stairs while muffled voices talked by the front doorway. Silently, he waited. Finally, he heard the front door open and close, and the one called Lily made her way down the hallway, turning off some of the lights as she went. He didn't want to rush upstairs. It would be better if the women were sound asleep.

The redheaded woman had turned off most of the lights; however, she had left one on in the entry hall. Its glow helped to partially illuminate the downstairs bedroom. Max looked around. One thing he noticed, the floors in this room didn't have the dust the floors of Presley House did. These looked as if they had recently been mopped and shined. There wasn't a single cockroach in sight. He wasn't sure if that was an improvement or not.

Closing his eyes, Max yawned, settling into the comfort of his new home. He would give the girls time to fall asleep before going upstairs. But first, first he needed to take a nap. It seemed as if it had been hours since he had been able to sleep.

"SO TELL me about this haunted house the chief was talking about," Walt asked when he appeared in Danielle's bedroom. She had just slipped into bed.

"I thought I told you about it." She scooted over to one side, making room for Walt.

"I think you mentioned something about it." Walt settled into the bed, lying next to Danielle. He leaned against the headboard and kicked off his shoes. They vanished before they hit the floor. "Did the chief call it Presley House?"

"I guess that's what they call it. Joe and Brian mentioned it to me a while back, but I really didn't pay much attention to it. Lily and I drove by it once. A big old Victorian, all boarded up, a couple blocks from here. I just sort of assumed it was nothing but an old vacant house that people made up stories about."

"And now what do you think?" Walt summoned a lit cigar and then instantly remembered smoking was off-limits in Danielle's bedroom. The cigar vanished as quickly as it appeared.

"Thank you," Danielle said when she noticed the cigar come and go.

Walt flashed her a smile. "So you think it may be haunted?"

"If Joe and Brian really did see that bulb light up, without electricity—sounds like it might be. Do you know anything about Presley House? Was it around back when you were…well…"

"You mean back when I was alive?"

Danielle shrugged.

"You can say it, Danielle. Back when I was *alive*. But no, I don't recall any Presley House."

"It looks old, but I don't think it's as old as Marlow House. A traditional Victorian. Really is a shame; the place is a mess. The other houses in that neighborhood are really nice. It must drive the people on that street crazy to have to look at that every day, with its boarded-up windows and sad yard with dying trees and weeds."

"While I've never heard of a Presley House—until today—I did know someone with that name who lived in Frederickport."

"Did he live in a Victorian House? I assume the house is named for the family that lived there. Maybe they didn't start calling it Presley House until after you…well, you know…"

Walt shook his head. "No, this Presley didn't own a house. Can't imagine him even buying one in later years."

"Why is that?"

"He worked for Eva's parents."

"Eva, as in Eva Thorndike?" Danielle asked.

"Yes. He lived in a little apartment over their garage. He was a caretaker for their property here. I never cared for him."

"Why is that?"

Walt shrugged. "There was just something about him I didn't trust. I mentioned it to Eva once; she told me I was being silly."

"Was it just a feeling you had about him, or did you see him do something he wasn't supposed to be doing?"

"Aside from being a drunk when the Thorndikes weren't here, nothing specific. I don't remember seeing him after Eva died, but I assume he was still working for her parents…and still drinking too much."

"Did he have family in the area? Maybe the house was owned by one of his relatives."

Walt shook his head. "As far as I knew, he didn't have any family in the area."

"Well, I assume someone named Presley lived in that old house. And it looks like he or she has stuck around. Although, according to legend, the ghost only haunts the place around Halloween and pretty much goes dormant the rest of the year."

"If that's true, then I suppose the chief's problem will be resolved in another week," Walt suggested.

"At least for another year." Danielle glanced over at Walt, who leaned back against the headboard, his eyes closed. "Can I ask you something?"

Walt opened his eyes and looked at Danielle. "Sure, what?"

"Have you ever hit a woman?"

Walt scowled. "Why would you ask me something like that?"

"Your comment earlier, about how in your day a sassy woman would be spanked."

"I thought you knew I was teasing."

"Well, I did...sort of..." Danielle shrugged.

"Sort of?"

"I've read how men from your generation saw nothing wrong with hitting their wives—punishing them like they might a child. I just wondered...well...if you ever did something like that."

Walt let out a deep sigh. "I thought you knew me better than that, Danielle."

"It's just that...I thought...I mean..." Danielle regretted her question.

"I will confess, there were times I was sorely tempted to give Angela the back of my hand. But no, I don't believe a man should ever hit a woman. Yet, you are right, had I felt it within my right to strike her, I doubt anyone would have intervened or thought less of me."

"I'm sorry I asked."

"I suppose I understand why you did, considering how different things are now compared to when I was alive. And for the record, had I ever been fortunate enough to have had children, I would not have raised my hand to them either. I would like to believe I would have found another way to teach my child."

"I think you would have been a wonderful father," Danielle said in a soft voice.

Walt turned to Danielle and smiled. "And someday you'll be a wonderful mother."

THE THUNDER WOKE HIM. Max lifted his head. He wondered how long he had been asleep. Inching from under the bed, he peeked out. It was dark save for the dim light coming from the entry hall. The house was quiet. Max guessed everyone was asleep.

Making his way out from under the bed, Max startled when light flashed across the bedroom window: lightning. He hated thunder and lightning. It was nights like these he was grateful to be indoors, safely under a roof. In the past, he had reluctantly stayed in Presley House, enduring Harvey's abuse and mischief. The only good thing about Harvey—he only came around in the fall. Where he went the rest of the year, Max had no idea.

Standing at the bedroom doorway, he looked out into the hallway. A part of him considered returning to his comfortable spot under the bed and going back to sleep. After all, he might be able to hide out in the house for days before anyone noticed him. But then his stomach grumbled, reminding him of how hungry he was.

Treading softly, Max made his way down the hallway toward where he believed he would find the stairs to the second floor. He could only guess. It was a logical guess, considering he had heard the dog pounding down them earlier and the women walking up them a short time later. In both cases it was noisy, something he would have to avoid. The last thing Max wanted was for one of the women to wake up before he could pounce. Fortunately, Max was both agile and quiet when the situation called for it—such as now.

He came to the staircase and looked up. It was dark. Unlike the first floor, there didn't seem to be a light on upstairs. The darkness didn't bother Max; he preferred it. With featherlight steps, he made his way up the staircase leading to the second floor of Marlow House.

Once on the second-floor landing a thought came to him. *What if her door is shut? That could ruin everything!* He thought about the noisy hinges of the door leading to the basement of Presley House.

Refusing to be deterred, he continued on, moving in the direction where he believed her bedroom to be. He stayed close to the floor to avoid being detected should the redheaded woman choose that moment to come out of her room. Then he saw it, an open door! He was certain it was the door to her room: the woman with the long dark hair.

WALT STOOD at the attic window, watching the lightning streak across the sky. He heard a clap of thunder—and then something else. Cocking his head, he turned from the window to the door. *It's probably just Lily or Danielle getting up to use the bathroom,* he thought. About to turn back to the window, he paused again. Something just didn't feel right.

The next moment, he stood at the base of the stairs leading from the second floor to the attic. Glancing around, he saw no signs of Lily or Danielle. All the lights were off; no one was in the bathroom. And then he saw it—something dark slinking across the floor toward Danielle's room.

Curious as to the intruder's intent, Walt decided to watch and wait. There would be plenty of time to harness his energy if necessary.

DANIELLE SLEPT SOUNDLY on her bed, unaware of the intruder who had just pushed his way into her room—or of Walt, who stood just outside her door. The intruder had no idea he was being watched. He looked around the room, searching for her bed. Lightning streaked across the window, briefly illuminating the room, followed by a clap of thunder.

Light from the storm enabled Max to see clearly how the room was laid out. The woman's bed—and the woman—were just a few feet away. *What now?* He began questioning his boldness in coming up to her room. Perhaps this was not the best tactic. Maybe he should have introduced himself first—on neutral territory—maybe at the beach. *No, not the beach,* he thought, remembering the man who had kicked him.

In the next moment, lightning lit up the window, followed by a loud clap of thunder, effectively ending Max's momentary reluctance. Without another thought, he raced toward the bed and leapt onto the mattress.

The moment Max jumped onto Danielle's bed, Walt turned on the overhead lamp, instantly flooding the room with light.

Danielle, startled awake by both the sudden light and the intruder landing on her bed, bolted up in a sitting position and opened her eyes. Before she had time to scream, the intruder jumped onto her lap, stared into her eyes, and started to purr.

"Holy crap!" Danielle shouted, her heart beating wildly. Staring into a pair of golden eyes, Danielle tentatively reached out and touched the black cat now sitting on her lap. "Where did you come from?"

TWELVE

W alt walked into the room from the hallway. "He must have slipped in when your guests left."

The cat's head jerked up, looking to the doorway, startled by Walt's sudden appearance. He hissed and moved closer to Danielle, trying to climb under the covers with her.

"I don't think he likes you." Danielle looked down at the furry intruder and gently stroked his neck, trying to calm him. She noticed he was not all black. White fur covered the tips of his ears.

"He seems to be making himself at home." Walt took a seat on the vanity's chair, turning it to face Danielle's bed.

The cat attempted to burrow under the blanket. He looked from Walt to Danielle.

"He's confused," Walt told her.

Danielle frowned. "Confused?"

"The fact you can see me. He doesn't understand that."

"I think you're scaring him." Danielle looked down and stroked the cat's back. "Don't be afraid. Walt's not bad for a dead guy."

"Dead guy? Really, Danielle?"

Danielle shrugged. "You don't like me saying ghost." She looked back at the cat, who seemed intent on crawling up her body, trying to get closer to her face. "We need to find out where he lives. Poor little fellow, I bet the storm's scared him."

Walt stared at the cat. After a moment, the cat stared back. They continued to look at each other for several moments.

"His name is Max," Walt finally said. "And according to him, he lives here."

"Here?" Danielle frowned.

"You know cats." Walt shrugged. "They choose you, you don't choose them. And apparently this one has chosen you."

"Well, he came from somewhere. I'm sure someone is looking for him."

"No. According to him, there is no one. Just you." Walt leaned back in the chair. "I wonder what Sadie is going to think about all this?"

Settling on Danielle's lap, Max's golden eyes stared intently at Walt.

After a moment Walt said, "No, Max, we are not getting rid of the dog. Or of Ian."

Danielle glanced from Walt to the cat.

"And no, Max," Walt said, "I'm not going anywhere either."

"What am I going to do with him?"

"You might start with feeding him. He's pretty hungry."

"Really?" Danielle ran a hand over the cat's body. He was rather thin, a bit underweight.

Gently pushing the cat off her lap, Danielle climbed out of bed. She looked down at him. "Well, if you're hungry, let's go down to the kitchen and get you something to eat."

Max made no attempt to jump down off the bed. He watched as Danielle headed for the door.

Danielle paused at the doorway and looked back at Max, who continued to stare at her. "Well? Are you coming?"

"He doesn't speak your language." Walt looked from Danielle to Max. "Go with her. She's going to get you something to eat."

Max jumped off the bed and followed Danielle to the kitchen.

"I DON'T UNDERSTAND," Danielle said as she sat in the kitchen with Walt, watching Max devour a chicken breast she had cut up for him. "How is it he can understand what you say and not me? I don't get it."

"I told you before, I could never communicate with animals like

I do with Sadie. Not until I died. But now I understand what she's trying to say and she understands me."

"But Sadie understands us. She must be able to, because when you first met she told you Ian wasn't a teacher. How else would she know that if she didn't understand what he was saying?"

"First, Sadie has been around Ian since she was a puppy. She's been around people. She's not stupid."

Max stopped eating and looked up at Walt. He let out a low growl.

"I'm not saying you're stupid," Walt told Max. "But you obviously haven't been around living people much. If you had, I imagine you'd understand more of what Danielle's saying."

Max looked at Walt.

"Her name is Danielle. Dani is a nickname," Walt explained.

"I don't get it!" Danielle said in exasperation.

"You don't get what?" Walt frowned.

"You're talking to the cat and he obviously understands what you're saying. But you're speaking the same language I am, yet you say he doesn't understand me."

"Because it's not what I'm actually saying he understands—it's my thoughts. The thoughts I choose to convey. I could just as easily communicate with him without uttering a single word. But that would be rather rude, wouldn't it? You would start feeling like Lily —how she feels when she can only hear your side of our conversation."

Danielle looked down at Max, who went back to eating. "So why me? Why did he choose me?"

Walt looked at the cat. "I really don't know the answer to that question. But he seems determined to make this his home—and he's staked his claim on you. You did say you wanted a cat."

"I said I was thinking about it. And just because he has staked his claim on me doesn't mean he doesn't belong somewhere. I don't want someone coming along claiming I stole their cat."

Walt watched Max, who was no longer eating but now meticulously grooming himself. After a few moments, Max paused and looked into Walt's eyes.

"He claims he's been hanging out in a vacant house. Grabbed meals from trash cans. Basically he's been living on the street."

"He is kind of thin." Danielle knelt by Max, who immediately started weaving back and forth around her legs, pressing himself into her. She could hear his loud purr. "And he does seem to like me."

"The little monster broke into the house and jumped into your bed." Walt chuckled. "Since he doesn't seem to understand much of what you're saying, I have to believe him when he says he's been living on the street. After all, Bella was able to pick up on some of what you were saying because she's been living with someone— someone like you."

"If I keep him, I should take him to a vet and get him vaccinated."

"This means you're keeping him?"

"Yes. And I should probably see about having him neutered."

Walt frowned. "What do you mean?"

Danielle glanced from Walt to Max. By Walt's question, she suspected neutering house cats wasn't done when he was alive. If she discussed neutering in front of the cat—and the cat understood Walt's side of the conversation…

"Nothing. I'm just thinking aloud." Danielle smiled sweetly.

"HE JUMPED INTO YOUR BED?" Lily asked incredulously the next morning. Danielle had just told her about the cat's unusual appearance.

"Walt said he chose me." Danielle glanced down at Max, who was greedily devouring his breakfast.

"That would have freaked me out, having something jump into my bed in the middle of the night."

"Even if it was Ian?" Danielle giggled.

"Ha-ha." Lily rolled her eyes. "Wouldn't matter who it was. It would still freak me out. So you think we let him in last night when everyone went home?"

"The door was open for a while. It was pretty dark outside. Not surprising no one noticed a black cat in the bushes outside." Danielle poured herself a cup of coffee and joined Lily at the kitchen table.

"Well, you did mention you wanted a cat." Lily sipped her coffee.

Walt appeared a few minutes later. Max was no longer eating his breakfast but curled up contently on Danielle's lap. Lily noticed a chair seemingly move as if someone was sitting down at the table.

"Good morning, Walt," Lily chirped.

Walt looked at Max. "I see he's making himself at home. And, Max, I came to warn you; Sadie and Ian are on their way over. I was looking out the attic window and saw them cross the street. They're cutting through the side yard and should be here in a minute. If you intend to stay, you have to accept them."

Max began to growl. Yet it wasn't a growl exactly, more an unholy gurgling sound.

Lily looked at the cat. "Is he growling?"

"I think Walt said something he didn't like." Danielle glanced over to Walt.

Lily scooted her chair away from Danielle and Max. "He's not going to attack or anything, is he?"

Before Danielle could answer, Ian knocked on the back door. It was still locked. Lily stood up and walked to the kitchen door, keeping a safe distance between her and the snarling cat as she made her way around him.

Lily opened the door and Sadie raced in, charging toward Walt. She came to a screeching halt when she noticed the hissing cat in Danielle's lap. Standing her ground, Sadie began to bark. Max stood up on Danielle's lap, his fur bristling. He snarled at Sadie, batting a front paw in her direction. Danielle looked down nervously, not wanting to get in the middle of a nasty dog and cat fight.

"Knock it off, both of you," Walt snapped, seeing Danielle's discomfort. Sadie and Max immediately looked to Walt. Sadie stopped barking and Max stopped hissing.

"Another cat?" Ian walked over to the table and looked down at the black cat perched in Danielle's lap. He pointed to the far side of the kitchen. "Sadie, go sit down."

Reluctantly, Sadie made her way to the other side of the kitchen and sat down, her eyes never leaving Max.

"Max, put those claws away. If you scratch Danielle, you'll be one sorry cat."

Supremely insulted, Max glared at Walt.

"I understand you would never intentionally scratch her," Walt said. "But it could happen if you start batting at Sadie."

"He just showed up last night," Lily explained.

"Where did he come from?" Ian poured himself a cup of coffee.

"He's a stray. I think I'm going to keep him," Danielle announced.

"You sure he doesn't have a home?"

"I don't think so." Danielle stroked Max's head and looked over at Walt. "He's kind of scrawny. Gobbled up the food I gave him last night and this morning."

"You want me to keep Sadie at my place?" Ian offered. "Maybe I shouldn't bring her over."

"Absolutely not. Max and Sadie will just have to get used to each other," Danielle insisted.

Ian cocked his brows. "Max? How did you come up with that name?"

"Umm...he looks like a Max to me."

Max looked up at Danielle and started to purr. He butted his head against her hand.

"He recognizes his name when you say it," Walt told her. "Now that I think about it, he knew your nickname, Dani, so he obviously understands some of what you say. He may understand more of what you say than I initially assumed."

Danielle glanced down at Max and thought about her announcement last night that she would have him neutered. She smiled. "No, I don't think he does."

Ian frowned. "You don't think he does what?"

THIRTEEN

"Max! Max! Get out here and stop playing games!" Harvey flew through the rooms on the second floor, checking out all the usual hiding places. "I won't make you go back up on the rafters today. We can do that tomorrow. Today I want to check out the vents, and I need you!"

After looking through all the rooms on the second floor, Harvey stood on the landing by the staircase, hands on hips. He looked around and then mumbled, "Damn cat." He considered checking the attic again, but he had been up there twice already. Instead, he trudged down the stairs in search of the elusive black and white cat.

He was passing the doorway to the kitchen when he heard an unusual sound—laughter. Frowning, Harvey paused by the door, cocked his head, and listened. He heard it again. But this time, the sound of feet stampeding in his direction accompanied the laughter.

Harvey moved into the kitchen and directed his attention to the boarded-up window. He leaned toward the plywood and peeked through a knothole, looking into the backyard. To his surprise, he found four teenage boys standing on the other side of the window.

He surmised they had entered through the vacant lot behind Presley House and had climbed over the wooden fence separating the two properties. The lot behind him had not always been vacant. At one time, there was a house, but it had burned down years earlier, and since that time, no one had rebuilt.

"Max, you really need to come out and see this," Harvey mumbled. "Or maybe you shouldn't. Is that why you're in hiding? You saw them coming? Smart cat. Yes, you better stay put. We don't want one of these nasty boys carrying you off. Or doing what mean boys do, stuffing you in a sack and tossing you in the ocean."

BRAD MILLER USED the claw end of his hammer to pry the plywood off the window opening while his buddies kept watch for nosey neighbors. Normally, no one would notice them entering from the rear of the property, but considering the time of year, people in this neighborhood tended to be on alert for any suspicious activity. The last thing Brad needed was to get busted and end up grounded for Halloween, which would mean today's escapade was for nothing.

Brad cursed when the hammer slipped and smashed his right thumb. He shoved the injured digit in his mouth and looked back at his friends. Kevin clutched a sack to his chest while Curt and Jeff looked around nervously. Brad wasn't sure if they were afraid of being caught by one of the neighbors or afraid of encountering the legendary ghost of Presley House. Since everyone knew ghosts only came out at night, Brad wasn't too concerned about running into one on Saturday morning. That was, of course, if he actually believed in ghosts—which he didn't. However, he wasn't so sure what his friends believed, considering their troubled expressions.

"Stop sucking your thumb and get that board off!" Kevin hissed. His eyes darted around nervously.

"You could help me!" Brad snapped. "They used a million nails on this stupid thing."

Kevin reached out, snatched the hammer from Brad, and then shoved the sack at him.

Brad accepted the sack and continued sucking his sore thumb. He watched Kevin, who was now wrestling with the plywood.

"Crap, you weren't kidding about this," Kevin huffed as he persistently tugged on a stubborn nail with the hammer.

"Not sure why we had to do this today. Halloween isn't until next Friday," Jeff said.

"It's either today or tomorrow," Kevin grunted as he wedged the hammer's claw end between the window frame and the plywood.

"Unless we come over here at night, which you guys didn't want to do," Brad reminded them.

"I can't believe none of you have ever been in here before." Kevin loosened one end of the board from the window frame.

"Well, neither have you!" Curt spat.

"Well, duh, I moved here nine months ago. You guys have lived here all your lives." Kevin moved the claw end of the hammer to the other side of the plywood.

"We were going to last year. In fact, Jeff broke this window," Curt boasted.

"Yeah, but don't say that too loudly." Jeff looked around, half expecting some nosey neighbor to jump out of the bushes. "Anyway, you guys were there too."

"So what happened? Why didn't you get inside?" Kevin asked.

"One of the neighbors appeared out of nowhere," Brad explained.

"Out of nowhere?" Kevin chuckled.

"Not really out of nowhere. It just seemed that way. She was out walking her dog; I guess she heard the glass break. Brad saw her running back to her house. We figured she was going to call the cops. So we took off."

"Was this at night?" Kevin asked.

"Yeah. The day before Halloween. But we never got inside," Brad explained, looking down to the sack.

"This is going to be so awesome on YouTube." Curt grinned. "Best prank ever. That lame Hell Raisers gang thinks they're so tough!"

"They're gunna run like crying little girls when we're done with them." Jeff laughed. "And everyone in school will get to see it!"

"Yeah, well, they won't if we can't get inside." Kevin tossed the hammer to the ground. "Come on, guys; help me loosen this some more. All we need is enough room to squeeze in the window."

Inside Presley House, Harvey silently watched as a sneaker-clad foot wiggled its way through the slim opening between the loosened board and the window frame. The four teenage boys each took turns wedging through the tight opening, each landing with a thud in the darkened kitchen. The room's only light came from slivers of sunlight peeking through the edges around the ill-fitted board covering the window.

In each boy's hand was a flashlight, which they immediately

turned on when entering the house. The boys waved the flashlights around, sending streaks of white light along the walls and ceiling of the dusty room.

"Sort of stinks in here," Curt said.

"What did you expect?" Brad asked as he set his flashlight on the counter and proceeded to empty the sack.

"Are we going to set it up in here?" Jeff asked, no longer exploring the room with his flashlight. His friends all stopped waving their lights and gathered around Brad.

"I just want to make sure we have everything," Brad explained.

"We need to check out the house first," Kevin suggested.

"Yeah, we can leave this stuff here." Brad picked up his flashlight. "Doesn't look like we forgot anything."

Harvey stood in the middle of the kitchen and watched the teenagers file out of the room. He could hear their voices as they explored the first floor of the house. Curious, he walked to the counter to see what the boys had brought with them.

Looking down at the counter, he frowned. He wasn't quite sure what he was looking at. Some sort of electrical gadgets perhaps? He picked up one item and then another. He turned knobs and pushed buttons. He had touched and inspected every piece on the counter when he heard the boys trudging up the staircase. Pausing, he listened. Smiling, he looked back to the items on the counter.

Minutes later—Harvey wasn't sure if it was five minutes or sixty, he wasn't good with time—he heard the boys tromping down the stairs and back toward the kitchen. They stood at the kitchen door, discussing where to install a camera they had brought with them. Harvey glanced back down to the peculiar items on the counter. *Surely one of these things isn't a camera.* Harvey then picked up one of the items.

"HEY, GUYS," Kevin called out. His friends stood by the kitchen doorway, debating where to install the spy cameras. "There's another door over here!"

The boys stopped talking and went to investigate.

Brad looked at the door where Kevin stood. "I think it leads to the basement. I remember hearing the house had one."

"Let's go check it out!" Kevin opened the door, revealing the dark stairwell.

"Might as well. This house isn't half as creepy as people say it is." Jeff followed Kevin and Brad through the doorway and down the rickety stairs.

"I know. But it is kind of gross, and there was that dead rat upstairs." Curt followed behind them.

"Yeah, without a head!" Kevin laughed.

"What do you think happened to its head?" Brad asked.

"I figure the other rats probably gnawed it off. I seriously don't think ghosts eat rats." Curt laughed.

"Kind of disappointing. Jeff is right; this house isn't as scary as everyone says it is." Kevin reached the bottom of the stairs and stepped into the basement. Moving the beam from his flashlight over the wall, he checked out his surroundings. His friends gathered around him.

Jeff wrinkled his nose and said, "Maybe it isn't that scary, but it sure stinks nasty!"

"Probably more dead rats," Curt said.

"This is kind of a cool-looking old trunk." Kevin looked down at the trunk.

"My grandma used to have one like that," Brad told them. "Mom sold it for like two hundred bucks at a garage sale."

Kevin looked from the antique trunk to Brad. "Are you serious?"

"Yeah. After Mom sold it, I went on eBay and found another trunk just like it. The bid was already up to two thousand bucks."

"Holy crap, two thousand bucks for an old trunk? Did you tell your mom?" Kevin asked.

"Yeah." Brad shrugged. "She just said something about shipping a trunk that size would cost a fortune."

"I bet it would cost way less than a thousand to ship, and if you sold if for over two thousand—damn—that's good money!" Kevin looked longingly at the trunk.

"What are you thinking, Kev?" Curt asked.

"This old trunk is just sitting here. No one wants it. If we sold it on eBay, that would be like more than five hundred bucks each!" Kevin said excitedly.

"But it isn't our trunk to sell," Brad reminded him.

"It doesn't belong to anyone. We might as well take it," Kevin suggested.

"Kevin is right," Jeff chimed in. "If they wanted the trunk, they would have taken it by now."

"It's not like someone dumped the trunk outside and just left it. It's here, inside the house," Brad said.

"Might as well be sitting outside." Kevin shrugged. "No one obviously wants it, or it still wouldn't be sitting here. I say we take it and sell it on eBay. I don't know about you guys, but I could sure use five hundred dollars."

"How are we going to get it out of here?" Jeff asked.

"I could always borrow my brother's truck. But we'd have to pick it up at night so the neighbors don't see us take it," Curt suggested.

"That's the same as stealing, guys," Brad argued.

"If you don't want to do it, no one is forcing you," Kevin said. "Just means a bigger share for us."

"You guys are never going to get it out of this house without one of the neighbors seeing you," Brad said.

"For five hundred bucks—I mean more than five hundred since you don't want a share—you bet I will find some way to haul this thing out of here." Kevin laughed.

"Let's get it open and see if anything is inside," Jeff suggested. "If it's filled with junk, we'll need to empty it first."

"Might be cool junk," Curt said. "More for us to sell on eBay!"

"How about it, Miller, are you with us, or are you going to wuss out?" Kevin challenged.

Brad silently considered a moment and then let out a deep sigh. "Fine. I'm in." He handed his flashlight to Jeff. "Hold this with yours and keep the light on the trunk while I help Kevin open it. The lid looks heavy. I know the one on the trunk Mom sold needed two people to open it."

Kevin handed his flashlight to Curt. Curt and Jeff, each holding two flashlights, pointed the beams at the trunk while Kevin positioned himself on one side of the trunk and Brad on the other, preparing to open it.

FOURTEEN

H arvey stood at the basement doorway, silently watching the four teenagers as they prepared to open the trunk. He was fairly certain he had heard them correctly. They intended to steal the trunk. Chuckling to himself, Harvey wondered how anxious they would be to take it with them once they got the lid open and discovered what he had tucked inside.

They really didn't look much different from the boys he once knew—back when he had been alive. He glanced down at his loose-fitting denim pants and rope belt, then back up to the boys, who each wore a pair of fitted denim pants. They must come from money, he thought, to be able to wear clothes tailored to fit their bodies, yet they intended to steal something. The thought made Harvey angry.

BRAD TUGGED on his side of the trunk. "Are you sure it isn't locked?"

Curt flashed a light beam over the front of the trunk "I don't see any lock."

"You want us to help?" Jeff offered.

"No, you just hold the lights on it. I think it's coming loose. Just stuck," Brad said with a grunt.

"It sure smells nasty. Hope we can get the smell out or no one will buy it." Kevin continued to tug on the lid, urging it to open.

"If we sell it on eBay, they won't know how it smells," Jeff said just before the lid gave way and flew open, exposing the trunk's contents.

Jeff and Curt saw it first. They each let out a scream worthy of a horror movie, dropped their flashlights, charged for the doorway, and raced up the stairs.

Confused and virtually plunged into darkness, Brad and Kevin grappled with the flashlights rolling around on the concrete floor while cursing their friends' hasty departure. They still did not know what had sent the two boys running.

Kevin managed to grab a flashlight first. He aimed it at the open trunk. Instead of fleeing as his friends had, he stood mesmerized, looking at the contorted body of the man shoved rudely into the wooden container. The dead man's eyes stared blankly up at Kevin.

"Bra-Bra-Bra-Brad…" Kevin stammered, unable to look away.

After retrieving a flashlight for himself, Brad stood up straight and turned to the trunk. His eyes widened. Like Kevin, he seemed riveted to the spot.

"Is it real?" Brad whispered.

"Sure looks real."

"Is he dead?"

"I think that's what we smell." Kevin gulped.

"You think we should check for a pulse?" Brad asked.

"I'm not touching it. Go ahead. You can if you want." Kevin took a step back from the trunk. The two boys stood there a moment in silence, just staring.

"I'm getting out of here!" Brad suddenly announced. He and Kevin turned from the trunk at the same time, bumping into each other. Each shoving the other one away, they scrambled to the doorway and up the stairs to the first level.

When they got upstairs, they noticed the front door wide open. Apparently, their friends had left by that exit instead of going back to the kitchen and squeezing through the window opening. They decided the open front door looked like a far better escape route. Without a second thought, Kevin and Brad rushed to the open doorway and out of the house. They couldn't get outside quick enough.

Kevin and Brad ran down the front walkway leading from

BOBBI HOLMES

Presley House to the street. They expected to find Jeff and Curt waiting for them. What they hadn't expected to find was the police car parked in front of the house, with their friends sitting on the curb, looking up into the faces of Officers Morelli and Henderson.

HANDS ON HIPS, Joe watched as Brad and Kevin raced in his direction. The boys halted midway. They stood mute and stared, looking from the officers to the parked patrol car, and then to their friends who sat quietly on the curb. Joe doubted they were aware of the police presence until that moment. Narrowing his eyes, he stared at the two boys and cricked his finger at them, motioning for them to come closer.

Brad rushed forward, asking, "Did they call you? How did you get here so quick?"

Kevin trailed behind Brad, yet kept looking over his shoulder, trying to figure out if it might be possible to make a run for it. Unfortunately, he knew both officers and they knew his parents. It was a small town.

"Sit!" Officer Henderson snapped, pointing to the curb. Obediently Brad and Kevin joined their friends and sat down.

Joe stood over the boys, glancing from them to the house. "So is this everyone?"

Before anyone could answer, a female voice called out, "You boys should be ashamed of yourselves!" Millie Samson shuffled over from across the street.

"We're taking care of this, Millie," Brian said with a sigh.

Ignoring Brian, Millie continued in their direction, waving her finger at the silent teenage boys.

"I know your parents! You should be ashamed of yourselves! Breaking in like common criminals!" Millie stabbed an angry finger in their direction.

"We've got this, Millie," Joe said patiently.

"You wouldn't have anything if I hadn't called you after seeing these four hooligans climbing over the fence!"

"And we do appreciate you calling," Brian said lazily. "But we have it all under control."

"There's a dead body!" Curt shouted. The three adults turned abruptly in his direction and stared.

82

"Excuse me?" Joe asked.

"There's a dead body in Presley House."

Millie gasped; her hand flew to her mouth. "Oh my!"

Brian glared at the boys. "Is this some Halloween prank? You've already upset Mrs. Samson enough. This is not funny."

Brad looked up into Joe's face. "He's telling the truth." Last summer the sergeant had dated Brad's sister. But the last time Brad had seen Joe had nothing to do with his sister. It was about another body found in Frederickport, one that might have been saved had Brad made other choices at the time.

"A dead body? Whose dead body?" Millie fiddled nervously with the zipper on the jacket of her jogging suit as she stared up at Presley House.

"There's a trunk in the basement," Brad explained. "We opened it. There's a body in there."

"Are you sure?" Brian asked.

"Oh yeah!" the four boys chorused.

"These two just left us," Kevin said angrily, elbowing Curt, who sat to his right.

Curt rubbed his now sore arm. "It just freaked us out. Figured you would follow us."

"Aren't you going to go in there? See who it is?" Millie asked.

"Yes, Millie. But first, we need to get all the information. It would probably be best if you go on back home so we can get this worked out. Chances are, it's not a real dead body, just a dummy some kids shoved in there to freak people out." Brian gently led Millie by her arm back across the street. She tried to argue with him, but he refused to back down.

Joe signaled for the boys to stay quiet. He would ask more questions when Brian returned and Millie was out of earshot. As it was, he imagined once she stepped inside her house, she would be on the phone calling all her friends, telling them about the so-called dead body in Presley House.

He silently watched Brian take Millie across the street. After leaving Millie at her house, Brian pulled out his cellphone and began making a call as he returned to Joe and the boys.

"Are you sure it was a real body you saw?" Joe asked when Brian returned and was off the cellphone.

"It wasn't no dummy," Jeff insisted. The other boys nodded in agreement.

The two officers stood over the boys, who remained sitting on the curb.

"Is there anyone else in the house?" Brian asked.

"Just the dead guy," Curt said.

"Did you guys come with anyone else? Just you four?" Joe asked.

"It was just us," Brad said.

"Okay, Brad, tell us what you think you saw," Joe told him.

Brad took a deep breath before answering. "We were checking out the house and went down to the basement. There's an antique trunk down there, and we just wanted to see what was inside. Jeff and Curt held the flashlights while Kevin and I opened it. The lid was kind of stuck."

"And it smelled bad," Jeff piped up.

"When we opened the lid, Jeff and Curt just took off. They saw the body; I guess it freaked them out."

"You can't say you guys weren't freaked out too!" Jeff interrupted.

"Maybe we were, but we didn't just run off like a couple of babies," Brad returned.

"Yeah, real nice of them to just run out on us," Kevin snapped.

"I told you—"

Joe interrupted Curt. "You boys can argue later. Let Brad finish."

"They dropped the flashlights," Brad continued. "When Kevin and I picked up a flashlight, we looked in the trunk and we saw him. He was all…well, sort of all folded up in the trunk…but his eyes were open. Real creepy."

"Brad wanted to check for a pulse, but I told him I wasn't gunna touch it, but he was welcome to."

"Did you take his vitals?" Brian asked.

Brad shook his head. "No. I could tell he was dead. And then… well, all I wanted was to get out of there as fast as possible. When we saw you out here, I thought the guys had called you. But it didn't make sense. I couldn't figure how you could get here so quick."

"Mrs. Samson saw you boys climbing over the fence. She called us," Joe explained.

"Yeah, I sorta figured that out," Brad said sheepishly.

"Can we go home now?" Curt asked.

Brian looked at Curt and shook his head. "I don't think so. I already called for backup. They should be here in a minute, and then a couple of us will go in and see what all the ruckus is about. Chances are you boys mistook a Halloween dummy for a body."

"It was real," Brad insisted.

"If it was real, can you describe what he looked like?" Joe said.

The boys sat quietly for a moment before Kevin spoke up. "I know who he looks like! One of those guys the cops are looking for!"

"Yeah," Brad looked over at Kevin. "I think you're right. He did kinda look like one of those guys."

"You mean Chuck Christiansen and Bart Haston?" Joe asked.

Kevin shrugged. "I don't know what their names are. Those dudes who killed that rich guy and his wife. I saw their pictures in the paper. The dead guy sorta looks like one of them."

Before they could ask more questions, backup arrived. The boys were instructed to stay put on the curb while Joe and Brian went into the house with several of the arriving officers.

BRIAN AND JOE stood in the basement of Presley House, with several other officers, looking into the empty trunk.

"Just what I thought, no dead body," Brian said.

"But they were right about one thing, this smells nasty." Joe wrinkled his nose.

One of the other officers, who had his flashlight pointed inside the trunk, moved the beam around, inspecting the trunk's interior.

"It looks wet. What is that? And on the side, is that blood?" Joe leaned closer.

"I don't know, but that smell is making me ill." Brian almost gagged. "But yeah, that does look like blood. Damn."

"Is it possible there was a dead body in here just a few minutes ago?" Joe asked.

Brian looked up from the trunk into Joe's eyes. "If so, then that means someone is still in the house."

FIFTEEN

C urled up on Danielle's lap, Max rested his chin on her arm. Considering his loud purr, Danielle was fairly certain he wasn't sleeping, in spite of the fact his eyes were closed, and he hadn't moved for over ten minutes. Her hand gently stroked his black fur and occasionally rubbed the white tips of his ears—the only part of him that wasn't jet-black. Occasionally a drop of spittle would escape his mouth, dampening the sleeve of Danielle's jacket.

They sat outside on the new swing Ian had installed in one of the trees in front of the house. Here she could watch the cars drive by—although, there was never much traffic on her street—and listen to the faint sound of the breakers as they washed up on the beach beyond Ian's house. Lily and Ian had taken Sadie for a walk on the beach. Walt was inside doing whatever Walt did when no one was in the house—what that was, Danielle had no idea.

She closed her eyes and breathed deeply, taking in the clean ocean scent. It was definitely fall with a hint of winter creeping in. The toe of her right shoe continually pressed against the ground, keeping the swing swaying gently in a steady and soothing motion.

The sound of an approaching car broke the silence. Danielle opened her eyes and was surprised to see a police car parking in front of her house. It wasn't until the driver got out of the vehicle did she know who it was: Police Chief McDonald.

"You look comfortable," MacDonald greeted her as he approached the swing.

"Morning, Chief."

Max opened his eyes and raised his head. He stared at the uniformed man who now stood several feet from the swing.

"Who's your friend?" The chief smiled down at the black cat.

"This is Max." Danielle nodded to the empty space on the swing. "Have a seat."

"I didn't know you had a cat." MacDonald sat next to Danielle.

"He sort of happened to me." Danielle smiled. Max closed his eyes and rested his chin back on Danielle's arm.

"Sounds about right." MacDonald chuckled and then asked, "Have you read the morning paper?"

"I would have, had someone not stolen it. Gee, maybe I need to file a police report?" Danielle joked.

"I suppose I could rouse up that character across the street. He looks like he might be a likely suspect."

"Yeah, normally it is Ian. Yet he's nice about it, lets us read it first…Well, maybe not always first. But no, he swears it wasn't him this time. So what's up?"

"It wouldn't have even been in the paper if Millie Samson hadn't called them." MacDonald leaned back in the swing.

"Millie from the museum?"

MacDonald nodded. "Yes."

"So what's going on?"

"Millie lives down the street from Presley House."

Max lifted his head and looked at MacDonald.

"Yesterday four teenage boys broke into the house. She saw them climbing over the back fence and called us."

"A Halloween prank?" Danielle asked.

"It started out that way. They were going to install some spy cameras, I assume to set up some pranks to play on their classmates and post it on YouTube."

"Gotta love what YouTube has done for today's youth."

"When Joe and Brian arrived, two of them were running out of the house like the devil himself was chasing them. They rounded them up, made them sit on the curb, and tried to get them to calm down. They weren't making any sense. Before they had a chance to find out what was going on, the other two came running out."

"Running out of the house? Don't tell me, Presley House's

ghost, the one who likes to dabble with electricity, played a few tricks on them?"

"I'm not quite sure."

Danielle continued to pet Max. "What do you mean?"

"They claimed there was a dead body in the house. Stuffed in an old trunk in the basement."

"Claimed? You mean there wasn't one?"

"When Brian, Joe and the other officers went down there, the chest was empty. But the boys swore they saw one. My men searched the property; they couldn't find anyone—alive or dead."

"That's weird."

"The thing is, they brought the trunk in. And according to the lab, it looks like there could have been a body in there—and fairly recently."

"How do they figure that?" Danielle asked.

"Body fluids—blood."

"Yuck." Danielle wrinkled her nose.

"The smell alone would knock you over."

"So what happened to the body?"

"I don't know. That's why I'm here."

Danielle smiled up at the chief. "Well, I certainly don't have it!"

"I was going to ask you if it would be possible for a spirit to make people see things that aren't there."

"I've never seen that happen. But it doesn't mean it's impossible. I suppose I could run it by Walt. But you said you were *going* to ask me?"

"After the lab results came back, I decided it wasn't some illusion. I think there really was a body in the trunk."

"Ahhh...well, a spirit—one who has harnessed energy—could be capable of moving a body. But hiding it? That might be a little more tricky."

"That's what I wondered." MacDonald leaned back in the swing again and gazed across the street, thinking of Presley House and not the view before him.

"Any idea who the dead guy might be? If we're talking fresh body fluids, I don't imagine it belongs to the spirit currently haunting the place."

"According to the boys, it could be either Christiansen or Haston."

"Either? Those two look nothing alike."

"I know." MacDonald turned to Danielle. He reached out to pet Max, yet retracted his hand when Max attempted to take a bite out of his finger.

"Max," Danielle scolded, running her hand over his head, "that wasn't nice."

"I don't think he likes me," MacDonald murmured, looking down at his fingers, grateful they had escaped the cat's razor-sharp teeth.

"So why do you say it might be either of them?" Danielle asked.

"According to the boys, the dead man looked like one of the men they saw in the paper—Christiansen and Haston. But they didn't know which one was which in the photograph."

"Couldn't you just show them the newspaper clipping, and let them point to the one the dead guy looked like?"

"I would have—yet at this point there is no body, and if I bring the boys in to identify a body we can't find—well, let's just say we've had more than our share of bad press over the last few months."

"Sorry about that."

"Hey, it wasn't your fault."

"I know…but still…What now?"

"I was hoping I might convince you to go over to Presley House with me."

"Why?"

"Maybe you could reason with the spirit, find out where he put the body and why he moved it."

"Spirits don't always do things for a specific reason. Sometimes they just like to mess with us."

"Well, this one is messing with me."

"I suppose I could try," Danielle offered.

Instead of a purr, Max began to growl, his gaze fixed on MacDonald.

"Is he going to attack me?" MacDonald asked nervously, looking at the angry cat sitting on the lap next to him.

"Wow, he really does not seem to like you." Danielle stood up and cradled Max in her arms. "I'll be right back."

MacDonald watched as Danielle took Max to the house and put him inside, closing the door so he couldn't get back out. A moment later, Max appeared at the parlor window. He sat on the windowsill, staring out at MacDonald, his tail swishing back and forth.

"I know where I've seen that cat before," MacDonald said when Danielle returned to the swing.

"Where?" Danielle glanced briefly to the parlor window and then sat back down next to MacDonald.

"At least a cat that looks just like him. Black as night with white ears. An unusual combination. And if you say he found you, then it could be that cat."

"What do you know about him?"

"A few years back, maybe five or more, one of my neighbors came to me, upset about a guy he worked with who was bragging about how he intended to drown a cat when he went fishing that weekend. Apparently, the guy's young daughter had been encouraging a stray, and when the cat brought her a gift of a dead mouse, she freaked out."

"Cats are known for bringing gifts. But drown the poor cat? I loathe people like that."

"My neighbor had called animal control, but he didn't think they were going to do anything, so he came to me. I stopped by the guy's house. He was kind of a jerk. Admitted to having the cat, but claimed he was taking it to the shelter."

"You rescued Max?" Danielle asked.

"If it is the same cat, yeah, I suppose, in a manner of speaking." MacDonald shrugged. "I got him to give me the cat."

"What did you do with him?"

"I turned him over to animal control."

"Maybe that's why he doesn't like you!"

"If it is the same cat, I seriously doubt he remembers that."

"You would be surprised what animals remember. I assume they adopted him out?"

"Actually, he was going to be euthanized."

"You were going to kill him!" Danielle shrieked. "I don't blame Max for wanting to bite your finger off!"

"I wasn't going to do it!" MacDonald said defensively. "It was animal control. Do you know how many unwanted cats they have down at the shelter?"

"Killing them is not the answer! Which is one reason I intend to make an appointment to have Max neutered when he gets his shots."

"If it is the same cat, he's already been neutered," MacDonald said. "I remember them telling me that down at the shelter. So obviously the cat I picked up belonged to someone before he met Victoria."

"Victoria?"

"The jerk's daughter."

"They were going to kill a neutered cat?"

"Don't yell at me. I don't work for animal control."

"Obviously they didn't do it, if you think Max might be the same cat. Do you know what happened?"

"I ran into one of the guys from animal control and asked him if by chance they found the cat a home, and he told me he had escaped."

"Escaped?"

"They suspect some shelter volunteer was responsible for a few of the cats escaping."

"It could be the same cat." Danielle glanced back to the parlor window. Max was still watching them from his perch on the windowsill. "He's been on his own for a while, living on the street."

"How do you know that?"

"Walt told me."

"How does Walt know?"

"Max told him."

"Max...never mind...I don't think I can wrap my brain around much more...talking ghosts...talking cats..."

"I didn't say Max talked. Don't be silly." Danielle laughed.

"But you said Max told Walt."

"Sure. But it's more a...a communications exchange. Everyone knows cats can't talk."

SIXTEEN

W alt walked into the parlor and found Max sitting at the window, staring outside. "Max? I thought you were with Danielle."

Max didn't acknowledge Walt's entrance. Instead, his tail continued to swish back and forth, his gold eyes fixed on Danielle and MacDonald.

Walt walked to the window and looked outside. "Ahh, she's visiting with the chief. He isn't such a bad guy."

Max let out a low growling gurgle.

Walt cocked a brow and looked down at Max. "So you don't like the chief?"

Max continued to growl.

"What do you mean he wants her to go to Presley House?" Walt frowned. "What exactly do you know about Presley House?"

"WHY ARE you working on a Sunday, anyway? Don't you ever take time off?" Danielle asked from the passenger seat of the police car. They drove toward Presley House.

"Actually, I'm leaving on Wednesday. I'll be gone for a week."

"Vacation?" Danielle asked.

"Yes. I could use some R and R."

"But in October? Don't your kids have school?"

"The boys aren't coming. They're staying with my sister."

"Ahh...you're going away with your lady friend!"

"Yep." The chief grinned.

"Where are you going?"

"Hawaii."

"Hawaii? You rat! You guys didn't say anything about it at the party!"

"We're not really broadcasting this. In fact, I haven't even said anything to Joe or Brian. Figured it's no one's business. They just know I'm taking off for a few days. And this is all pretty new for me...getting serious with someone who isn't the boys' mother."

"I'm flattered you told me."

"I know your secrets; I figure you can keep mine."

"Well, I won't tell anyone. I hope you have a wonderful time. You deserve it."

"Thanks, Danielle. I'm looking forward to it. Which is why I would love to wrap this up before I take off on Wednesday."

"Yeah, I can see where you wouldn't want to worry about some random body popping up while you're in Hawaii."

"I'm not even going to answer my phone when I'm over there. Unless, of course, it's my sister."

The chief pulled up in front of Presley House and parked. He sat with Danielle in the car and looked up at the weathered Victorian, its windows boarded save for one lone window on the second floor

"So what's the story on Presley House? I asked Walt if he knew anything about it, and he didn't."

"Presley House was built after he died, I think in the early thirties, so it doesn't surprise me that he hadn't heard about it. From what I understand, the same family has owned it since it was built."

"I assume their name was Presley?" Danielle stared at the house.

"Yes."

"Umm...any relation to..."

"Elvis?" The chief grinned.

"Yeah. Any relation?"

"No. I asked that question myself when I first saw the house."

"Drat. I was kinda hoping I'd be meeting Elvis's ghost today." Danielle sighed.

"Sorry, kid," the chief said with a chuckle.

"So what do you know about its history? When Brian and Joe mentioned it, they didn't seem to know anything about it or who the ghost might be."

"I don't think either one of them considers there is a ghost."

"Not even after the magic lamp?"

"Joe figures there's a logical explanation for everything."

"What about Brian?"

"I don't know what Brian thinks these days."

"So what do you know?"

The chief studied the house. His fingertips lightly tapped the steering wheel. "The house was built by the Presley family. I don't know too much about them, just what Ben, from the museum, once told me. I know they had two boys—twins. The only other thing Ben could really recall about the family was that his father was surprised when they just upped and moved about a month before the boys graduated from high school. I guess it was all very sudden and unexpected."

"Would it have been during the war?"

"Yeah. I think a couple years before the end of the war. Maybe the sons decided to enlist before graduation. I just know the family moved yet kept the house. It's been rented out off and on over the years."

"It obviously hasn't been rented for some time. It's a shame how run-down it is."

"Just keeps getting worse and worse with each passing year. They couldn't keep it rented, so they just stopped trying. It hasn't been rented since I've been here."

"I'm assuming it has something to do with the ghost?" Danielle asked.

"I just know that every Halloween people report strange things happening at the house. I don't know the details of those early tenants or why they didn't stay. I just know the house has been a major pain for me over the years. But until this year, the only thing I ever witnessed was malicious mischief from the local teenagers."

"What do you mean until this year?"

The chief turned to Danielle. "If you would have asked me last month if the house was haunted, I would have laughed and said no. Even considering what I've learned from you, I never really thought Presley House was haunted. But with that lamp Brian and Joe swear turned on without electricity and the body the boys swear they saw, I'm beginning to wonder."

Danielle unbuckled her seatbelt. "Well, should we go in?"

DANIELLE AND MACDONALD stood in the entry hall of Presley House, each holding a flashlight. They had left the front door wide open to let in the sunlight. Yet even with the door open, it was too dark to see clearly.

The entry flowed into the living room; its ceiling reached to the ceiling height of the second floor. Random beams of sunlight cut through the space, breaking in from the edges of the windows, those not covered completely with sheets of plywood.

Danielle looked up, noting the cobwebs and floating dust particles glistening, illuminated by the shafts of light slipping into the house. It smelled dusty, stale. When she had first stepped into Marlow House, she had felt an instant harmony—good feng shui some might call it—in spite of the fact it was haunted and had been closed up for decades. She did not experience the same positive sensation with Presley House.

"This is not a happy place," Danielle blurted out.

"Happy? No, I wouldn't call it that."

"What I mean…I don't like it here. It makes me feel…let's just hurry up and do what we have to do and get out of here." Danielle felt a chill go up her spine.

"Are you okay?"

"Yeah…let's just do this." Danielle cleared her throat and called out, "Hello? Is anyone here? We are here to help you."

Silence.

"You want to follow me?" the chief asked as he pointed his flashlight toward the living room.

"I suppose so…" Danielle wanted to go home.

"Hello?" Danielle called out again.

No response.

MacDonald led her through the living room, kitchen, dining room, and small parlor.

"I know the boys found the body. Why don't you show us where you put it? You put it somewhere, didn't you?" she asked the elusive spirit.

Silence.

"The basement is down here." The chief opened the door leading to the basement stairwell.

"Basement?" Danielle squeaked. *I lied to the ghost; I really don't want to find the body.* Reluctantly, she followed MacDonald down the rickety wooden stairs. Once in the basement, they moved the beams of their flashlights over the walls of the small cement room. It was empty.

"The trunk was here." MacDonald used the light from his flashlight to show her where the trunk had been. A rectangular stain marred the concrete floor.

"We know there was a body down here. In the trunk. You moved it, didn't you?" Danielle called out. "Please show us where you put it, and then we'll leave you alone. Unless you want to talk to me. Maybe I can help you."

Silence.

"I have a gift," Danielle called out. "I can often see spirits. But you have to show yourself to me. If you stay hidden, I can't help you. Why are you here? Why do you come back to this house every Halloween? Or are you always here? People only notice you on Halloween?"

Silence.

Danielle sighed. "I don't know, Chief. I'm not getting anything. Other than the fact this place is creeping me out big time. Can we go back upstairs? I'm getting claustrophobia down here."

"Sure."

MacDonald let Danielle go up the stairs first. When they got to the first floor, he suggested they check out the second floor.

"Maybe he's up here," MacDonald said as they made their way up the staircase leading to the second floor.

"I just hope I don't trip over the dead body. Maybe you should go first." Danielle stepped aside when they reached the second-floor landing, letting the chief lead the way. Together they explored every room on the upper level, even making it to the attic. Yet there was not a glimmer of paranormal activity. Even the few remaining light-bulbs screwed into the chandelier over the entry hall remained unlit.

"I thought it was worth a shot," MacDonald said with a heavy sigh when they were back outside again.

Danielle watched as he locked the front door. "Where did you get the key?"

"We had the locksmith come over yesterday. Still haven't been able to get ahold of the owners of the property."

"I'm really sorry I wasn't able to help. But like I told you before, I can't necessarily communicate with all spirits. I was never able to see my parents or my husband."

"I just appreciate you giving it a shot."

They were halfway down the walkway—leading from Presley House to the street—when they heard someone shouting for the chief. They looked up. It was Millie Samson.

"Damn," the chief grumbled. "I wonder what she wants now. I'll meet you at the car."

"Okay." Danielle paused a moment and watched as MacDonald walked down the street, meeting Millie halfway. As the two talked, Danielle turned and faced Presley House again, giving it a final look.

She was just about to turn away and walk to the car when she noticed movement on the second floor. Using one hand to shield her eyes from the sun, she looked up into the bedroom window.

Their eyes met—Danielle and the ghost of Presley House. He looked much younger than she had imagined he would look. For some reason she had expected a spirit of an older person, not that of a teenage boy. The way he stared at her, she wondered if he knew she could see him. Smiling, she raised her right hand and waved at him. The gesture caught him by surprise. He clearly had not expected that.

Excited, Danielle glanced over her shoulder at the chief. He was still talking to Millie some distance away. Anxious to tell the chief about the ghost and thinking they could return to the house and find the body, she looked back at the window.

The ghost looked at her and shook his head, as if to say no. Danielle frowned, not knowing what he meant. The ghost then pointed to the chief and then raised a finger to his lips as if to silence her. He shook his head again—*no*.

It was clear to Danielle; the spirit did not want the chief to know he had shown himself.

"SORRY THAT TOOK SO LONG," the chief said when he met Danielle back at the car.

Danielle glanced up at the house. The spirit was no longer standing in the window. "Is everything okay?" she asked.

"Yes. Millie just wanted to rehash yesterday. She's still upset about what the boys said about a dead body in the house."

"Yeah, I can imagine," Danielle said dully, getting into the car. Her gaze continued to focus on the upstairs window of Presley House.

"Is everything okay, Danielle?"

"Yeah, fine."

SEVENTEEN

Max greeted Danielle the minute she walked into Marlow House. He wove in and out between her legs, rubbing against her while purring loudly. Smiling, she leaned down and picked him up.

"Someone is happy to see you," Walt said when he appeared the next moment.

"I see that." Danielle grinned, rubbing the side of her face against Max's neck. "Lily back yet?"

"No. I imagine Sadie's enjoying her walk on the beach."

"I love when Sadie greets me, but this is nice too." Danielle kissed Max on the head.

Walt waved his hand. A lit cigar appeared. "He was worried about you."

Danielle looked up to Walt as she carried Max to the parlor. "Worried about me, why?"

Walt followed Danielle. They both sat down—Danielle in the love seat with Max, and Walt in the chair across from her.

"He didn't want you going to Presley House."

Danielle glanced down at the cat now curled up on her lap. "Presley House? What does Max know about Presley House?"

"That's where he's been living for the last few years."

"Really?" Danielle looked down at Max and scratched his ear.

Max opened his eyes, yawned, and closed his eyes again. "What does he say about the resident ghost? I assume he could see him."

"According to Max, his name is Harvey. Did you meet him today?"

"I went into the house with the chief, but he wouldn't show himself. Harvey, you say? That's an old-fashioned name. Makes me think of that giant invisible rabbit."

"Invisible rabbit?" Walt frowned.

Danielle chuckled. "It's an old movie. I'll find it for you to watch sometime. It's a classic."

"So your little trip today was a waste?" Walt took a drag off his cigar and then blew out a series of smoke rings. He watched them float upwards and disappear.

"When I said he didn't show himself—that wasn't exactly true. He didn't show himself when the chief and I were going through the house, but when we were outside, getting ready to leave, I saw him in the window."

"And you didn't go back in?"

"No. I had the feeling he wouldn't communicate with me if I went back in—at least not with the chief there. In fact, I didn't tell the chief I saw him."

"Hmm...interesting. I take it you didn't find the body?"

"How did you know about a body?"

"Max, of course. Did you find it?"

"Some teenage boys found it yesterday." Danielle went on to tell Walt the entire story the chief had told her, ending with the disappearing body and the smelly trunk. Walt, in his own way, communicated Danielle's story to Max, who responded by meowing loudly.

"He doesn't understand why Harvey moved the body," Walt explained. "He was under the impression Harvey wanted the boys to find it."

"Well, they did find the body," Danielle pointed out. "Harvey looks like a teenager, by the way. Which probably means he died when he was young."

"You think that's always the case?" Walt waved his hand; his cigar vanished.

"What do you mean?"

"I wonder...if I had lived to—let's say Marie's age—would it be possible for my spirit to appear as a younger version of myself, or would I have to remain for eternity as an old man?"

"For one thing, your eternity isn't here on this plane. If you're capable of changing your clothes—which we both know is nothing but an illusion—then I would have to assume it's possible."

"Interesting thought…So what now? Are you going to tell the chief about the body?"

"I suppose I should. But I wonder what Harvey did with it. And why is he haunting the house? Did Max tell you?"

Their conversation was interrupted when Danielle heard the front door open and Sadie race into the house, sliding as she turned to make her way into the parlor. Skidding on her way in, she continued at full speed, charging straight for Danielle before coming to an abrupt halt and barking at Max, who was now standing on Danielle's lap, hissing, his paw extended, batting Sadie's nose.

"Sadie, stop that barking!" Ian said as he entered the parlor with Lily. "Or I'm going to leave you at home."

"No, you aren't!" Danielle reached out and petted Sadie, who was no longer barking but standing at attention, her tail and butt wagging energetically. Danielle had gently pushed Max back, preventing him from smacking Sadie. "These two are just going to have to learn how to get along. In fact, I see them becoming best buds."

"Did you hear that, Sadie and Max?" Walt asked. "Danielle expects you two to become friends."

Sadie and Max looked at Walt for a moment and then back to each other. They each sat down while never breaking their stare.

"See, they like each other," Lily said cheerfully as she stood by Ian and looked down at the dog and cat. Max responded by giving Sadie a final smack on the nose, to which Sadie replied with a grunt before flopping on the ground, her chin resting on her paws as she looked up to the cat occupying Danielle's lap.

"I hope Sadie isn't going to be too much trouble," Ian murmured.

Danielle looked up to Lily inquisitively.

"Ian has to fly to New York on Tuesday. I told him he could leave Sadie here."

"Of course." Danielle looked from Lily to Ian. "Business?"

"Yes. I was hoping to get out of this one. I won't be back until the first."

"You'll miss Halloween?" Danielle asked.

Ian looked at Lily, reached out, and squeezed her hand. "Unfortunately."

"You know Sadie is always welcome." Danielle reached down and patted Sadie. "These two will get used to each other."

"Lily told me you were going to try to get Max into the vet I use for Sadie."

"Yeah, I'm going to call in the morning. But I need to pick up a cat carrier."

"You could always just borrow one," Lily suggested.

"Who do we know around here who has a cat?"

"Our new neighbor?" Lily suggested.

MAX CROUCHED NERVOUSLY in the cat carrier Danielle had borrowed from her neighbor Heather. He peeked out from the small jail door into the examining room, where Danielle waited for the vet. She had placed the carrier on the examining table but left Max locked inside while she took a seat a few feet away. He meowed pitifully.

The vet assistant entered the room, introduced herself, and removed Max from the carrier, giving him a brief exam. She asked Danielle a few questions and then returned Max to the carrier and told Danielle the vet would be in shortly. She left the room. A few minutes later, she returned with the vet.

"Ms. Boatman, nice to meet you. I'm Dr. Lenard," the vet said as he entered the room, extending a hand to Danielle, who accepted it and gave it a brief shake. "I understand you've taken in a stray and want to make it official." He turned his attention to the cat carrier.

"Yes, he sort of adopted me. His name is Max." Danielle stood up and watched as the vet removed Max from the carrier.

"Max?" The vet sounded surprised. He stared at Max, who now sat on the exam table, curiously looking around the room.

"I know this cat," Dr. Lenard said. "It has to be him, the markings are so unusual." He gently pushed Max down on the table and proceeded to examine his belly. "I know I neutered this cat. This is Max," he said to Danielle.

"Are you saying he isn't a stray? He has an owner out there?"

Danielle felt her heart sink. She had already become attached to the quirky and affectionate cat.

"I don't doubt he was a stray. I'm just surprised you chose the name Max. That was what she named him."

"I don't understand, does he have a home or not?"

"He does now." Dr. Leonard smiled. "I always wondered what happened to him. Hoped someone had picked him up and taken him in. But Max...I still can't get over that...the same name!"

"Can you please tell me what you're talking about?" Danielle was confused.

"I'm sorry." The vet laughed. "This just caught me by surprise. Mrs. Bentley, a sweet little old gal, had just lost her cat; she was heartsick. One of my friends had taken in a pregnant stray and was trying to place the kittens. I told Mrs. Bentley and she picked out a little black fellow with white ears. She named him Max."

"You think he's my Max?"

"The markings are unusual. He appears to be about the right age—and he's been neutered. I neutered Max for Mrs. Bentley."

"So where is she?"

"About two years after she adopted Max, she broke her hip, and her family put her in a nursing home. It was supposed to be temporary while she recuperated. One of the neighbors fed Max. There was a doggy door in the house, so he was used to coming and going, but he always stuck around the house. Unfortunately, Mrs. Bentley came down with pneumonia while she was in the nursing home and died."

"Oh, that's so sad." Danielle reached out and stroked Max. "So what happened to Max?"

"From what I understand, the day after she died, her daughter came to pick up the cat. She was going to take him to the shelter. But Max wasn't at the house. He had disappeared."

"So they didn't take him to the shelter?"

"No. It was really strange, because Mrs. Bentley was in the nursing home for almost a month, and during that time Max stuck around the house. Neighbor saw him every day when she'd come over to feed him. Yet right after Mrs. Bentley died, the cat vanished. It was like he knew."

Danielle looked down at Max; her thumb rubbed his right ear. "I imagine he did."

"If he is the same cat, and I would swear he is, I wonder where he's been all this time."

"You aren't the only one who recognized Max. Police Chief MacDonald had a story about him too."

"Really?"

"He turned a cat over to animal control that looked just like this one. I guess Max was hanging out somewhere where he wasn't wanted, and the guy who nabbed him had plans to toss him into the ocean."

The vet shook his head. "People can be cruel when it comes to dealing with stray cats. I don't understand that. If he was turned over to animal control, he must have been adopted out."

"No. According to the chief, he escaped."

The vet chuckled. "That sounds like the Max I remember. It's almost as if he knew Mrs. Bentley's daughter planned to take him to the shelter. I wonder where he's been living."

Danielle suspected the late Mrs. Bentley had visited Max one final time—before moving on. She was probably aware of her daughter's intentions and knew of the high kill rate of the local shelter, so she may have urged Max to leave before her daughter arrived. Yet she kept that thought to herself. Instead, she said, "I think he's been hanging out at Presley House."

"Presley House? You mean that old boarded-up house on the north side of town that everyone says is haunted?"

"Yeah. Someone I know says she remembers seeing this cat hanging around there," Danielle lied.

"That would explain where he's been. I imagine there are enough rodents over there to keep him from starving." The vet smiled up at Danielle and said, "I guess you have a cat."

EIGHTEEN

When Danielle left the vet's office on Monday morning, she couldn't help but think about Presley House. She still hadn't told the chief what Walt had told her about the body—according to the cat.

The day before, Lily and Ian had talked her into driving over to Astoria with them on Sunday afternoon; Ian needed to meet with Emma Jackson before he took off on Tuesday for New York. On Sunday evening, after she returned from Astoria, she had another private chat with Walt about Presley House and its resident ghost. The only thing Walt could discover from Max was that the ghost was named Harvey, and he returned to the house each year around Halloween, searching for something. What he was looking for, Max didn't know. Nor did Max know Harvey's last name, although Danielle suspected it was Presley. She was certain he was one of the twins.

The first thing she had done on Monday morning was call the vet to book an appointment. It turned out they had just had a cancellation so they told her if she could bring Max right in, they could see him. She had taken Lily's suggested and asked Heather if she had a cat carrier she could borrow—which she did.

Danielle got back from the vet around ten in the morning on Monday. Still thinking of Presley House, she decided to do a little sleuthing before calling the chief with what she knew. After dropping Max off at home, she returned the cat carrier to Heather and headed off to the museum. If she were lucky, Ben Smith would be on docent duty. If not, there might be someone else at the museum who knew about Presley House's secrets.

———

WHEN DANIELLE WALKED into the museum late Monday morning, she found Ben Smith standing behind the counter at the museum gift store, ringing up an order for a visitor. Still spry in his eighties, Smith regularly volunteered at the museum.

Just as he handed the small paper gift sack to the customer, he spied Danielle. "Danielle Boatman, what brings you to the museum?"

The customer he had been waiting on nodded a thank you and went off with her package to see what else she might find at the gift shop.

"I wanted to see you." Danielle grinned.

Ben's blue-gray eyes twinkled. "You know how to flatter an old man."

Danielle stepped up to the counter, standing where the customer had been just moments before. "I was hoping you'd be working."

"I'm off today. Just stopped in for a minute."

"I have some questions for you," Danielle explained.

"I hope I have the answers you need."

"Thanks, Ben," an elderly woman called out as she hurriedly shuffled into the gift store from the direction of the restroom. She took her place behind the counter.

"No problem." Ben told her. "I rang up a couple postcards and a book."

The woman gave Ben a pat on the shoulder as he made his way from behind the counter to Danielle.

"So how can I help you?" he asked Danielle.

Danielle glanced around. The elderly docent behind the counter seemed more curious than Ben to hear her answer. The customer who had just made a purchase lingered nearby, also listening.

Impulsively, Danielle said, "If you're not working right now, how about I treat you to a cup of coffee and a donut at the coffee shop? We can talk there."

"Sounds great."

DANIELLE SAT across from Ben at the diner. The waitress had just filled their coffee cups and had left to get the donuts.

"I have some questions about Presley House," Danielle explained.

"Ahh...Presley House. I heard about the dead body."

"Dead body?" Danielle sipped her coffee.

"From Millie. Said something about teenage boys breaking in, swearing there was a dead body in the house." Ben shook his head. "Every year it's the same thing. Kids pulling some silly prank. I told Millie not to get all upset. If there had been a dead body, Henderson and Morelli would have found it."

"I understand you know a little about the house's history."

"A little. The house was built by the Presley family in the early thirties. Moved when the boys were still in high school."

"Was one of them named Harvey?" Danielle asked.

"You mean one of the twins?"

"Yeah. I was curious about their names. I thought someone said one was named Harvey," Danielle lied.

Ben shrugged. "Not sure. Might have been. I really didn't know them. They were older than I was. Closer to Marie's age."

"Marie Nichols?"

Ben nodded. "Yes."

"Would Marie have known them?"

"I'm sure she would have. Don't know if she'd remember them now or their names. I've a devil of a time remembering names myself."

"Do you remember anything about the family?"

"I know they left abruptly. Heard that from my sister. Family moved about a month before the boys were to graduate from high school."

"You think I might be able to talk to your sister about it?"

"I'm afraid she's been gone over ten years now."

"Oh...I'm sorry."

Ben shrugged and took a sip of coffee. The waitress came to their table with the donuts. After she left, Danielle continued.

"Do you know anything else about the family?"

"At one time, Mr. Presley—the twin's father—worked for the Thorndikes."

"Eva Thorndike's family?" *So this was the Presley Walt knew*, Danielle thought.

"Yes. He was a caretaker for their house here, and he'd do some odd jobs for them. This was before he was married. He left the area for a while after Eva died and her parents sold their house here. Not sure if he was still working for the Thorndikes after they all left. But he returned with his family in the thirties, bought some property, and had a house built."

"Who did he work for when he moved back?"

"I don't think he worked for anyone. He must have done something to make some money when he was gone, because according to my father, his financial situation seemed vastly improved when he returned."

"Where did they go when they moved again?"

"I have no idea. They just upped and moved. As I said, they must have had some money, because they didn't sell the house. But I never heard what happened to them."

"So what about the story of the house being haunted?" Danielle asked.

"What do you mean?" Ben sipped his coffee.

"How long have people been saying it's haunted? How did those stories start?"

"I know some strange things happened before they moved. Maybe that's why they left."

"Strange? How?" Danielle tore off a piece of donut and popped it in her mouth.

"A few of the people who worked there claimed the place was haunted. There were things like doors closing on their own and furniture moving. But my dad always said it was probably the twins."

Danielle picked up a napkin and wiped the corner of her mouth. "The twins? Why did he assume that?"

"For one thing, those types of things only happened around Halloween."

"So why would that mean it was the twins pulling pranks?"

"You believe in ghosts, Danielle?" Ben grinned.

Danielle blushed. "Of course not. I'm just curious why your father thought it was the twins when others thought the place was haunted."

"Back then, Halloween wasn't like it is now. It was mostly about teenagers getting into mischief, pulling pranks. Since the strange occurrences only happened around Halloween, Dad figured it was probably the twins messing with people."

"But the stories continued after they moved?"

"I know the house sat vacant for years. Then one day, must have been in the seventies, someone came in, cleaned up the place and put it up for rent. But each year, never fail, the tenants would move out around Halloween, claiming the house was haunted. This went on for years. Finally they just boarded up the place and stopped trying to rent it out."

"So they claim paranormal activity only happens around Halloween?"

"That's what they claimed. I never saw it. The only thing I've ever seen is mischief by local teens—like those boys who broke in the other day and claimed to see a body. Just Halloween nonsense, if you ask me."

"So how do you explain the tenants seeing paranormal activity? Especially if more than one claimed to have seen something?"

"I figure part of that was nothing more than a renter wanting out of a lease."

"And the other part?" Danielle asked.

"An overactive imagination." Ben glanced at his watch. "I've enjoyed our chat, but I didn't realize it was so late. I really need to get going. I have a doctor's appointment in about fifteen minutes."

"No problem. I really appreciate your time."

"Sorry I don't know more about the family. You might ask Marie Nichols about it. Like I said, the boys were closer to her age."

"Thanks, Ben, I think I'll do that."

DANIELLE SAT ALONE in the booth, thinking about what Ben had told her. She was just about ready to get up and pay the bill when Adam Nichols walked into the diner. He immediately spied her sitting alone.

"Morning, Danielle." He glanced at the two coffee cups on the table. "I was going to ask if I could join you, but I see you aren't alone."

"Go ahead and sit down. I was just having coffee with Ben Smith. He just left."

"Isn't he a little old for you?" Adam snickered as he took a seat.

"Ha-ha." Danielle rolled her eyes.

"And I think he's married too."

"Cute, Adam…real cute."

"Yes," Adam said with a sigh. "The ladies are always telling me that."

The server arrived the next moment. She took Adam's order, refilled Danielle's coffee cup and removed Ben's cup.

"What do you know about Presley House?" Danielle asked.

"Presley House? Ahh, so you heard about the dead body?"

"Things get around this town fast."

"It was in the paper. Although, from what I hear, the dead body was more a figment of those boys' imaginations. What do you know?"

"Nothing." Danielle fiddled with her coffee cup. "I'm just curious about the house. They say it's haunted, and it is almost Halloween."

"I used to property manage it for a while. I never saw anything to support the ghost stories, just a bunch of broken windows every year. Nothing paranormal in that. The owners got tired of replacing them and had me just board them up. I don't manage the property anymore."

"What do you know about the Presley family?"

"Nothing really. I was contacted by their attorney to manage the property. I figure the estate must have run out of money because they stopped paying me."

"Ben Smith said your grandmother might know the family who used to live there."

"Yeah, I think she did. I remember her mentioning something to me about it around the time I took over the property."

"Is your grandmother home today? I'd like to talk to her about it."

"Knowing Grandma, she'd love to see you. But she's in Portland until Wednesday."

"Portland? What's she doing there?"

"Little trip to see some of her friends."

"Did you take her?" Danielle knew Marie no longer drove.

"No. Daughter of one of her friends took her." Adam grinned.

Danielle arched her brows. "You look awful happy."

"You know I adore my grandmother. But sometimes…well, she can be a little demanding. Let's just say I'm enjoying this break."

"You're a good grandson," Danielle told him. "In spite of everything else."

"Hey." Adam frowned. "What is that supposed to mean?"

"Well…let's see…there was that little matter of breaking and entering at Marlow House…"

"And I didn't take anything!"

"You broke the window."

"In all fairness, Bill broke the window. But we did fix it."

"We? I didn't see you repairing the window."

"I helped Bill pay for the glass."

"That was generous of you."

"Danielle, if you aren't nice, I won't bail you out of jail the next time you get hauled in for murder."

Danielle laughed. "Fair enough."

NINETEEN

A fter Danielle left Adam at the diner, she headed home. Before she reached her street, she impulsively took a detour, heading for Presley House. A few minutes later, she pulled up in front of the old boarded-up Victorian and parked her car.

Staring up at the house, she thought about its ghost—Harvey. Was it Harvey Presley? she wondered, and why did he return to the house each Halloween season? One thing Danielle did know, according to some folklore, Halloween was a time when spirits could more easily revisit the earth and make themselves known.

With her hands gripping the steering wheel, Danielle studied the house and debated getting out of her car. After a few minutes, she unhooked her seatbelt and opened her door. She knew the house was locked, so she didn't imagine she'd get inside. But she figured it was always possible Harvey might meet her outside.

Walking up the stone pathway leading to the front door, Danielle noticed how quiet it seemed. The only sound was that of the breeze blowing through the treetops. She couldn't even hear the breakers hitting the nearby beach. Tucking her fingertips into her pants' back pockets, she nervously approached the house.

"Harvey?" Danielle called out in a low voice. "You here?"

No reply.

Danielle glanced over her shoulder to see if any neighbors were outside. The street seemed as desolate as Presley House's yard. She walked closer to the house, reaching its front porch. While she knew the chief had locked the front door, she decided to try opening it anyway.

Stepping up on the porch, she walked to the door and reached out for its knob. Giving it a turn, she discovered her assumption was correct. It was still locked. Standing on the porch for a moment, she looked around.

"Harvey? Let's talk. Maybe I can help you."

The doorknob rattled unexpectedly. Danielle jumped at the unexpected noise and looked at the door. The tarnished brass knob turned to the right and then the left. Danielle's eyes widened as the front door slowly opened. She just stood and stared.

Gulping nervously, Danielle called out, "Hello? Is that you, Harvey?"

Silence.

The front door was now wide open, but there did not appear to be anyone there. Glancing around, wondering if anyone was watching, Danielle slowly walked to the open doorway. She peeked inside. She didn't see anyone in the entry.

Taking a deep breath and mustering her courage, Danielle stepped through the doorway of Presley House. Once inside, the door slammed shut behind her. She turned to the door and stared at it.

"Well, hello to you too, Harvey," Danielle called out.

Overhead, the lightbulbs in the vintage chandelier twinkled off and on.

"That's really a cool trick, since this house doesn't have any electric meter hooked up."

The lights went out.

"You could leave them on. It would help me see. This place is pretty dark."

The lights went back on.

"Thanks. That's better." Danielle forced herself to sound brave and calm. "Why don't you show yourself so we can talk?"

No answer.

"You showed yourself to me yesterday. I saw you in the window upstairs. I waved to you."

Silence.

"Why didn't you want Chief MacDonald to know you're here?"

Still no answer.

"I came by myself. Don't I get points for that?" She remained standing in the entry hall, the overhead lights of the chandelier flickering off and on.

"Will you help me?" a male voice called out.

"That's better. Are you Harvey?" she asked.

"How do you know my name?"

"Umm…a friend told me."

"What friend?" he asked.

"Max."

"Do you have Max?" he asked angrily.

"You know cats, they sort of do their own thing." Danielle questioned her wisdom of revealing the fact she knew his name—and that she knew Max. By his tone, he didn't seem happy at the thought she had the cat.

"Max belongs here!" Harvey shouted.

"I imagine Max keeps you company."

"I need Max to find it."

"Find what?"

"I don't understand. How can you communicate with Max? You aren't like me."

"Max sent me," Danielle lied impulsively. "Max thought I could help you."

"He did?" Harvey sounded hopeful.

"Yes, he didn't feel he could help you. He thought I might be able to."

"I still don't understand how he told you that."

"How about we not worry about Max right now. Tell me why you're here, Harvey. Why do you come every year?"

"I'm trying to find it," Harvey said.

"Trying to find what?"

"So they'll know what happened. It's here somewhere. I know it is. But I can't find it."

"And if you find it, then you're going to move on?"

"I don't like to come back here," Harvey insisted.

"Maybe I can help you find it, but first, what did you do with the body?"

Harvey laughed. "You should have seen those boys' expressions. That was the most fun I've had in a long time."

"Why did you hide the body?" Danielle looked around the room, hoping to see Harvey. She disliked talking to just a voice.

"I don't know. It just seemed like a good idea at the time. Figured that way the police might start tearing this place apart looking for him, and then they would find it for me."

"You wanted them to look for the body?" Danielle asked.

"Of course. Why else would I hide it?"

"Where did you hide it? That was a pretty neat trick of yours."

"They didn't look very hard. Those cops are useless."

"In all fairness to the cops, they assumed the boys made up the story."

"They took the trunk with them," Harvey reminded her. "I'm not sure what good an empty trunk is going to do them."

"Harvey, why don't you tell me where you hid that body, and then I can help you find whatever it is you're looking for."

"Why would you help me?"

"Because you seem as if you need someone to help you."

"I still don't understand. No one has ever been able to see or hear me before. Only Max. I miss Max. I want him to come back; he belongs here."

"I would like to see you now. Why don't you show yourself to me, like you did when you were in the window yesterday?"

"Would you really help me if I tell you where the body is?"

"Yes, Harvey, I would really help you."

Harvey didn't respond. Instead, the room seemed even stiller than it had been just moments earlier. The lights overhead dimmed; they were barely lit.

"Harvey? Are you still here?"

There was no answer. The lights went out completely, plunging Danielle into virtual darkness. The only light came from shafts of sunlight breaking in through the edges of the boarded-up windows.

Then she heard it, a slamming sound, like doors opening and closing. Silence again. And then she smelled it. The unmistakable stench of rotting flesh. Pinching her nostrils closed, she reluctantly walked toward the smell leading her to the kitchen.

Once she walked through the doorway, she saw it: the bloated body of a man sprawled on the kitchen floor, his face turned away from her.

Light spilled into the room from the partially boarded-up window. The plywood—most of its nails removed by the teenage boys on Saturday—had that morning slipped from where it had been hung and now only covered half of the opening.

"Who is it?" Danielle found herself asking.

"I don't know." Harvey appeared before her. He looked even younger than when she had seen him standing in the window. If this version of his body represented who he was shortly before death, Danielle figured he was barely a teenager when he died.

"What happened to him?" Danielle asked.

"Some man shot him." Harvey shrugged. "Ran out of the house. Must have taken the gun with him because I never found it. I would like to have a gun."

"Why would you want a gun?"

Harvey smiled. "Imagine if I could learn to use a gun like I've learned to do other things."

Harnessed energy, Danielle thought. The idea of a loaded pistol in the hands of an unstable ghost with harnessed energy sent chills up Danielle's spine. *Hopefully the universe would intervene,* she thought.

"Will you help me now?" Harvey asked brightly.

"I think it might be a good idea to take care of the body first. He doesn't look like he's in such good shape." Danielle walked closer to the corpse and knelt down. According to the boys, the man looked like one of the missing fugitives. From the angle of the body and its condition, Danielle didn't feel capable of making an identification one way or the other.

"I'm surprised his spirit isn't lingering nearby." Danielle looked up at Harvey. "Or is he?"

"I told him he couldn't stay."

"So he was here?"

"Of course. But I told him he had to go."

Danielle stood up and walked around the dead man. Kneeling down again, she got a clearer view of his bloated face.

"So it's you," Danielle murmured. She silently studied the body for a few moments. "I guess I'll have to do something with your body."

"Danielle Boatman, why am I not surprised?" Brian Henderson said from the doorway.

Startled, Danielle looked up into Officer Henderson's face. He shook his head as he walked into the room. She quickly stood up.

"I was just getting ready to call the chief," Danielle explained.

"Yeah, I bet you were." Henderson stood over the body, hands on hips, looking down. "Who is it?"

"Looks like Bart Haston to me. But I'm not sure. He's not in the

THE GHOST OF HALLOWEEN PAST

best condition." Cocking her head slightly, she looked at Brian and asked, "What are you doing here, anyway?"

"I was patrolling the neighborhood, saw your car. Wanted to see what you were up to."

Danielle glanced around. She could no longer see Harvey.

"So how did he get in the kitchen? We searched this place yesterday," Brian asked.

"I have no idea," Danielle lied. "I walked into the kitchen and found him on the floor."

"Old habits are kind of hard to break, huh?" Brian asked.

"Old habits?" Danielle frowned.

"Breaking and entering. This is private property."

"I was just curious."

"Someone dragged him into the kitchen." Brian removed his gun from his holster. "Whoever it is might still be here."

"I don't think so. This place seems pretty empty to me."

Brian grabbed Danielle by the forearm as he led her outside while keeping his gun at the ready for a potential attack from some unknown stranger.

DANIELLE LEANED against the hood of her car, waiting for Brian. Once he had taken her outside, he told her to wait by her car and not to go anywhere. He had called for backup and then returned to the house without waiting for reinforcements.

The responders arrived at the same time Brian came back outside. Danielle watched as he told the responders what was going on, after which he turned his attention back to her.

"I'm flattered," Danielle said with a grin when Brian approached her.

"Flattered?" Brian frowned.

"That was all very knight-in-shining-armor back there. Getting me out of the house in case the killer was still lurking around, and then going back in. You're kind of my hero right now."

"Danielle, I'm still arresting you," Brian told her as he pulled out his handcuffs.

"Of course you are." She obediently extended her wrists, waiting for him to slap on the handcuffs. "But you can skip the Miranda rights; I think I know them by heart."

TWENTY

anielle sat alone in the interrogation room, thinking about
lunch. She was ravenous. The donut she'd eaten at the diner
had just whetted her appetite. Leaning back in the chair, she looked
over to the two-way mirror and gave it a little wave. She had no idea
if anyone was in the other room, watching her, but she figured she
might as well be friendly.

Brian had confiscated her iPhone—he told her it was protocol.
Which, of course, she already knew. After all, this wasn't her first
arrest. Instead of making a phone call, she told Brian she just
wanted to see the police chief. When she compared this arrest with
her priors, she found this one less stressful, in spite of the fact Brian
found her hovering over a dead body.

When thinking of the dead body—which she now knew
belonged to Bart Haston—Danielle was fairly certain who had killed
him: Chuck Christiansen. Chuck had been furious with Bart for
spilling everything to the cops after their arrest. The two had disappeared on the same day, and Bart's car had been found in Frederickport, where Chuck lived.

Danielle wondered if Chuck had made it to Canada. She was
the only one—except for the chief—who didn't assume the killer
was hanging around Presley House, playing hide-and-seek with
Bart's smelly corpse.

When the door to the interrogation room opened, Danielle expected to see Chief MacDonald. Instead, Joe Morelli walked in.

"Hey, Joe. Where's the chief?" Danielle greeted him.

Joe tossed the legal pad he was carrying, along with a pen, onto the table and sat down across from Danielle. "You look pretty laid back, considering you were just found with the dead body of Bart Haston."

"It's not like I killed him or anything. Where's the chief?"

"He's not here."

"What do you mean he isn't here?" Danielle sat up in the chair, no longer feeling as smug as she had been a moment ago.

"He's on vacation."

"What do you mean he's on vacation? He's not supposed to leave until Wednesday."

Joe cocked his brow. "I didn't realize you were so familiar with his schedule."

"I'm not." Danielle shrugged. "He just mentioned he was going on vacation starting Wednesday." Actually, Danielle thought, he just said he was leaving for Hawaii on Wednesday—he didn't say when his vacation leave started.

"I'm in charge while he's gone," Joe explained.

Danielle almost asked why Brian wasn't in charge, yet then remembered Joe outranked his partner. She always wondered why, considering Brian was much older than Joe and had more years on the force. She kept her questions to herself.

"So what am I being charged with, breaking and entering?" Danielle asked.

"Who says I'm charging you with anything?"

"I don't know. Just seems that's what typically happens around here."

"How did you get into Presley House? I know the door was locked, but there was no sign of a break-in. And why were you there?" Joe leaned back in his chair and studied Danielle.

Silently, Danielle met Joe's intent gaze. He was a handsome devil, she thought. It was too bad it hadn't worked out between them. For a brief moment she wondered if she might be willing to overlook some of his flaws—after all, he had those sexy brown eyes, great abs, smoking hot Italian good looks—after an extended moment she let out a sigh and thought—*Nah, not happening.*

"I really hadn't planned to go into the house." Which was true,

Danielle thought. "I was on my way home, was curious, decided to stop by Presley House and have a look. I didn't figure it would hurt —or that I would be breaking any laws—if I just had a look around. After all, that house is pretty infamous around here."

"Brian found you in the house."

"When I got there—well, I confess I did try the doorknob. I figured it would be locked."

"So why did you try it?"

"I don't know." Danielle shrugged. "Haven't you ever tried a doorknob that you assume is locked and you really don't plan to go inside?"

"Not really."

"Well, it was locked."

"But you were inside."

"Obviously," Danielle said impatiently. "But then the door... well, it just opened."

"Just opened? Uh-huh." Joe shook his head.

"Well, it did!" Danielle insisted. "And then I saw the lights."

"The lights?" Joe frowned.

Danielle smiled to herself. She remembered what the chief had told her about Joe and Brian finding the lamp—the magic lamp, she liked to call it. "Oh yes, the lights from the chandelier, they kept flickering on and off."

"But that house isn't hooked up to electricity," Joe said dully, his expression unreadable.

"Exactly," Danielle said with a grin, leaning over the table toward Joe. "Isn't that just creepy?"

"Your eyes must have been playing tricks on you."

"Think so?" Danielle asked sweetly. Abruptly she let out a sigh, sat back in the chair, and said, "And then I smelled it—poor Bart. I followed that nasty stench, went into the kitchen, and well, Brian showed up about then."

"You don't seem very upset about finding a dead body."

"Would you prefer I cry hysterically?" she asked.

"It might be more normal."

"Come on, Joe, you figured out a long time ago I'm not exactly normal."

The door to the interrogation room opened and Brian entered, carrying a cellphone.

"The chief wants to talk to Danielle. Alone," Brian announced.

He handed the cellphone to Danielle.

She stood up and smiled at the two officers. "I'll take this in the hallway. Don't worry; I won't make a run for it. Brian still has my car keys, purse, and cellphone."

"She's damn cocky," Joe muttered after Danielle stepped out of the room.

"I think there's something going on between her and the chief," Brian said.

Joe scowled. "What do you mean?"

"I don't know. They just seem real chummy these days. Did you know he went to that party she had Friday night over at Marlow House?"

Joe stared at the closed door. "I didn't even know there was a party."

"HI, Chief, I didn't think you were leaving until Wednesday." Danielle wandered into the break room and sat down. She was the only one in the room.

"Our flight's not until Wednesday, but technically my vacation started today. I'm in Portland picking up some things for the trip. So you found the body?"

"Yeah. I didn't tell you before, but I saw our ghost standing in the upstairs window when we left the house yesterday." Danielle stared at the open door leading to the hallway. She didn't want anyone walking in on her phone conversation.

"Why didn't you say anything?"

"I had this gut feeling if I went back inside with you, he wouldn't show himself. When I saw him in the window and then looked over at you, he put his finger to his lips."

"Finger to his lips?"

"Yeah, you know, like when you're telling someone to be quiet or keep a secret."

"So why did you happen to go over there today?"

"I went over to the museum earlier, trying to find out more about Presley House and its resident ghost. Oh, by the way, Max was hanging out there."

"Max?"

"Yeah, the cat that adopted me."

"The ferocious one who wanted to chomp my finger off?"

"Be gentle with Max, he has issues. But yeah, that one. He told Walt a little about the ghost and Walt told me."

"I don't really understand."

"Spirits can communicate with animals. And I can communicate with spirits. You figure it out."

"Okay, so what did Max tell Walt?"

"Only that the ghost's name is Harvey. He's just a kid. Or he was when he died. A teenager. I talked to Ben Smith from the museum, but didn't find out too much. On my way home, I decided to stop by the house. When I got there, the door flew open."

"I locked it."

"I remember. I jiggled the doorknob when I got there; it was still locked. Then suddenly it seemed to turn on its own and the door flew open. I walked inside."

"And you found the body?"

Danielle told the chief about her faceless conversation with Harvey, the lights flickering, and then the strange sounds coming from the kitchen.

"So you think he took the body to the kitchen when you were there?"

"I think so. I know I didn't start smelling it until I heard all that noise."

"But where was he keeping it?"

"I have no idea. Maybe there's some secret room in that house."

"Secret room? Hmmm…I hadn't considered that."

"Do I have to spend the night here?" Danielle asked.

The chief laughed. Then in a serious tone he said, "My bet is on Chuck being the killer."

"Me too. I wonder if he's in Canada."

"I suspect he is, but there's no way to explain how that body got moved around. The only plausible explanation is that the killer came back and moved it."

"And you believe that?" Danielle asked.

"Of course not." The chief sighed. "Let me talk to Joe."

"I will say one thing," Danielle said as she stood up with the phone.

"What's that?"

"When Brian arrested me this time, well, he didn't seem to have that same old gung ho spirit. It was almost like he regretted arresting me."

"Brian believes he owes you for what you did for him. If it wasn't for you, he might be in prison for Darlene's murder."

"Yeah, I suppose. But for some reason, it makes that little thing we had—well, less fun."

"Fun?"

"Maybe fun is the wrong word. But I was rather getting into loathing Brian, and he makes it difficult these days for me to stay mad at him."

"Oh, I'm sure one of you will do something to piss the other one off and whatever truce was on the table will be out the window."

"One can hope." Danielle sighed. "Although, if I'm honest and not being a smartass, I rather like this new Brian. Getting arrested can be exhausting. And expensive."

"You're rich. It's not like you can't afford an attorney." The chief snickered.

"True. You have a point. I'm going to give the phone back to Joe, and you can tell him to let me go."

Danielle walked back into the interrogation room and handed the phone to Joe. She and Brian silently listened to his side of the conversation.

When Joe got off the phone, he said, "The chief told me to cut you loose."

Danielle smiled. "Can I have my things now?"

"Joe, it might be a good idea to assign someone to Marlow House," Brian suggested.

"What do you mean?" Danielle frowned.

"For your own protection," Brian explained.

"You have a point," Joe agreed.

"My own protection? From what?"

"If our hunch is correct, Chuck Christiansen killed Bart, and since someone moved that body—twice—the killer is probably still in the area. If it is Christiansen, he also had an issue with you. You could be a target."

"I'll be fine. I'm sure Christiansen is in Canada by now."

"Really?" Brian snapped. "And who moved that body?"

"I don't know." Danielle shrugged. "Teenage pranksters?"

"Brian is right," Joe agreed. "I'll get someone to keep an eye on Marlow House."

Danielle groaned inwardly. "Okay, but can I please have my stuff back."

"Yes, then I'll drive you back to Presley House to pick up your car," Brian said.

Danielle shook her head. "You don't have to do that. I can get someone to pick me up."

"Don't argue with me, Boatman," Brian snapped. "Come with me. You'll need to sign for your things."

Danielle looked from Brian to Joe.

"He's just trying to help you, Danielle," Joe said.

"Yeah, I know." Danielle groaned. Reluctantly, she followed Brian. "This time, can I sit in the front of the squad car?"

TWENTY-ONE

"Where've you been?" Lily asked when Danielle finally returned to Marlow House late Monday afternoon.

"Long story. But first, where is everyone?" Danielle tossed her purse on the desk in the parlor.

"I'm here," Walt said as he appeared in the room.

"Ian and Sadie are across the street. Ian's doing some laundry for his trip. Then he has a few errands to run before he picks me up for dinner. You're welcome to join us."

"No, thanks for asking, I'm pretty exhausted."

"I don't know where Walt is, but your cat is sleeping on your bed, last I looked."

"Walt's here." Danielle pointed to what appeared to be an empty chair.

"Hi, Walt," Lily greeted him. She then turned her attention back to Danielle. "Where have you been? I knew you took Max to the vet this morning, but when I saw him napping on your bed and your car wasn't here…"

"For starters, I found Bart Haston," Danielle announced.

"Where? Was Christiansen with him?" Walt asked.

"What do you mean you found him?" Lily said at the same time as Walt posed his question.

"He's dead. Looks like Chuck killed him."

Lily gasped. "Does this mean you talked to his spirit?"

"Never saw his spirit, just his dead body at Presley House."

"So there was a dead body?" Lily asked.

"Yep. Looks like Chuck—assuming he's the killer—shot Haston at Presley House. Not sure what they were doing there, but I assume they broke in. Maybe they were hiding out; I don't know. But Chuck shot him, left the body, and the resident ghost of Presley House decided to put the body in the trunk. He moved it when the cops went looking for it, and today when I went over there and made contact with him, he put the body in the kitchen."

"Did you go over there alone?" Walt asked.

"Did you go alone?" Lily asked.

Exasperated, Danielle said, "It sure would be a lot easier if you two could hear each other."

"Walt can't hear me?"

"I can hear Lily."

Danielle groaned. "I mean I wish Lily could hear Walt so you weren't always asking the same questions."

"I don't know why that's a problem," Lily said. "I think you're avoiding my question. Did you go over there alone? If so, do you really think that was such a good idea?"

"Lily's right, Danielle. I don't like the idea of you tromping around alone in houses with strange ghosts."

"Strange ghosts?" Danielle looked at Walt.

"What strange ghost?" Lily asked.

"Uggg…" Danielle groaned again.

"Oh, stop that! What strange ghosts?" Lily demanded.

"Walt said he didn't think I should be tromping around alone in houses with strange ghosts."

"I agree with Walt."

"Thank you, Lily."

"Whatever…" Danielle sighed. "If you two want me to finish telling you what I did today, then you'll have to both be quiet."

Walt and Lily each resisted the temptation to ask any more questions. Danielle then proceeded to tell them about the day's events.

"I can't believe you were actually arrested again," Lily said when Danielle finished telling her story.

"I wasn't arrested exactly."

"You said he put you in handcuffs," Lily reminded her.

"True. But he didn't have his heart in it."

"Did they put those boys in handcuffs?" Lily asked.

"What boys?"

"The boys who broke into Presley House and said they found the body," Lily reminded her.

Danielle frowned for a moment, considering Lily's question. "Hmm, now that you mention it, according to the chief, they didn't take the boys in. They let them go after they searched the house."

"Ahh, Dani, see, you still have a special spot in Officer Henderson's heart." Lily smirked.

AFTER BRIAN RETURNED from taking Danielle to pick up her car, he found Joe in his office, staring at his computer screen.

"I'm back," Brian called out.

Joe looked up and waved him into his office. "Come here, I want to show you something."

Brian walked into the office and started to sit down. Joe stopped him, asking him instead to walk around his desk so he could look at the computer monitor. A moment later, Brian stood behind Joe and looked at the monitor. It was black.

"What am I supposed to be looking at?" Brian asked.

"Just a second, let me get it back." Joe fiddled with his mouse. "Remember that computer stuff we confiscated from Presley House?"

"You mean the surveillance cameras and stuff the boys left in the kitchen?"

"Yes. I just got this off one of the cameras. Here…watch this…" Joe stared at the monitor as he strategically moved the mouse.

A video began playing. The scene was dimly lit, but Brian could make out the setting.

"That's the kitchen doorway at Presley House."

"Yes. Listen to the voices. Wait a minute, let me start at the beginning and you listen." Joe pointed to the monitor. "You see the three boys standing by the doorway."

"It's pretty dark. I can't really make them out. But yeah, I guess I see them."

"Listen to their conversation," Joe told him.

Squinting his eyes, Brian listened carefully to the voices on the screen. "They're talking about where they want to plant the cameras. So?"

"You see three of them, right?" Joe asked.

"Yeah, so what?"

"Tell me who each one is by their voices."

Brian shrugged but continued to listen. "That was Brad…"

"Yes."

"Curt, without a doubt," Brian said.

Joe nodded.

"That was Jeff."

"Yes." Joe smiled. "So tell me who is taking the movie."

"Obviously Kevin. I see the three boys standing in the doorway. I can't see their faces, but I recognize their voices. It has to be Kevin filming them."

"Wait a second. Let me start it over again. I want you to keep listening and tell me what you hear," Joe said.

Brian shrugged again but continued to listen.

"Hey, guys! There's another door over here!"

Brian frowned. "That sounded like Kevin."

"It was. I've played that over at least a dozen times. It's coming from down the hall. Someone else took the movie."

"That's impossible. They must have left the camera on."

"That might make sense if the camera was stationary. But look…" Joe replayed the video while Brian watched. "Someone is holding the camera, and they're moving it around."

HARVEY WONDERED if she had lied to him. She had promised to help him, yet after the cops showed up, everything went crazy. He had to admit it wasn't completely her fault. He had watched her from the upstairs window after the cop forced her from the house. He had hoped she would come back after they took the body away. Instead, he helplessly watched as the cop put her in handcuffs and loaded her into the back of the police car. Perhaps he should have done something before the cop took her back outside.

He wondered if she was in jail. If so, then there was no way she could help him. Frustrated, Harvey made his way downstairs. He was halfway down the staircase when he saw him—standing at the doorway of the kitchen, snooping around.

"What are you doing?" Harvey asked angrily as he flew down the staircase.

The man looked up at Harvey and smiled. "I forgot what an interesting place this is. Much more so than where I'm staying."

"You need to leave," Harvey ordered.

"I want to know what you did with the body. You did something with it, didn't you?" the man asked. By the way he was standing, it was obvious he had no intention of going anywhere in the near future.

"What do you care?" Harvey snapped.

"I just want to know where it is. Can I see it?"

"The police took it."

The man raised his brow. "The police? They took it, when?"

"Today. It's not here."

"What time today?"

Harvey frowned. "I don't know."

"This morning or afternoon?"

"I guess this afternoon." Harvey shrugged.

"Hmmm…interesting. That might explain things," the man murmured.

"Explain what?" Harvey asked.

"You did something to get them to find it, didn't you?" the man asked.

"I suppose I did. So what?"

"What did you do?"

"Why are you asking me these questions?" Harvey wanted the man to leave. He made him uncomfortable.

The man stared at Harvey for a moment before answering. "I get the feeling you've been at this for a lot longer than me."

"Yeah, so what?" Harvey snapped.

"I want you to help me."

"I don't want to help you. I want you to leave!"

The man chuckled and then walked into the living room. He glanced around. "This is a nice place you have here. Much nicer than where I'm staying."

"So?"

"Maybe I'll stay. Move in."

"You can't do that!"

"Why not? You can't make me leave. If I want to stay, there really is nothing you can do about it." The man walked over to the sofa and flopped down, making himself at home. Leaning against one arm of the couch, he rested his feet on the opposite arm.

"You killed that man, didn't you?" Harvey asked.

"Took you long enough."

"Why do you want the body back?"

"I don't really want it. I just wanted to know what happened to it. I figured something had to have happened."

Harvey eyed the stranger suspiciously. "Why?"

"One minute he was there, annoying the crap out of me. And the next—he just vanishes. Goes away. I rather liked that."

"I still don't understand what you want from me."

"I just figured there had to be some connection between his body and why he's no longer hanging around driving me nuts."

"If you didn't like him, you should just be glad he isn't here anymore. I want you to leave."

"You aren't listening to me," the man said angrily. "I need you to help me."

"How can I help you?" Harvey eyed the stranger.

"Ahh…now you're asking the right questions!" The man smiled. He pointed to a chair. "Sit down. I'm going to tell you what I need, and you're going to tell me how you might be able to help me."

Reluctantly, Harvey sat down. Silently, he listened as the man explained his problem.

"Are you sure this is what you want to do?" Harvey asked when the man finished.

"I don't like what I have now."

"But it could be worse. In fact, I'm fairly certain it will be worse."

"Maybe. But at least I'll be going forward to wherever I'm supposed to go."

"I don't think you're going to like it," Harvey warned.

"Are you going to help me or not?"

"If I don't?"

The man glanced around the dimly lit living room. He then looked back to Harvey. "Then I suppose you'll just have to get used to me, because if I'm stuck here, I might as well keep you company."

Harvey silently stared at the man. Finally, he said, "All right. I'll help you. But you'll see I was right. You were better off lost."

"How are you going to do it?"

Harvey considered his options a moment. "I could see if she'll help me." *If she's not in jail,* he thought.

"She? She who?"

"Just a woman I know."

"A live woman?"

"Of course. You don't think someone like us could help, do you?"

"I don't know. I've come to you for help and you aren't alive."

"If I help you, I want you to leave. There's no reason for you to stick around here. You'll know when I've done what needs to be done."

"Why can't I stay here?"

"If you want me to help you, then you need to leave."

Reluctantly the man stood up. "Fine. But I'll be back in the morning."

"Give me until tomorrow night. This will take a little time."

The man stared at Harvey for a moment and then said, "Fine. I'll give you until tomorrow night." The man vanished.

TWENTY-TWO

C urled up on a kitchen chair, his head peeking out from under the hem of the tablecloth, Max watched as Bill Jones installed a pet door in the door going from the kitchen to the side yard. Walt sat in the chair next to him.

"That's kind of a big kitty door, isn't it?" Lily asked. She stood with Danielle in the side yard, watching Bill.

"I figure that way Sadie can use it too," Danielle said. Her and Lily's conversation drifted through the doorway to Max's and Walt's ears.

Max let out a gurgling growl.

"Stop that," Walt scolded. "Sadie is not going anywhere."

Max stopped growling. He looked at Walt and blinked. Reluctantly he rested his chin on his paws and watched the man finish installing the door.

"OKAY, IT'S DONE," Bill muttered as he gathered up his tools.

"You did a nice job, Bill," Danielle praised. "Thanks." She reached into her pocket, pulled out some cash, and handed it to him.

Pausing for a moment from gathering the tools, he accepted the money and shoved it in his back pocket. "Thanks," he muttered under his breath.

Danielle and Lily flashed him a smile before going back inside the house, entering through the kitchen door—now equipped with a newly installed pet door.

Bill gathered up the rest of his tools and tossed them in the back of his truck. He gave the kitchen door one final look before climbing into the cab of his truck and grabbing his cellphone off the dashboard.

"I finished the job," Bill told Adam after Adam answered his call. Bill drove down the driveway toward the street, holding the cellphone to his ear.

"Did she pay you?" Adam asked with a chuckle.

"With cash, just like you said. I don't get it. Why did she call me?" Bill pulled onto the street.

"She asked me who could install a doggy door and needed the job done as soon as possible. Who else would I recommend?"

"But why would she hire me. She knows we broke into her house."

"I told you, that's all water under the bridge."

"I still say she is one ditzy chick," Bill told Adam as he drove down the street away from Marlow House.

"I CAN'T BELIEVE you used Bill Jones," Lily said as she took a seat at the kitchen table.

"He does good work. Adam recommended him."

"That's another one. I remember when you couldn't stand Adam."

"Lily has a point," Walt chimed in.

"Yeah, I know." Danielle sighed. "I would feel totally different had they broken in after I found the Missing Thorndike and tried to steal it from me."

"They did try to steal it from you!" Lily reminded her.

"Not exactly. They saw it as treasure up for grabs. Back then, no one really knew who owned it, and I didn't even know it existed."

"I sorta understand what you're saying. But still..." Lily grumbled.

The next moment the sound of Sadie hitting the doggy door from outside interrupted their conversation. The golden retriever flew into the kitchen. Max immediately leapt off his chair into Danielle's lap.

"Nice door," Ian said as he entered the kitchen, checking out the new doggy door. "But isn't it kind of big?"

"That's what I said," Lily chimed in.

"I wanted Sadie to be able to use it too."

"Well, she obviously knows how." Ian looked over to Sadie, who sat by Danielle's chair, staring at Max, who stared back. "Those two becoming friends?"

"Well, Sadie isn't trying to eat him." Danielle grinned.

Ian eyed the two animals. "My money is on Max. Don't let him hurt my little girl when I'm gone."

"I promise she'll be fine." Danielle scratched Sadie's ear. Max responded by reaching out with a paw, attempting to bat Danielle's hand away from the dog.

"You sure you don't want to go with us?" Ian asked.

"No, I've had a big day. But thanks for asking," Danielle said.

"She was arrested today," Lily said when she stood up.

"Arrested?" Ian frowned.

"I'll tell you all about it over dinner."

LILY WAS STILL OUT with Ian when Danielle climbed into bed that night. She was exhausted. The moment she pulled the blankets up over her, Sadie jumped onto the mattress from one side of the bed and Max from the other. The two animals stared at each other.

Weary, Danielle glanced from Sadie to Max. Neither animal made an attempt to lie down or move off the bed. They both stood, locked in a stare down.

"You two are welcome to stay, but no arguing! I need my sleep!" Danielle reached over and pushed Sadie down, and then she did the same to Max. The two animals curled up on the bed, each inching closer to Danielle, determined to stake their claim.

Hugging her pillow tightly, Danielle closed her eyes and ignored the animals. Within ten minutes, she was fast asleep.

Walt appeared by the bedside. He looked down at Danielle, who made a little snoring sound. He smiled. Looking from Sadie to Max, he noticed neither one was asleep but intently watching each other.

"Listen up, you two," Walt said in a whisper.

Max and Sadie looked up at him.

"Danielle needs her sleep. No shenanigans."

———————

DANIELLE ROLLED over in the bed, hugging her pillow. She was about to change positions again when someone abruptly snatched the pillow from her grasp and yelled, "I said wake up!"

Danielle bolted upright in her bed and looked around. Wild eyed, she tried to get her bearings. But she was no longer in her bed...or in her bedroom. She sat on a cold concrete floor in a dark and dingy room. She had been in this room before.

"How did I get here?" Danielle asked frantically. She was in Presley House.

"You sure are hard to wake up!" Harvey said from the corner.

Startled, Danielle looked to the voice. Suddenly it made sense.

"I'm dreaming. I'm not really at Presley House."

"You catch on quick." Harvey sat on the floor next to Danielle.

"This isn't a regular dream. You've dream hopped, haven't you?"

"Is that what they call it?" Harvey grinned. "I wasn't sure I could do it. I've never tried. You're the first."

"What do you want?"

"I need you to do something for me."

"Is this about whatever it is you're looking for?"

Harvey started to answer and then paused. Cocking his head, he studied Danielle. "Are you in jail?"

"Excuse me?"

"I saw him arrest you. I wondered if I hopped in your dream while you're locked up."

"No." Danielle shook her head. "They let me go."

"Why didn't you come back, then?"

"If I came back, they would arrest me again. I can't just walk into Presley House whenever I want. It's breaking and entering."

"You said you'd help me."

"So that's why I'm here?" Danielle asked.

"I still want you to help me find it. But that's not why you're here. I need you to do something else first. I need you to drive to Pilgrim's Point and walk to the cliff."

"Why would I do that?" Danielle asked.

"Because I want you to. I want you to do it tomorrow."

"Why?"

"I don't have to explain myself to you!" Harvey said angrily. "You will do what I tell you to!"

"Go away," Danielle said wearily. "I want to go back to sleep."

"You are asleep."

"You know what I mean." Danielle yawned.

Harvey glared at Danielle. Finally, he said, "Girls are afraid of snakes."

"Excuse me?" Danielle frowned.

The next moment Danielle found herself in a deep pit in the middle of a jungle, surrounded by hundreds of snakes. They slithered and rolled, inching closer to her. Jumping to her feet, she looked around frantically.

Wearing only her nightgown, her feet bare, she stood in mud and could feel it ooze between her toes. While she knew it was only a dream, it felt more real than anything she had ever experienced. She loathed snakes—she hated everything about them. The way they moved, the way they slithered and coiled.

"Harvey! Get me out of here!" she shouted frantically.

Harvey laughed. A menacing laugh. He didn't show himself. "This is the most fun I've had in a long time!"

HER CRIES WOKE MAX. He crawled up to her face and sniffed her nose. She was asleep. Butting his head against hers, he tried to wake her. Instead of waking up, Danielle's head moved frantically from side to side as she cried out in her sleep.

Max meowed pitifully. Sadie opened her eyes and looked at the mewing cat. She almost closed her eyes and went back to sleep, but Max leapt at her, swatting her nose with his paw. Jerking awake, Sadie started to growl at Max but then noticed he seemed preoccupied with Danielle.

Danielle cried out in her sleep again. Sadie leapt up and nosed her ear while Max persistently butted the side of her face. Yet neither one was able to wake her.

Max looked at Sadie and let out a loud meow. Sadie jumped off the bed, racing to the attic to find Walt. Max stayed by Danielle's side, his damp nose pressed against her cheek.

Walt made it to Danielle's room before Sadie, who had to run back down the attic stairs and down the hall. He found Danielle tossing in her sleep, tears running down her face.

Sitting on the side of the bed, Walt looked down at Danielle. "Wake up, Danielle, you're having a nightmare. Wake up."

She refused to wake up. Instead, her head tossed from side to side as she let out pitiful sobs. Walt had never seen her this way before. Closing his eyes, he tried to hop into her dream. But it was as if a door was firmly closed and he couldn't enter her sleep. Frustrated, he looked to Sadie.

"Go get Lily. Wake her up. Bring her in here. Let's see if she can wake Danielle up."

Sadie leapt off the bed and raced to Lily's room.

LILY HAD ONLY BEEN asleep for thirty minutes when Sadie jumped onto her bed.

"What the—" Lily bolted upright, rubbed her eyes, and looked around the room.

Sadie nipped at Lily's blanket, pulling it from the bed.

"Sadie! Stop that!" Lily jerked on the blanket, inadvertently entering into an unwanted game of tug-of-war with her boyfriend's dog. She was about to yell at Sadie again when she heard a loud meow at the doorway. It wasn't quite a meow—more a cat's tortured battle cry.

Confused, Lily muttered, "What is going on?"

Sadie released the blanket and raced to the door. Looking back at Lily, she barked and then dashed from the room. When Lily did not get out of the bed, Sadie returned and barked again, Max by her side.

Shaking her head, Lily stumbled out of bed and made her way from her room into the hallway. Once in the hallway, she noticed the light on in Danielle's room. Sadie and Max sat by Danielle's bedroom door, waiting for her. Unease washed over Lily. She raced to Danielle's room and found her asleep, yet obviously in the throes of a violent nightmare.

Without a second thought, Lily jumped onto Danielle's bed and started shaking her. It took a few minutes, but finally Danielle woke up. She looked at Lily and broke into a fresh round of tears. Throwing her arms around Lily, Danielle held on tightly; tears soaked Lily's shoulders.

"There were snakes, Lily! So many snakes!"

TWENTY-THREE

D anielle sat alone on the porch swing, wrapped in a quilt. Sadie and Max slept together on the ground by her feet. She looked up when she heard the front door open and close.

Lily walked to her, carrying two cups of coffee. "Here." Lily handed Danielle a cup and then sat next to her on the porch swing.

"Sorry about last night." Danielle held the cup between her hands, soaking up its warmth.

"You don't have anything to apologize for," Lily insisted.

"Did Ian get off okay?"

"Yeah. He left really early this morning for the airport, that's why I had him leave Sadie with us last night."

"I'm glad you did." Danielle looked down at the animals by her feet and smiled.

"What are you going to do?"

Danielle looked over to Lily. "What do you mean?"

"You're never going to get any sleep if you have to worry about some maniac spirit hopping in your dreams and giving you nightmares."

"I figure the only thing I can do is drive out to Pilgrim's Point." Danielle sipped her coffee.

"Why do you think he wants you to drive out there?"

Danielle shrugged. "I don't know. The only thing I can think of, it's where Darlene was killed."

"Do you think Harvey has some connection to Darlene?"

"Just that one of her co-conspirators was found murdered in the house he haunts."

"So you think this has something to do with her?"

Danielle shook her head. "I really don't know what to think."

"The idea of going out there is kind of creepy. I wish Ian was here so he could go with us."

"You don't have to go with me, Lily."

"Are you kidding?" Lily frowned. "I'm not going to let you go out there by yourself. Although, maybe you should give the chief a call and let him know what's going on."

"I really can't do that."

Lily looked at Danielle. "Why not?"

"The chief is on vacation leave, and he's leaving tomorrow. I don't want to bother him with all this."

"Bother him? If he hadn't asked you to help him, you would never have gotten involved with that Harvey monster and had that horrible nightmare!"

"I don't think Harvey is a monster exactly." Danielle took another sip of coffee.

"Not a monster? Dani, you were terrified last night."

"Harvey may have been born decades ago, but mentally he's nothing more than an immature adolescent, one with serious unresolved issues, considering he's been haunting Presley House for years. I should have handled it differently last night."

"I am surprised about one thing." Lily stared down at the coffee in her hands.

"What's that?"

"Last night you were aware it was a dream hop. You knew the snakes weren't real, and still, you were utterly terrified."

"Yeah…" Danielle sighed. "I guess with some phobias even imaginary can be frightening."

"I never knew you were so afraid of snakes."

"It's not really something I talk about."

"I'll share a little trick with you, just in case something like this happens again and we aren't around to wake you."

"I sure hope that doesn't happen again!" Danielle groaned.

"If you can get yourself to yell, it'll wake you up."

"Lily, whenever I try to yell for help in a dream, no sound comes out."

"Exactly." Lily nodded. "But if you really concentrate and focus and force yourself to yell, you'll do it. And it'll wake you up. I know. I've done it a few times."

"Really?"

"Yeah, the last time freaked out Mom." Lily giggled. "I was staying at my parents' house and having this dream where I was being chased. I managed to scream, woke myself right up. Only problem, it also woke my parents."

"That must have shaken them up."

"Pretty much." Lily glanced back to the house. "You know, he was really worried about you."

Danielle looked to the house. "Walt?"

"I knew he sent Sadie to wake me up. I could feel his presence in the room last night. It was—this feeling of urgency, concern—I can't really explain it, but I know it came from Walt."

Danielle smiled. "I tell you what, Lily, I feel very blessed this morning, in spite of that horrid dream I had last night. I've you and Walt, special friends like Ian, wonderful furry protectors like Sadie and Max…"

"You're a regular Pollyanna," Lily teased.

LILY FIDGETED with the controls on Danielle's car radio. She sat in the passenger seat of the Ford Flex while Danielle drove toward Pilgrim's Point.

"The book is in the glove compartment." Danielle pointed to the dash area in front of Lily. "You'll find a list of the different Sirius stations somewhere in there."

Lily opened the glove compartment and pulled out a booklet. "Can't you control the radio from your steering wheel?"

"Yeah." Danielle glanced down at the steering wheel. "I just haven't figured out how to do it exactly."

Lily sat back in her seat and thumbed through the booklet. "I wish you would have called Joe."

"Joe? Why would I call him?" Danielle continued to drive the car down the highway.

"You could have had him come with us today."

"Oh yeah, right," Danielle said with a snort. "And exactly what would I tell him? *'Gee, Joe, I had a dream last night.'* I don't think so."

Lily shrugged and flipped a page in the booklet.

"Almost there," Danielle announced.

Looking up, Lily leaned forward and opened the glove compartment again. After tossing the booklet back inside, she closed the glove compartment and leaned back in the seat. "It is pretty up here."

"Yeah." Danielle slowed down and looked to the west. Running parallel to the highway was the Pacific Ocean. Up ahead, they could see Pilgrim's Point. "There it is."

Just as Danielle was about to pull off on the view point, she spied a woman standing along the side of the road.

"I wonder if something is wrong," Danielle said as she pulled off the highway.

"What?" Lily looked around.

"There's a woman walking along the bluff. I don't see a car anywhere." Danielle glanced around as she turned the steering wheel.

"Maybe her car broke down and she's walking for help," Lily suggested. "We should probably see if she's okay."

Danielle parked the car. "I could always call someone for her if she needs help."

Lily looked around. "Where is she?"

Danielle pointed up the road. "Right there. See, a few feet in front of those trees."

Lily looked in the direction Danielle pointed. "Where? I don't see her."

Danielle pointed again. "Right there." The woman stood about two hundred feet away from their car.

Squinting her eyes, Lily looked around. "Where?"

"Dang, Lily, do you need glasses?" Danielle laughed. She pointed to the woman again, yet stopped laughing when the woman turned and faced her.

"Oh crap," Danielle muttered, clutching the steering wheel tightly.

"What is it?" Lily frowned. She still didn't see the woman.

"I know now why you don't see her."

"What do you mean?"

"It's Darlene." Danielle stared at the ghost.

Darlene's blond hair and the skirt of her long white dress seemed to be fluttering in the wind—yet the air was still. There was no breeze. The ghost, her back to the cliff overlooking the ocean, stared at Danielle, her face expressionless. She stepped backwards once and then again, moving closer to the edge of the cliff while never looking away from Danielle.

Danielle let out a little gasp when Darlene took one final step backwards, dropping effortlessly off the side of the cliff, disappearing from sight.

"What happened?" Lily asked.

Danielle's heart raced. Although she knew Darlene was already dead, witnessing her dramatic exit was more than a little unnerving.

"She just stepped off the cliff," Danielle explained. "Backwards. She was just standing there, staring at us, and then took several steps backwards and dropped out of sight."

"Is this why Harvey wanted you to come up here?"

"I don't know. But I think I have to go look over the cliff."

"Dani, do you think that's a good idea?"

"That's why we came, isn't it?"

"Is it?" Lily asked. "Maybe we should go home."

"I don't think there's anything to be afraid of. Darlene wants to show me something. I'd bet on it."

"But she was killed when she fell off that cliff the first time! I don't think we need to be walking along that bluff!"

"Lily, Darlene was killed when Chuck smashed her skull with a paperweight. I imagine if I fell off the cliff—which I don't intend to do—there are enough shrubs and bushes to help break my fall. You stay here." Danielle unhooked her seatbelt.

"No, I'm going to go with you," Lily insisted as she too unhooked her seatbelt.

"I'd rather you stay here with the car. Just in case." Danielle opened her car door.

"Just in case of what?" Lily asked nervously.

"I really don't know. But here are the keys." Danielle tossed Lily her key ring. She opened the car door and started to step out. Pausing, she looked at Lily. "You have your cellphone with you?"

"Yeah, why?"

"I don't expect anything to happen but just in case. Well, you know what to do." Danielle got out of the car and slammed the door behind her. Taking a deep breath, she started walking in the direction of the cliff.

The sound of waves hitting the rocky beach below filled her

ears. It grew louder with each step she took toward the bluff. When she was about twenty feet from where Darlene had dropped off, she paused a moment and looked back at her car. Lily sat in the passenger seat, anxiously watching her.

Turning back to the cliff, Danielle startled when she came face-to-face with Darlene, who stood less than two feet away.

"You again," Darlene said.

"I thought you had moved on."

"I had something I needed to do first." Darlene smiled.

"And did you do it?"

"Yes." Darlene glanced back to the cliff.

"Then why are you still here?"

"I've just been waiting for someone to come by. I had no idea it would be you—someone who could actually see and hear me."

"Why did you need someone to come by?"

"To see what I did, of course." Darlene cocked her head to one side as if she were thinking of something. Finally, she asked, "Have you seen Todd?"

"Not since he left. Why? Have you seen him?"

"He's angry with me. He moved on without me. When marriage vows say *until death do you part*, it's true."

"You did kill him," Danielle reminded her.

"So? I'm dead now too, you would think that would even things out."

Danielle glanced back at the car. Lily was still watching her. She looked back to Darlene. "Okay, what do you want to show me?"

"It's over there." Darlene pointed to the edge of the cliff where she just a moment before had stepped off.

"Fine, but no funny business," Danielle warned.

"What is that supposed to mean?" Darlene frowned.

"Don't be trying to shove me off the cliff or anything."

"Shove you off the cliff?" Without warning, Darlene leaned forward and pushed at Danielle. Effortlessly, her hands passed through Danielle's body. "You mean like that?"

Danielle smiled. Darlene, like Angela, was unable to harness her energy in the same way Walt had.

"I don't know why that makes you smile," Darlene snapped. "Even if I could push you off a cliff, why would I? How could you help me then? And don't you think I'm in enough trouble already?"

"Fair enough. Okay, show me what you want me to see."

In a huff, Darlene turned from Danielle and marched to the cliff. She pointed down the hill. Taking a deep breath, Danielle walked to the cliff and looked down.

Teetering precariously on a shelf midway between the top of the cliff and the shore was an upside-down black sports car, its cab so severely smashed Danielle could not imagine anyone had survived the accident.

Danielle looked back to where Darlene had been standing; she was going to ask if anyone was in the car, but Darlene was no longer there.

TWENTY-FOUR

The air had been still when they had first arrived at Pilgrim's Point, yet now the breeze sent the treetops to dancing and repeatedly blew Lily's hair into her face, which she stubbornly brushed back over and over again. Danielle, whose hair was neatly confined in a fishtail braid, was spared the annoyance.

"If someone was in that car, I don't see how they could still be alive," Lily said as she and Danielle stood by the red Ford Flex, waiting for the police to arrive.

"I keep thinking, maybe whoever was driving flew out before the car landed, and they got out of there alive. Maybe they just haven't returned to get their car."

"Don't you think the police would have told you that when you called?" Lily asked.

Danielle sighed sadly. "Yeah. You're probably right."

"I wonder whose car it is."

"I can't think of anyone around here who drives a black sports car." Danielle pulled her cellphone out of her back pocket and checked the time. "I wish they would hurry up."

"Is this why Harvey wanted you to come here? Is there some connection between him and Darlene? Or whoever owns the sports car? And why is Darlene still here?"

"If Darlene hadn't said what she did, I would make two assumptions. One, that she is currently haunting this place because it's where she died. And two, she just happened to witness the accident. So seeing her today wouldn't necessarily have anything to do with Harvey or the black sports car."

"What did she say?"

"She said something about wanting me to see what she had done. As if she was responsible for the accident."

"Well, that's just creepy." Lily shuddered.

"Although that doesn't make sense either. There is no way a spirit—one who is unable to harness her energy—could cause a car accident."

The sound of sirens roaring up the highway in their direction momentarily silenced them. They both looked in the direction of the sound. A moment later, several police cars, followed by an ambulance, came into view.

———

"DO you have some special radar that homes in on dead bodies?" Officer Brian Henderson asked almost forty minutes later as he walked up to Danielle and Lily, who continued to stand by Danielle's car, out of the way of the commotion. He had just been with the rest of the responders, who were currently working to bring the battered car up the side of the mountain to the highway.

"I guess this means someone is in the car?" Danielle asked, still leaning against her vehicle.

"Yes, but until they can lift the car up, it's impossible to get to him."

"A male? Just one person? Any idea who it is?" Lily asked.

Brian shook his head and looked back to where all the activity was taking place on the side of the hill. "None. One interesting fact. The car is registered to Stoddard Gusarov."

"Really?" Danielle frowned and glanced back to where she'd seen Darlene earlier. "I knew he had a lot of cars; wouldn't they have gone to the trust? And if so, who would be driving it?"

"I just got off the phone with their attorney. Seems they've already sold all Stoddard's cars—or at least they thought they had. He checked the inventory list to see who purchased that one, but it wasn't on the list. They didn't know about it."

"Who would be driving around in Stoddard's sports car?" Lily asked.

They had their answer twenty minutes later when the responders were finally able to access the cab of the sports car. Danielle and Lily watched as the car was hooked up to the tow truck and the body loaded into the ambulance.

"Chuck Christiansen?" Danielle repeated after Joe Morelli told her the identity of the deceased driver.

"Coroner says it looks like he was killed on impact," Joe told her. "We found a gun in the car. It's the same caliber as the one that killed Haston. But we won't know if it's the same one until it's tested."

Brian, Joe, Danielle, and Lily stood by the Ford Flex while the team continued to process the scene.

"He had a considerable amount of cash on him," Brian added. "Along with a false ID in his wallet. There were packed suitcases in the car. Looks like he was heading out of Frederickport when he drove off that cliff."

"So you think he shot Bart and then took off? Heading to Canada, maybe?" Lily asked.

"Canada would be my guess," Joe said. "Considering the direction he was driving."

"Wow." Danielle shook her head as she stared off toward the cliff. "They're all dead now. Darlene, Stoddard, Bart, Chuck…"

"Don't forget Isabella," Joe added.

"None of this would have happened had Isabella not had that brain aneurysm," Danielle murmured.

"Or if I hadn't pulled into that rest stop," Lily added.

Brian shook his head and watched his team. "It was all so senseless."

The four stood in silence for a few moments, each considering the strange series of events that had brought them to this place. Finally, Joe looked at Danielle and asked, "How did you happen to come here today? What made you walk out and look down the side of the hill? That car could have gone undetected for days."

Danielle considered her choice of words before answering. She looked at Joe and shrugged. "I just had this gut feeling. Can't really explain it. I told Lily I wanted to drive out here this morning, and she agreed to come with me."

Joe studied Danielle for a moment. "A gut feeling?"

"The same gut feeling you had when you broke into Presley House?" Brian asked.

"I didn't break in exactly," Danielle argued.

"Or when you found your cousin in that beach shack?" Brian added.

"Maybe I do have some sort of radar," Danielle conceded.

"You have some sort of something, that's for sure," Brian muttered.

"I HAVE TO SAY, Brian seems friendlier these days," Lily said as she got into the passenger side of the car while Danielle climbed into the driver's side. Joe and Brian had returned to the other officers.

"I suppose he did soften up a bit when I helped him get those murder charges dropped against him." Danielle slammed her car door shut.

"He should be grateful to you." Lily buckled her seatbelt. "If it wasn't for you, he could be facing the death penalty right now. Heck, he owes you his life."

"I'm not sure about that."

"I am," Lily huffed.

"It's Joe I wonder about." Danielle hooked her seatbelt as she watched Joe in the distance.

"What do you mean?" Lily leaned back in the car seat.

"Just that I wonder what he thinks about me now. There was a time he was convinced I was some mental case."

"Do you care?"

Danielle shrugged. "I don't know. I guess not." She slipped her car key in the ignition yet made no attempt to turn on the engine. Instead, she and Lily leaned back in their seats and watched the responders finish up.

"Assuming the gun they found with Christiansen was the same one that killed Haston, then it's safe to assume Haston's murder has been solved," Lily said.

"We always figured it was probably Chuck." Danielle watched as the ambulance pulled out onto the highway.

"So what do you figure happened?"

"I don't know…It's pretty obvious Haston drove himself to Frederickport, considering where they found his car parked. I wonder, was the plan to meet with Chuck before they went to court in Astoria, or were they intending to skip town together?"

"It's possible Haston assumed they were leaving together, but Chuck had different plans, maybe first to settle a score with his partner in crime for rolling over on him." Lily suggested. "Or perhaps Christiansen asked Haston to meet him here under the pretense he wanted to discuss the case before they went to court. Considering how Haston spilled everything to the cops, can't really see him as someone who intended to live as a fugitive on the run."

"I don't know about that. When he first started talking, he probably assumed they would go lighter on him if he cooperated. But all it did was dig his hole deeper. And considering he obviously met with his killer at Presley House, he doesn't sound like someone who planned to make it to court."

"Okay. So let's assume the two decided to meet up here. Somehow, Chuck got his hands on one of Stoddard's cars. I guess that wouldn't be so difficult, considering everything. The cops are going to be looking for a car registered to Chuck when he doesn't show up at court. They decided to meet at Presley House. It's possible Bart parked his car where the cops eventually found it, and he walked over to Presley House, assuming Chuck was going to pick him up there so they can drive off to Canada together. But Chuck has different plans. When they get there, Chuck kills Bart, knowing it will be a while before someone finds the body—and by then he'll be in Canada."

Danielle looked to Lily. "Sounds like a likely scenario."

"But my question—how does Harvey figure into all this? Why did he send you up here?"

"Not sure. I wonder how Harvey would even know Chuck had been killed in a car accident. It looks like Chuck left Presley House after he shot Bart and then headed out of town, probably going to Canada...unless..."

Lily looked to Danielle. "Unless what?"

"Maybe his spirit went back to Presley House after the accident. That would make sense. Shortly after death, a spirit can be confused. Wouldn't be out of the question for him to go back to the last place he had been."

"Are you saying he and Harvey became some sort of spirit buddies? Harvey is passing on information Chuck gives him?"

"It has to be something like that. But I'm still trying to figure out Darlene's role in all this—if she has one."

"Looks like they're done." Lily nodded toward the responders, who were all returning to their vehicles, preparing to take off. The two women watched as Brian and Joe headed to their car. Just as the officers opened their car doors, they glanced toward Lily and Danielle. Joe gave them a slight wave before getting into the vehicle while Brian nodded in their direction and then climbed into the car.

"You want to go get some lunch?" Danielle asked, still not making an effort to start the engine. She watched as each of the responders' vehicles pulled out onto the highway. When Lily didn't answer her question, Danielle repeated it while turning on the engine.

"Lily?" Danielle looked at her friend, who stared off toward the bluff. "Do you want to stop and get some lunch or not?"

Lily continued to stare off into the distance. Licking her lips, she said, "Umm...Dani...I think I know how Darlene might have been responsible for Chuck's accident."

"I told you, she can't harness her energy. There is no way she could make him drive off that cliff."

Lily nodded toward the cliff. "What do you see, Dani?"

Danielle frowned and then looked from Lily to the cliff, where Darlene had been standing earlier that day. She froze for a moment and then looked back to Lily. "What do you see?"

"I asked you first. What do you see, Dani?"

Danielle swallowed nervously and then said, "Darlene. She's standing by the edge of the cliff. Don't tell me you can see her too."

Lily nodded. "Yep. I can see her."

TWENTY-FIVE

I nstead of going out for lunch, Danielle headed back to Marlow House.

"If Chuck could see Darlene, like I did, then maybe she was responsible for him driving off that cliff," Lily suggested.

"It is a sharp turn. If he had just left Presley House after killing Bart, his adrenaline would be pumping...and then the woman he murders suddenly appears out of nowhere."

Lily shuddered. "No wonder he drove off that cliff."

"If Darlene has been haunting that spot, she probably recognized the car. After all, it did belong to her husband. Who knows, maybe she's been waiting for Chuck to drive along Pilgrim's Point so she could get her revenge."

"How is it that I could see her? I didn't see her the first time when we drove up."

"I don't know." Danielle considered the possibilities. "Although, you hear about some haunted places where people report seeing ghosts—not people like me—normal people."

"You saying you aren't normal?" Lily teased.

Danielle smiled. "You know what I mean."

"Do you think Darlene chooses who can see her? Or is it random?"

"If she scared Chuck and got him to drive off the cliff, I wouldn't think it was random."

"Then would it be possible for me to see Walt if he wanted me to see him?"

Danielle silently considered the question a few moments before answering. "Interesting idea. But I don't think so. If ghosts could just make anyone see them if they wanted, then wouldn't more be hanging around? Think about it, young mothers who die suddenly and don't want to leave their children. Or anyone who wanted to stick around. Think how much easier it would be if you could get people you loved to see you—maybe even hear you. And then if they could also harness energy…" Danielle shook her head. "No I don't think that's in the universe's grand plan."

"But I did see Darlene. And chances are, so did Chuck before he drove off that cliff."

"I just think it's one of those isolated, limited things. Some spirits find a way to make people see them—it might only be for brief glimpses. Others, like Walt, harness energy so they can move things around, yet he's confined to a limited area, and people can't see him, other than someone like me. Although, most people seem to be able to smell the cigar smoke. And then there's Angela, who can control electric gadgets to some extent but can't move a solid object."

Lily shook her head. "Sounds all very random to me."

They were quiet for a few minutes. Finally, Danielle said, "Perhaps it is simply all about energy."

"Energy? In what way?"

Gripping the steering wheel as she drove down the highway, Danielle stared ahead. "I've been looking at this all wrong. Maybe it's not about Walt harnessing energy—he is the energy. All spirits are energy."

"Okay, so? What would that mean?"

"Think of a flashlight battery; it will run your flashlight, but it isn't strong enough to power an electric car. Darlene is using what energy reserves she has to get people to see her. I bet she can only do it in bursts; otherwise someone would have reported seeing her by now. Maybe Walt really could leave Marlow House and wander the countryside if he wasn't already using his energy to move objects around and dream hop."

"Sounds very confusing. It would sure make it a lot easier if there was a rule book!"

Danielle laughed. "You mean like in *Beatlejuice?*"

"*Beatlejuice?*" Lily frowned.

"Yeah, remember they had some sort of book of the dead…let me see…what was it called?"

"Oh, you mean the *Handbook for the Recently Departed*," Lily said with a chuckle.

"Was that what it was called?"

"I think so. Maybe we should get a copy."

"Wouldn't hurt," Danielle said with a snort.

When they pulled up into the drive at Marlow House a few minutes later, Lily asked, "Are you going to tell Walt your energy theory?"

Danielle parked the car and turned off the ignition. "I don't think so. He's always reminding me that I don't really know how all of this works—that I'm only guessing."

"Yeah, you don't want to do anything to make him think he was right," Lily teased.

"Exactly! Why would I do that?"

They both laughed. Just as they reached the back door leading into the kitchen, they heard a woman call out from the side gate. "Oh, Danielle! Danielle Boatman!"

Pausing at the back porch, Danielle and Lily looked toward the caller. It was Heather Donovan.

"I've been watching for your car!" Heather said in a rush when she reached them, out of breath from running. "I've been dying to talk to you!"

"Watching for my car? Is something wrong?" Danielle asked.

"I heard all about that dead body you found!" Heather explained.

Danielle frowned. "How could you have heard? I just got home."

"It was on the radio."

"On the radio? That's awful quick."

"Dani"—Lily nudged her friend—"I think she's talking about the *other* dead body."

"Other dead body?" Confused, Heather looked from Lily to Danielle, who was now staring at Lily.

"Bart Haston, Dani. She's talking about Bart," Lily said under her breath.

"Of course I'm talking about Bart Haston. Who else would I be talking about?" Heather asked.

"Oh, duh," Danielle said, feeling foolish. "What did you need to talk to me about?"

"Do you have a few minutes, I was wondering if I could come in and talk to you for a minute." She then glanced at Lily and then back to Danielle. "Alone, if you wouldn't mind."

"Hey, no problem," Lily answered for Danielle, snatching the key from her hand so she could unlock the door. "I have some things I need to do."

Just as Lily unlocked the door, Sadie came charging into the kitchen to greet them.

WHEN LILY and Sadie stepped into the library a few minutes later, she was greeted with the scent of cigar. Shutting the door behind her, she said, "Walt, if you're in the library, let me know. I want to talk to you."

She had her answer when a book fell from the desk.

"Danielle is in the parlor with our new neighbor. I thought you might be interested in knowing what we found today."

Lily went on to explain what had happened at Pilgrim's Point, while hoping the book dropping to the floor was the result of paranormal activity and not an earthquake. Because if Walt wasn't really in the room, she was going to feel ridiculous if she had been talking to herself.

"I HOPE I didn't hurt your friend's feelings," Heather said when Danielle led her into the parlor a few minutes later.

"I'm sure Lily is fine. Why did you need to talk to me alone?" Danielle took a seat on a chair while Heather sat on the sofa. "I don't really have any secrets from Lily."

"Well, I do."

"Excuse me?" Danielle frowned.

"Oh, I don't mean Lily exactly. But like I explained when we first met, I'm a writer and I'm working on a book. I got the impression Lily was rather close to Jon Altar."

"Jon—or Ian as we call him—is also one of my close friends."

"It's just that I feel uncomfortable discussing my work with another writer."

"In case they might steal it?" Danielle joked.

"Exactly." Heather was not joking. "I was hoping you would agree to keep this discussion between the two of us."

"Okay, between the two of us." *Liar, liar. The minute she leaves, I'll probably tell Lily everything.*

"First, what did Lily mean when she said *other body?*"

"It's sort of a long story." Danielle wasn't prepared to share what had happened to them at Pilgrim's Point with a woman she barely knew. "Why don't you tell me what you wanted to talk to me about."

Heather looked disappointed that Danielle wasn't going to answer her question, but she continued.

"I heard on the radio about the dead body you found at Presley House."

"Yes. He was in the kitchen. But I'm sure you've heard some teenage boys actually found him first."

"Yes. I understand that when they found him, he was in a trunk in the basement. And when the police checked, the trunk was empty."

Danielle studied Heather. "That sounds about right."

"I was wondering, how did you happen to get into Presley House?"

"Well—" Danielle smiled "—I suppose if you asked Officer Henderson, he would say I broke in."

"Did you?"

"Well, technically speaking, I suppose I did."

"Was the door locked?" Heather asked.

"Actually it was when I first tried it."

"So did you break a window to get in?"

"Of course not. I don't go around breaking windows. Anyway, every window in that house—except one—is already broken."

"I understand the broken windows are all boarded up to keep people out."

"True, although the window in the kitchen was only half boarded up. According to Officer Henderson, it had been boarded up the last time he was in the house. The plywood was pretty much just hanging there."

"So that's how you got in?"

"No. I went through the front door."

Heather frowned. "I thought you said the door was locked?"

Danielle studied Heather a moment and finally said, "You might say the door…it just sorta opened on its own."

Heather's eyes widened. "Someone—or something let you in?"

"Is this about the story you want to write? Is this why you're asking me all these questions?"

Heather sat back in the sofa. "What do you mean?"

"You said you wanted to write about a haunted house."

"Do you think Presley House is haunted?" Heather asked.

"According to local legend it is."

Heather smiled. "But you've actually been in the house—you say the door opened by itself and let you in."

"I didn't say that exactly."

"Then how did the door open if it was locked when you first got there?"

"What is it you really want?"

Heather took a deep breath and then looked Danielle in the eyes. "I want to know if you saw a ghost when you were at Presley House."

"Why would you ask something like that? I know many people who've gone into Presley House and have never seen a ghost. Like the boys who broke in, the police officers who checked out the property and even Adam Nichols, who used to manage Presley House for its owners. None of them claimed to have seen a ghost."

"Yes, but when you went there by yourself, you managed to get into the house without breaking in. And you found the body."

"So?"

"I'm thinking if those boys really did find a body and it disappeared, then something had to have hidden it."

"And you think a ghost hid it?"

"Maybe."

"And just where did the ghost hide it?" Danielle asked.

"Umm…probably a secret room in the house."

"A secret room?" *Interesting, the chief and I discussed the possibility of a secret room.*

"Yes."

"So because I found the body, you assume the resident ghost must have helped me find it?"

"That's pretty much what I'm thinking, yes."

Danielle laughed. "And if I was to say *yes, I saw a ghost,* you would think I was crazy."

"No, I wouldn't. I would ask you another question."

"Really? What would you ask me?"

"I'd ask you if the ghost told you his name."

"His name?" Danielle frowned.

"Yes. I want to know if the ghost's name is Harvey."

TWENTY-SIX

D anielle and Lily sat in the parlor, eating tuna fish sandwiches:
Lily on a chair facing Danielle, who sat on the sofa. Max
perched on the back of the sofa, his paw gently patting Danielle's
shoulder, begging for a taste of tuna.

"She knew his name and she wouldn't say how she knew it?"
Lily asked before taking a bite of her lunch.

Danielle removed a bit of tuna fish from her sandwich and
offered it to Max. He nibbled it daintily from her fingers. On the
floor, Sadie sat at Lily's feet, glaring up at Max. Just moments
earlier, she'd tried begging for a bite of sandwich, only to have Lily
scold her.

"I didn't admit to seeing a ghost, so she didn't tell me how she
knew his name."

"She just blurted out his name and then didn't explain
anything?" Lily took another bite of her sandwich.

"At first I assumed she was just being nosey. You know, had
heard on the radio about me finding a body and wanted the juicy
details. But then she started asking about ghosts, and when she
mentioned his name, well, that kinda threw me for a loop."

"I bet it did. I would like to know why *Harvey*—how she came up
with that name."

"I did ask her. She said something about hearing that was the
ghost's name, which I don't believe for a minute."

BOBBI HOLMES

Lily looked up from her half-eaten sandwich. "You think she was lying?"

"Without a doubt. Heather Donovan is not a very good liar."

"Hmmm…well, when you first met, she did tell you she intended to write about a haunted house, and Presley House is the only house in town with the reputation of being haunted. So perhaps you and those boys aren't the only one who visited the house this past week."

"You suggesting she may have also seen Harvey?" Danielle asked.

"If she knew his name, I'd say she must have also talked to him. If so, I wonder, does she have some psychic abilities like you? Or is Harvey like Darlene, using his energy to make his presence known to people who aren't normally sensitive to these sorts of things?"

"What does Lily mean by that?" Walt asked as he appeared in the room.

Danielle glanced over to Walt. "Hi, Walt. Where have you been?"

"Around." Walt walked over to the sofa and sat down next to Danielle.

Lily looked to the door, where Danielle had just directed her greeting. "Hi, Walt."

Danielle nodded at what appeared to be an empty spot on the sofa. "He's over here now."

Max jumped down from the back of the sofa, landing in the space occupied by Walt's lap. Sadie immediately leapt up and went to the couch, nosing Max, who swatted her nose.

"Stop, you two!" Walt scolded.

"Don't tell me, the animals are both converging on Walt?" Lily asked.

Danielle glanced to Walt and the competing pets and nodded. "Pretty much."

"So what were you talking about?" Walt asked. Sadie now lay by his feet while Max leaned over the sofa's cushion, occasionally batting the dog's head.

"We saw Darlene today," Danielle began.

Walt leaned back in the sofa and looked at Danielle. "Lily told me what happened at Pilgrim's Point."

"Lily did?" Danielle looked from Walt to Lily.

160

"I did what?" Lily frowned.

"Walt said you told him what happened to us this morning."

Lily let out a brief laugh. "I wasn't sure he was in the library with me. Glad to know I wasn't talking to myself."

Walt flashed an unseen smile to Lily and then turned his attention to Danielle. "So what now?"

"Well, the police are no longer looking for Christiansen and Haston. We don't have to worry about going to court, which I suppose is a relief. I wasn't looking forward to that. It's pretty crazy that all the parties directly involved with what happened to Lily are gone now."

"Do they know for sure Christiansen killed Haston?" Walt asked.

"I think it's just a formality, having the gun checked. I can't imagine who else would have killed him. The way Darlene was talking this morning, I get the feeling she might be moving on now. It sounded as if she was just sticking around so she could even the score with Christiansen."

"Are you going to do anything about Harvey?" Walt asked.

"I don't know what I need to do." Danielle shrugged.

"What you need to do about what?" Lily asked.

"Walt wanted to know if I was going to do anything about Harvey."

"Dani, you told us Harvey wanted to help you find something. Something that didn't have anything to do with all this other stuff—at least that was the feeling you got."

Danielle frowned. "So?"

"Harvey obviously has figured out how to dream hop. If he still wants your help, you can't exactly ignore him. He could easily take over your dream again."

Danielle groaned. "You're right. I would like to think all of this was finished, what with finding Haston's body and Christiansen."

"You know Dani, you virtually stopped taking reservations when I moved in to recuperate—aside from Will Wayne. These last couple of weeks, with me off the IV treatment, we've both gotten used to sort of coming and going without any demands of the B and B."

Danielle looked at Lily. "Not sure I understand your point."

"Without guests, it makes it easier for you to deal with certain annoyances—like a dream-invading ghost—or to venture off on side trips, like breaking into an old haunted house or taking a drive up to Pilgrim's Point. Beginning the second week of November, this place is going to be taking a lot of your time. You already have reservations booked pretty solid through Christmas and into the New Year."

"I think what Lily is saying is"—Walt spoke up—"you need to resolve the Harvey problem before your guests start arriving."

"You're both right." Danielle sighed.

"Oh? What did Walt say?"

"Pretty much what you did." Danielle set her now empty plate on the end table and leaned back in the sofa.

"So what is the plan of action?" Lily asked.

"I suppose the first thing I need to do is try to find out more about Harvey. Who is he, and what is he looking for?"

Max stopped batting at Sadie and looked at Walt.

"According to Ben from the museum, Marie probably knew the Presley twins; they were about her age. I'm pretty sure Harvey is one of the twins."

"I assume you're going to go talk to Marie and see what she knows," Lily said.

"Would be a good place to start. According to Adam, she should be back from Portland by tomorrow. I'll give her a call in the morning."

"And then there's Max," Walt reminded her, looking down at the cat.

"Max? Oh, that's right. Max was living in Presley House." Danielle reached out and stroked the fur along Max's neck. He began to purr.

"Unfortunately, Max doesn't really know anything about Harvey's history—when he was alive. He may or may not be one of the twins. Harvey has never mentioned his family or last name to Max. When Max moved into Presley House a number of years ago, the house was empty. There was no Harvey."

"I'm assuming that's because when he moved into the house it wasn't October?" Danielle suggested.

"Precisely." Walt nodded.

"I hate these one-sided conversations," Lily grumbled.

"I promise to fill you in on everything that we say—afterwards," Danielle told her.

"Sure…whatever." Lily popped the last bite of sandwich into her mouth.

"Max initially moved into the house during the summer. It was fall—I am assuming October—when Harvey showed up. He seemed surprised to see Max but told him he was welcomed to stay, providing he helped him look for it."

"Look for what?" Danielle asked.

"Max doesn't know. But every year Harvey would show up and start going through the house, from top to bottom, looking for something. What it was exactly, he never said. And when kids would periodically break into the house—normally as some Halloween prank or dare—he would do things to scare them. Max got the impression he initially did it to scare them away so he could search the house without them underfoot, but over time, Max came to realize Harvey enjoyed frightening the teenagers."

"Harvey is a teenager himself," Danielle reminded him.

No longer able to contain herself, Lily begged, "Please tell me what you two are talking about."

Danielle took a moment to fill Lily in on Walt's side of the conversation.

"What I'm trying to figure out, why Halloween? Now if Max wasn't there to verify the fact—" Lily paused a moment and let out a groan. "Good lord, I'm talking about a cat." She shook her head before continuing. "Then I would assume Harvey was always haunting that place, but people only noticed on Halloween. Because after all, it is Halloween —ghosts and stuff. And if Harvey is the spirit of a teenage boy, then it kinda makes sense he might be more active that time of year."

"But we know he's only there during October. He isn't there the rest of the year," Danielle reminded her.

Leaning back on the sofa, Walt silently listened as he watched smoke rings drift up toward the ceiling and disappear.

"Exactly! But why?" Lily asked.

Danielle silently considered the question for a moment. "I've thought about this a lot and have come up with two possible scenarios."

"Which are?" Lily asked.

"Perhaps, whatever he is looking for has something to do with Halloween. Something lost on Halloween, maybe?"

"And what is the other possibility?"

"Some people believe Halloween is a time when dead souls can return to the earth. To see their love ones—for their love ones to see them. Maybe there is some truth to that. Perhaps the Halloween season opens some doorway between our world and the spirit world," Danielle suggested.

Lily looked to where she was sure Walt was sitting on the sofa. She could smell the cigar smoke. "What about it, Walt? Do you think Danielle has something there? About the spirit doorway?"

Preparing to take a puff off his cigar, Walt paused a moment. Lifting his head, he looked from Lily to Danielle. Shaking his head, he said, "A bunch of hooey. Danielle is just making this stuff up. She doesn't know how any of this really works."

LILY REACHED into the pumpkin and pulled out the slimy innards. It was late Tuesday afternoon and she sat with Danielle on the side patio while they prepared jack-o'-lanterns.

"How can Walt say that?" Lily asked. "That you're just making this stuff up?"

"I suppose he's right, in a way." Danielle scraped the inside of her pumpkin out after dumping pulp and seeds on a sheet of newspaper. "Although I wouldn't call a theory the same thing as making stuff up."

"Did he say what he believes?" Lily asked.

"I imagine what he believes would not be as interesting as what he knows."

Lily looked up from her pumpkin. "What do you mean?"

"Think about it, Lily. When Walt left here the first time to follow the light, he went somewhere. He saw something."

"Has he told you what that was?"

"No, not really. I know just what I've told you. That Walt can leave when he's ready, but until then he's confined here at Marlow House."

"Do you think that's true?"

"True? You mean, do I think Walt lied?"

"Not lied exactly. But what you said about the energy thing— how Walt is using up all his energy to move things and dream hop, but if he focused his energy elsewhere, he might be able to leave here and wander the countryside if that's what he wanted."

Danielle shrugged. "I don't know. Maybe…maybe not."

"So what now?" Lily positioned her knife on her pumpkin and began carving features.

"First thing, I'm going to finish this jack-o'-lantern. Then I'm going to put it by one of the front windows—with yours. Later I'll serve us some of that yummy chili I have simmering in the slow cooker, and in the morning…I'm calling Marie Nichols."

TWENTY-SEVEN

A dam Nichols propped his newly polished leather shoes atop his desk as he leaned back in his office chair, newspaper in hand. Without looking away from the front-page article he was so engrossed in, he leaned forward and reached for his cup of coffee, which sat on the edge of the desk. Just as he grabbed it, a knock came at his door, breaking his concentration. He glanced up. Standing at his door in the hallway was Danielle Boatman.

"No one was in the front office," Danielle explained, nodding behind her. "Didn't think you'd mind if I just came in." She stepped into Adam's office.

Setting his mug back down and awkwardly removing his feet from the desk to the floor, he sat up straight and tossed the paper aside. "Well, if it isn't the never-a-dull-moment Danielle Boatman. I see you found another dead body. What is that, two in one week for you?"

Danielle walked to the two empty chairs facing Adam's desk. "Well, you know me, I'll do practically anything to avoid going to court." She tossed her purse on one of the chairs and sat on the other one.

"Careful, if Henderson hears you say something like that, he might get it into his head you put Christiansen and Haston in their current states."

Danielle smiled. "You have a point."

"So why were you and Lily at Pilgrim's Point?"

"We were just taking a drive. Ian took off early yesterday morning for New York. We don't have anyone staying at Marlow House this week. I suppose if we hadn't found Christiansen's car, someone else eventually would have."

"According to the newspaper, it was Stoddard's car."

"Yeah, I guess it was. According to the attorney for the trust, that vehicle wasn't included on the inventory list."

"I imagine it was parked at one of Stoddard's properties, somewhere that Chuck still had access to," Adam suggested.

"That's kind of what I figured. Although, I would have thought whoever was in charge of the trust would have inspected all the properties."

"Doesn't surprise me. I remember Isabella telling me her uncle had a number of corporations he expressly used to hide assets."

"Hide from who?"

"I imagine Uncle Sam and probably Darlene."

"Chuck obviously knew about the car and where it was stored. From what I understand, his car is still missing."

"He probably left it wherever Stoddard's car had been parked."

"Yeah, that's pretty much what I'm figuring."

"So tell me, Danielle, what brings you here today? I can't imagine you came just to gloat about your newest discovery."

"Gloat? Am I gloating?"

Adam chuckled. "Not really. But you have to admit, you are a regular Nancy Drew. Either that or a diabolical serial killer who has convinced everyone you just happen to trip over these dead bodies."

"Fortunately for me, they have the murder weapon that killed Haston, and Christiansen's fingerprints were all over it."

Adam picked up the newspaper and glanced at it for a moment, then looked up to Danielle. "According to the newspaper, they don't know if the gun they found shot Haston."

"I imagine they didn't know when they wrote that article. But I spoke to Joe this morning, and he told me it was. Looks like Chuck killed his partner in crime and then planned to hide out in Canada, but then had his misfortunate accident."

Adam shook his head and tossed the paper back on the desk. "I never cared much for Chuck and thought Haston was kind of a weenie."

"Tsk-tsk, to speak ill of the dead," Danielle teased.

"You don't seem too heartbroken over their deaths."

"Considering the fact they tried to frame me for Stoddard's murder, Chuck tried to kill me—and they both were involved with hiring that hit man to kill Joe and me, not to mention they were involved with abducting Lily...no, I'm not particularly crying over their deaths. Anyway, I don't believe death is the final frontier."

"Understandable."

"Anyway..." Danielle leaned forward. "I had some errands to do this morning and I thought I'd stop by and ask you when your grandmother is going to be back in town. You mentioned the other day she was going to be gone until Wednesday."

"Does this have something to do with what you were asking me about the other day, Presley House?"

"Yes. I'm just very curious about the house and its history. Like I told you, according to Ben, your grandmother probably knew the family who originally lived in that house. I just figured the story of Presley House—considering locals have been saying it's haunted for years—might be interesting for my guests."

"Ahh, sort of a tourist attraction?" Adam smiled.

"I suppose...not that I intend to be a nuisance to the neighborhood. But it wouldn't hurt to have colorful stories to share with our guests."

"Clever idea." Adam smiled. "If you're free to take a drive in about—" Adam paused and glanced at his watch "—twenty minutes, I'm heading out to meet my grandmother at a diner about half an hour from here."

"What is she doing there?"

"The woman who took her to Portland is dropping her off there instead of coming all the way in to Frederickport. She has to be at Salem this afternoon, so I told her I'd pick Grandma up to save her some time. If you want to drive with me, keep me company, I'm sure Grandma would love seeing you. We'll be having something to eat at the diner before we head back."

"Sure. Sounds great. Let me call Lily and tell her where I'll be going."

"IT WAS REALLY sweet of you to keep Adam company this morning." Marie eyed Danielle and Adam, visions of matchmaking dancing in her head. The three sat at a booth in the diner. Marie was already at the restaurant when they had first arrived. The moment Marie had seen them walk through the doorway together, she had scooted over in her bench seat, making it impossible for either one to sit on her side of the table. Determined, she made sure they sat next to each other.

"When Danielle mentioned she wanted to talk to you, I suggested she drive out with me today," Adam explained.

Marie leaned forward and patted Danielle's right hand. "Sure she did."

Danielle smiled and glanced over at Adam, who looked in her direction. He silently shook his head and rolled his eyes.

Marie picked up a menu from the table and opened it up. "You will never believe what I heard on the radio. Chuck Christiansen is dead. I didn't get the details; it was just a quick news flash."

"Danielle can tell you all about that," Adam said as he picked up his menu.

Twenty minutes later, after the server took their order, brought their food, and Danielle told Marie about her and Lily's discovery at Pilgrim's Point, Danielle broached the subject of the original owners of Presley House.

"I remember the Presley boys. Those three were always getting into trouble. My father told me to stay away from them. Of course, I never wanted anything to do with them, anyway."

Danielle set her iced tea glass on the table and looked at Marie. "Those three? Were there three brothers? I thought there was just a set of twins?"

"I meant the twins and Harvey Crump."

Danielle felt her heart race at the mention of Harvey. "Harvey Crump? Who was he?"

"Local boy, same age as the twins. They were friends for as long as I can remember. Harvey lived with his uncle—the town drunk. I remember my mother saying if she were Mrs. Presley, she wouldn't allow her boys to associate with someone like Harvey."

"Was Harvey a bad boy?" Danielle asked.

Marie pondered the question for a moment before answering. "To be perfectly honest, I'd say the twins were just as bad, if not worse. All three of them got into their share of mischief over the years—some say they were responsible for the fire on Main Street that took out a number of the local businesses."

"You mean the fire that burned down the newspaper office?"

Marie nodded. "Yes. Those three boys were caught about a week earlier, setting some fires along the beach. Burning up things they'd taken from people's back porches, like wooden chairs. And at the time of the fire downtown, some claimed to have seen the boys hanging around—not far from where the fire was set. Of course they couldn't prove anything, and then Harvey was killed."

"Harvey was killed? How?"

"Most say his uncle did it. Especially since they found the uncle's body a short time later. Jumped off a bridge."

"Nice family," Adam muttered as he took as sip of coffee.

"He was killed by his uncle?" Danielle couldn't imagine such a thing.

"That's what they say. Harvey's body was washed up on the beach a few days after the fire. His head was bashed in. Authorities figured whoever did it dumped his body into the ocean to get rid of it, but the ocean apparently had a different idea."

"Did they say why the uncle did it?" Danielle asked.

"Some say he was probably drunk, heard about the fire, and lost his temper. Probably didn't mean to kill him. Then after he realized what he had done, he took his own life."

Danielle shook her head. "How tragic...so what happen to the Presley boys after that? They weren't investigated for the fire?"

"I have my suspicions." Marie finished her orange juice and then set the glass on the table. "I imagine after they found poor Harvey's body, the Presley boys were quick to blame him. And since the boy was dead, the local authorities didn't pursue the matter."

"Do you know what time of year this all happened?" Danielle asked.

Marie shook her head. "No. I can't remember."

"Do you remember when the Presley family moved from the area?"

"A couple of years later." Marie pushed her now empty plate to the end of the table. "Although, now that I think about it, those two boys seemed to be a little more...difficult...after Harvey died."

"Difficult how?"

"Their troublemaking escalated. I recall my mother once mentioning how they seemed very—angry."

"If they practically burned down half the town, I'd say they were already angry," Adam quipped.

"No, Adam, that's not what I mean. As you know, young boys often do stupid things because they're young and immature."

Adam narrowed his eyes and glared at his grandmother. "What do you mean *as I know?*"

Danielle laughed and patted Adam's shoulder. "Aww, come on, you know exactly what she means."

Marie continued. "But later, their motives for doing certain things seemed more...spiteful, angry. They got into some very public rows with their father, which my parents witnessed. And then one day, they just upped and left town."

"Do you think they moved away because they were having such problems with the twins?" Danielle asked.

"That's what my parents assumed."

"Any idea why they never sold the house? Why it's been vacant for all these years?"

"No. I was never friends with the boys, so I never kept track of them. My parents didn't particularly like the twins' parents, so they didn't keep in touch with them either."

"Do you remember any of their names?" Danielle asked.

"You mean the twins?" Marie asked.

"And their parents. I might want to do a little Internet search, see what comes up. It would help if I knew their names."

BEFORE LEAVING the diner to return to Frederickport, Danielle excused herself to visit the restroom. A few minutes later, she stood at the sink to wash her hands when her purse slipped out of her grasp and fell to the floor, scattering the purse's contents all over the bathroom floor.

Cursing, Danielle quickly got to her knees and gathered her belongings, shoving them back into the purse.

"So gross," she muttered a few moments later as she rewashed her hands.

Ten minutes later, after Danielle had returned to Adam and Marie, a woman entered the now empty restroom. She walked into the first stall and closed the door behind her, locking it. Just as she was about to sit down, she glanced at the floor and noticed some-thing sticking out from under one of her shoes.

Lifting her foot, she looked to the floor: a credit card. Reaching down, she picked up the credit card and inspected it. The name on the card read Danielle Boatman. Smiling, the woman tucked the credit card into her back pocket.

TWENTY-EIGHT

Danielle sat at the parlor desk, logging on to her laptop computer. Just as she pulled up the page for Google search, Max jumped up on the desk and proceeded to walk on the keyboard. Gently, Danielle pushed him away from the computer. Undeterred, he persistently attempted to stake claim to the open laptop, only to be pushed back again.

"Why do cats always do that?" Lily asked as she walked into the room, carrying two mugs of green tea. One she set on the desk. She kept the second mug for herself and sat down on a chair. "I have a friend whose cat always does that."

"Next time Walt hops into one of your dreams, ask him to ask Max why he does that," Danielle suggested with a chuckle.

"Hmmm, maybe I'll do that." Lily took a sip of tea. "Did you find anything yet?"

"No. I just logged in."

"So Harvey wasn't one of the twins after all."

Danielle kept her gaze on the laptop's screen. "Apparently not… oh, this is interesting."

"What did you find?"

"I decided to start with the local newspaper website. Under its *About* section, it gives a little history of the newspaper, such as who started it. It also mentions the fire and how all the records were lost."

"I wonder if Marie was right and those boys were responsible for the fire." Lily sipped her tea.

"I don't know, but according to the website, the newspaper office burned down a week before Halloween."

"Does it say anything about who they think started the fire?"

"No. Nothing." Danielle looked up at Lily. "But if Marie is right and Harvey was killed right after the fire, that puts his death around Halloween."

"Which may explain why he shows up every year at this time."

"I want to know why he haunts Presley House. Why there?"

"I might suggest you just ask him. But considering he gave you that creepy dream, I don't think that would be such a terrific idea."

"If I can figure out why he's haunting Presley House—what he's looking for—then maybe he'll move on and I won't have to worry about him trying another dream hop."

"Do all the Internet searches you want, but promise me you won't go back over to Presley House. I don't think you should go over there."

"Don't worry, I won't go back over there—at least not until the chief comes back from vacation."

"Why would that make a difference?"

"For one thing, if I go back over there now, the way the local cops are keeping an eye on that place, I would just get myself arrested again. And with the chief in Hawaii, I'd probably end up spending his vacation in jail. No, thanks."

"I'm glad to hear you aren't going back over there."

"I will eventually, Lily. First, I intend to find out all I can about Harvey and the Presleys. And the next time I go back to the house, I'm going with the chief."

"What are you searching for now?" Lily stood up and walked around the desk, looking over Danielle's shoulder.

"Seeing what I can find about Harvey's death."

"You know how Marie told you people felt his uncle didn't mean to kill him—which is why he then took his own life."

Danielle glanced over her shoulder at Lily. "Yeah, what about it?"

"If he didn't mean to kill his nephew and he was so distraught, why did he bother dumping Harvey's body in the ocean before he jumped off that bridge?"

Danielle shrugged. "I have no idea. Marie said he was the town drunk. Maybe he was drunk when he did it and, when he sobered up, couldn't face what he had done."

Before Lily could respond, her cellphone began to ring. She picked it up from where she had set it earlier, on the coffee table by the parlor sofa.

"It's Ian," Lily said as she answered the phone and then walked into the hallway.

When Lily returned to the parlor ten minutes later, she asked, "Dani, I have a huge favor to ask you. Can I borrow your car?"

"Sure, why?" Danielle looked up from the computer.

"I need to drive over to Astoria for Ian. He left a flash drive at Emma's on Sunday that he needs for his meeting. I have to pick it up and then bring it back here and upload it to his Dropbox so he can access the information before his meeting."

"I don't suppose Emma could do it for him," Danielle teased.

"She is a pretty amazing woman for her age, but using a computer, I don't think so."

"Would you like me to go with you?"

"No, you stay here and see what you can find out about Presley House. But I might take Sadie with me. She loves car drives and Emma is fond of her."

"Okay. Say hi to Emma for me."

DANIELLE SAT on the parlor sofa, Max curled up on her lap, sleeping. Absently stroking the feline's neck, Danielle played back in her mind all that she had learned about Harvey Crump while searching the Internet.

It wasn't until Lily left that Danielle realized waiting for the chief to return from Hawaii before she went to see Harvey again would not be an option. Unless, of course, she planned to wait until next October. When she told Lily she had no intention of going to Presley House alone, she failed to consider Harvey's past history. Each year, he showed up at Presley House in early October, and he left right after Halloween.

"What was I thinking?" Danielle berated herself. "Duhh...he'll be gone by the time the chief comes home."

Danielle might feel better knowing Harvey was leaving in three days, if she believed his mischief would end with his departure, which she didn't. All it really meant—it would be difficult for her to track him down should she need to find him again. There was no guarantee he couldn't dream hop from wherever he spent the rest of his time. She would prefer to settle the matter now instead of waiting for his return next October. Even if he stayed out of her dreams over the next year, it wouldn't alleviate her anxiety over worrying about Harvey's return and what he might do when he showed up again.

"Did you learn anything interesting?" Walt asked when he appeared in the parlor.

Danielle looked up from the sofa. Walt stood by the bookshelf, cigar in hand.

"I found some articles on Harvey's death."

"So was he murdered by his uncle?"

"Nothing was ever proved one way or the other. But the police seemed to believe he did it."

"Because of the fire?" Walt sat down on the chair facing Danielle. Max continued to sleep on her lap.

"The articles didn't say anything about the fire. But they did say the uncle killed himself the day before Harvey's body washed up on the beach."

"I thought Marie said something about the boys being under suspicion for starting the fire."

"She did, but there was nothing in the paper about it. Yet there were a couple references to interviews the police made during their investigation. According to Harvey's neighbors, he and his uncle seemed to get along, and neighbors never heard them fighting, even when the uncle was on a drinking binge. If anything, the uncle seemed rather indulgent of his nephew. As if the boy could do no wrong."

Walt rolled the unlit cigar between his fingertips, his expression thoughtful. "If there was no mention of the fire and the neighbors claimed the two never fought, why did the police peg the uncle for the murder?"

"The neighbors' interviews weren't the only ones cited by the newspaper. According to one article, Harvey's best friends—the Presley twins—claimed the uncle used to beat Harvey when he was drunk. According to the twins, the uncle had a violent temper."

"I have seen good men turn irrationally violent after consuming too much booze."

Danielle shrugged. "Perhaps. But the Presley family seems a little odd to me."

"Odd how?"

"I have to wonder how they got their money. I asked Marie about that this afternoon. I know he used to work for the Thorndikes, but that was before he was married. According to Marie, when he returned to town with his family, he never had a job. I guess Marie's mother once asked Mrs. Presley what her husband did for a living, and according to Mrs. Presley, her husband didn't have to work, he had come into a significant family inheritance."

"Perhaps he did. It would explain why he didn't work." Walt popped the unlit cigar into his mouth.

"I don't know who he could have inherited money from. He didn't have any family."

"How do you know that?"

"During my Internet search, I did a little sleuthing over on Ancestry.com."

Walt frowned. "What's that?"

"It's a genealogy research site. Members can create accounts and upload their family trees and information they've collected. I found Ephraim Presley's family tree."

"Ephraim Presley? He's the one who worked for the Thorndikes."

"Yes. And he's the twins' father."

"Was there any mention of how he earned his living?"

"No, there was nothing about that or an inheritance. But according to the information, he was orphaned at a young age. His mother died during childbirth and his father worked for the coalmines, died in some accident. He didn't have any siblings or any family to speak of. Ephraim ended up on the West Coast at a young age—on his own."

"I wonder where he got his money, assuming he had some if he owned a home and didn't have a job after he left the Thorndikes."

Danielle shook her head. "I don't know, but his life seemed rather tragic. One of his sons committed suicide. It was a few years after they left town."

"The twin who killed himself, did he have children?" Walt asked.

"I doubt it. He was never married. I don't know what happened,

177

but after he killed himself, his brother never talked to his parents again. The remaining twin moved to Colorado, where he met his wife, married and had a daughter."

"Is that twin still alive?"

"No. In fact, his daughter and wife are also both deceased. But he has a grandchild, and I assume that's who owns Presley House."

"I thought you said the remaining twin never talked to his parents again?"

"Yes, but that doesn't mean Ephraim Presley disinherited his remaining child or grandchild."

"Grandchild—does that mean you don't know if he had a son or daughter?"

"The family tree doesn't say, I suspect because the child is still alive. The website doesn't normally display living people unless you have permission to view the tree."

"So what does all of this have to do with Harvey?" Walt asked.

"I don't know. Maybe nothing."

"There is some reason he's haunting their house."

"Perhaps." Danielle looked up at Max, who was beginning to stir.

Walt smiled down at the yawning cat. "He seems fairly attached to you."

Danielle grinned. "Yeah, he does, doesn't he? I wonder why."

"Why what?" Walt frowned.

"Why me? Why did Max choose me?"

Walt shrugged. "He is a cat, Danielle. It's what cats do."

Max stood up abruptly and jumped down to the floor. Without looking back, he sauntered out of the parlor.

Danielle chuckled. "I think I was just dismissed."

"Like I said. He is a cat."

TWENTY-NINE

D anielle sat at the desk in the parlor, watching Walt, who lounged on the small sofa, his feet propped up on one of the armrests while his head leaned back on the opposing end of the couch, his attention riveted to the television set as he watched a Jimmy Stewart movie. It was just the other day she had mentioned the old movie *Harvey* about an invisible talking rabbit. She had promised to find it for Walt, which proved easier than she had expected. Danielle planned to look for it on a subscription site, yet discovered one of the television stations was running the old movie on Wednesday afternoon.

While Walt seemed engrossed in the old movie, Danielle's attention was elsewhere. She couldn't get Harvey and Presley House out of her head. She had questions for Presley House's ghost. There was always the possibility Harvey would dream hop again, and she could ask him the questions then without her ever having to go back to Presley House, yet there was no guarantee he would come—and it was always possible he would bring the snakes.

She had no desire to get hauled into jail again, but if she walked over instead of taking her car, she had a better chance of getting into Presley House without being detected. The only thing she had to worry about were nosey neighbors watching the abandoned house, and according to the chief, there was only one who seemed to be keeping an eye on the place—Millie Samson.

Silently, Danielle stood up and started walking toward the door. Walt looked up. "Where are you going?"

"I have to make a quick phone call."

"Don't you want to watch the movie?"

"I've seen it a dozen times."

Walt shrugged and turned his attention back to the television.

Once in the hallway, Danielle placed her phone call.

A woman's voice answered. "Frederickport Museum, Millie Samson speaking."

"Oh, hello, Millie. This is Danielle Boatman."

"Danielle! Oh my, we were just talking about you! I was just on the phone with Joanne. I can't believe you were the one to find both Bart and Chuck!"

"Umm…you heard?"

"It's all anyone has been talking about."

Millie proceeded to ask Danielle a dozen questions or more. After getting her answers, she finally asked why Danielle had called.

"I was just going through the information I give our guests—you know on local places of interest to visit while here—and wondered if the museum hours are the same all year round or if they change during the off-season."

"It's always the same."

"Thanks. I guess I won't have to make any changes to that part of my handout. So you're doing docent duty today?"

"Yes, Wednesday is my long day."

"Long day?" Danielle asked.

"I'm the only one here on Wednesdays. So I'll be closing up. We're a little short on docents this time of year."

"I should tell Lily about that, might be something she'd enjoy doing."

"Oh, that would be wonderful! Isn't Lily a teacher?" Millie asked.

"Yes, but because of her recent medical issues, she had to take the year off."

"How is she doing now?"

"Great, feeling much better. I think she would like to go back to work, but I don't think she's quite ready for a full-time class yet."

"The reason I asked if she was a teacher, we could really use a docent who is good with children. The board is trying to get together a program with the local schools to bring students over once a week. Having a docent with experience working with young children would be ideal for that project."

"I'll be sure to mention that to Lily."

When Danielle got off the phone a few minutes later, she considered her newly hatched idea: go over to Presley House now. It would take her maybe fifteen minutes to walk over, and with Millie at the museum, there was less chance she would be noticed. Smiling to herself, she walked over to the parlor and peeked her head through the doorway.

"I'm going out for a while."

Walt looked up. "I thought Lily took the car?"

"I'm going to visit our new neighbor and then take a little walk on the beach. I should be home before Lily gets back."

"Have a nice visit," Walt called out as he looked back to the movie.

BEFORE LEAVING, Danielle made a quick trip to the bathroom and then grabbed a jacket and wool cap from the hall closet. The days were getting progressively cooler, and walks along the beach this time of year required warmer clothing. Of course, she didn't intend to actually walk on the beach, yet Walt didn't know that.

When Danielle stepped onto the sidewalk and glanced back to Marlow House, she noticed Max sitting in the attic window, watching her. Instead of turning right and taking the direct route to Presley House, she turned left, heading in the direction of Heather Donovan's house. She wasn't really sure to what extent Max and Walt communicated—although considering the things Walt told her about Max, it seemed the two were rather chatty. She didn't want Walt wondering why she was walking away from Heather's house and in the direction of Presley House. She saw no need to worry Walt.

When Danielle reached Heather's house, she noticed the blinds were all shut and there was no car in the driveway. Danielle had no intention of actually stopping at Heather's, yet if she had, it looked as if she would have discovered her new neighbor was not home.

Picking up her speed, Danielle hurried down the street and then turned left, away from the ocean. She planned to double back on the street behind Marlow House. Glancing upward, Danielle noticed gray clouds gathering overhead. It looked like it might rain.

It wasn't until Danielle arrived at Millie's street and reached for her phone to check the time did she realize she had left her cell-phone sitting on the bathroom sink back at Marlow House. Cursing herself for the oversight, she didn't even consider going back for it.

If any of the neighbors were home, none of them was outside. The street looked rather desolate. Danielle didn't expect to encounter any teenagers out for Halloween mischief, considering it was a school day and the sun was still up. Halloween wasn't until Friday; of course, that didn't mean some tricksters wouldn't be pranking Presley House Wednesday or Thursday night. Yet that didn't concern Danielle, as she intended to return home before nightfall.

The moment she reached Presley House's property line, she looked around anxiously, checking for prying eyes. Convinced no one was watching her, she slipped into the yard and into the shelter of the overgrown trees. While there were a number of dead trees on the property that needed to be removed, there were still a sufficient number of thriving evergreens for Danielle to use as cover. Making her way to the front door, she hastily stepped onto the porch, once again looking over her shoulder.

She knew the door was locked but assumed if she gave it a try, as she had before, Harvey would hear her and let her in. Just as she reached for the doorknob, it turned on its own volition, and slowly the door creaked open, revealing the darkened entry hall.

Stepping through the doorway, she looked around. "Harvey?" Just as she got all the way into the house, the door slammed shut behind her. Startled by the sudden movement and loud slamming sound, she jumped. Silently, Danielle told herself she should have expected that, considering he had slammed the door the last time she had visited.

"I wanted to tell you I went to Pilgrim's Point like you asked me to do." Danielle looked around the dimly lit room. Shafts of sunlight slipping through the edges of the boarded-up windows provided minimal lighting.

In the next moment, Harvey showed himself. He stood about six feet from Danielle, still wearing his ill-fitting denim pants, tied at the waist with a rope, and bloodstained shirt. "Yes, I know. Thank you."

"We found a car there; it had driven off the cliff. The man

inside—the dead man—he's the one who shot the man I found here, isn't he?"

Harvey nodded. "Yes. I didn't see him do it, but I heard them shouting at each other. They had broken into the house. At first, I assumed it was just some more kids. Then I heard the gunshot. I found the man standing over his dead body. I guess the man who shot him had already run out of the house with the gun."

"How did you know he was at Pilgrim's Point?"

Harvey laughed. "When he left here he had a little accident. Funny, he had gone to all that trouble to get rid of the man called Bart, only to have Bart show up after he died."

"You mean they were together?"

Harvey laughed again. "I told Bart he couldn't stay here. I guess he must have bumped into his old friend after he left here—refused to leave him. Rather ironic, don't you think?"

"I still don't understand how you knew he was at Pilgrim's Point, and why you wanted him found."

"Once you found Bart's body, Bart moved on. Not sure where he went exactly, but he left his old friend—the friend who killed him."

"I don't mean to sound dense. How did you know he was at Pilgrim's Point? Why did you care if he was found?"

"Isn't that obvious?" Harvey said impatiently. "After Bart moved on, his friend came here, looking for him."

"I would assume Christiansen would be glad Bart was gone, considering he murdered him."

"Christiansen, is that his name? He didn't say."

"Chuck Christiansen."

"I suppose when one steps over to this side of the curtain, you start rethinking past relationships. I didn't get the impression Chuck missed Bart as much as he was curious what happened to him. When he realized Bart moved on about the same time his body was found, he figured it might work for him too. He couldn't figure out how to do anything—so he threatened to move in here if I didn't help him. I didn't need him sticking around, and the only thing I could think of was getting you to find his body."

Danielle frowned. "I'm rather surprised Chuck would be so anxious to move on."

"You mean because he shot his old buddy Bart?" Harvey laughed.

"That and the fact he murdered another woman besides Bart and was accomplice to another murder."

"Nice guy," Harvey said with a snort. "I knew I didn't need him moving in here."

"If finding his body actually helped him move on, I suspect he may be regretting it about now."

Harvey shrugged. "As long as he doesn't come back here. By the way, why did you come back? I'm rather surprised. Figured I'd need to—what did you call it, dream hop?—to get your attention again."

Narrowing her eyes, Danielle glared at Harvey. "If you want me to help you, leave the snakes out of it."

Harvey laughed. "Why? They weren't real. You knew that."

"In spite of the snakes, I would like to help you."

"Do you still have Max?"

"I don't have Max, per se. He is free to come and go as he wants. But Presley House is not the best place for him. He needs regular food and water. He wasn't getting that here."

Harvey stared at Danielle for a moment. "Then I suppose you'll have to do instead of Max."

"Why do you haunt Presley House? What is it you're looking for?"

"Do you really want to help me?"

"Yes, I'm here, aren't I?" Danielle told him.

"I need you to help me find something."

"What is it you're looking for?"

Harvey shook his head. "I don't like all these questions. He asked all these questions."

"Who?"

"There you go again! You're just like Mr. Presley! Questions, questions, questions! Max never asked me questions, he just helped me."

"If I can't ask questions, then I'm not sure how I can help you."

Harvey stared at Danielle a moment, his expression serious. Finally, a smile turned the edges of his mouth. "Let me show you something. Follow me." Harvey turned and started walking toward the kitchen.

Danielle followed Harvey. They walked past the kitchen door to the far end of the hallway. To Danielle's surprise, a hidden door—tucked into the wall's paneling—opened, revealing a hidden room.

"What's this?" Danielle asked, peeking into the dark space.

Inside the secret room, an overhead light flickered on, dimly illuminating the space.

"Go inside. You'll see what this is all about."

Hesitantly, Danielle stepped inside the room. The moment she was completely inside, the door slammed shut and the light flickered off. She was trapped.

THIRTY

L ily wasn't having a good day. Her troubles began with the
missing flash drive. When Ian had discovered he had left it in
Astoria, he immediately called Emma to see if she could find it. The
flash drive was exactly where he thought it would be, sitting on a
bookshelf in Emma's study. Unfortunately, the elderly woman
decided to move it to a safer location. When Lily arrived to pick it
up, Emma forgot where that safe location might be. After searching
with Emma for over two hours, Lily finally found it.

She wanted to get back on the road, but Emma insisted she stay
for dinner. Lily called Danielle to tell her she was running late, but
there was no answer, so she left a message. By the time she finally
got back on the road with Sadie, the sun was beginning to set.

The next obstacle Lily encountered was an accident on the highway. All traffic stopped. Anxious to get home, Lily kept looking at
the time. Fortunately, Sadie snoozed quietly in the backseat. Once
again, Lily tried calling Danielle to let her know what was going on.
There was still no answer, so she left another message.

By the time Lily got back to Frederickport, she went straight to
Ian's house to use his computer to upload the information to his
Dropbox.

"It's not showing up here, but it sometimes takes a few minutes
to upload," Ian told her when she called him from his house to let
him know she'd uploaded the information to Dropbox.

THE GHOST OF HALLOWEEN PAST

"I'll stick around here for ten minutes. If it doesn't show up, give me a call and I'll check it."

"You want me to call you either way?" Ian asked.

"No. It's late. I'm exhausted." Lily yawned. "If I don't hear from you in ten minutes, I'll know you got it okay."

"I'm sorry you had to do this, Lily."

"No problem. I'm just tired. Emma is a sweetheart, but she can be exhausting."

Ian laughed. "Isn't that the truth? Okay, if you don't hear from me in ten minutes, you'll know I got it. Thanks a lot. I love you."

"Love you too. Stay safe in that big city."

"Not sure I'll be able to call you tomorrow; I'll be in meetings all day."

"No problem."

After Lily got off the phone, she wandered through Ian's house, looking for Sadie. She found the golden retriever on Ian's bed, sprawled out for sleep.

"What are you tired about? You didn't have to drive," Lily grumbled, climbing onto the bed with Sadie. Yawning, she closed her eyes.

WALT STOOD at the attic window, looking across the street. The lights were on in Ian's house and Danielle's car was parked in his driveway. He glanced down at Max, who sat on the windowsill, his black tail swishing back and forth.

"I don't know where she is, Max. She should have been home hours ago. I just wish Lily would hurry up. What is taking her so long over there?"

"OH CRAP," Lily groaned when she woke up in Ian's bedroom. Rolling off the mattress, she glanced at the clock on the nightstand. It was almost 3 a.m. Sadie was still sound asleep.

Combing her fingers through her hair, she stumbled out of the bedroom. Assuming Danielle had seen the car parked across the street at Ian's, Lily didn't question why Danielle hadn't called her to see where she was.

Grabbing her purse, cellphone, and keys from the living room coffee table, Lily decided to leave Sadie sleeping. She'd come back and get her in the morning. If she took Sadie over to Marlow House now, the dog might wake Danielle, especially if she decided it was a good time to play with Walt.

WALT STOOD at the attic window and watched as Lily backed out of Ian's driveway. He didn't see Sadie.

"Well, Max, it looks as if she has finally decided to come home!" When Max failed to give a response, Walt glanced down. Max was no longer sitting on the windowsill.

"Max? Max?" Walt called out. He glanced around, but there was no sign of Max in the attic.

LILY HAD JUST USED her key to unlock the back door when Walt appeared in the kitchen.

"What took you so long?" Walt roared.

Quietly slipping into the kitchen, Lily gently closed the door behind her.

"Danielle isn't here!" Walt told her.

Turning on the kitchen light, Lily locked the kitchen door and then set her purse and keys on the counter.

"Why were you over at Ian's so long? Where is Sadie?"

Lily walked to the refrigerator and opened it. She looked inside.

"You need to call the police!"

Lily shut the refrigerator door and yawned. She opened an overhead cabinet and grabbed an empty glass.

"I think Max is gone too. He was in the attic with me. But I don't think he's in the house."

Lily took the glass to the sink and filled it with water. After taking a sip, she turned toward the door leading to the hallway.

"Lily you have to hear me! Danielle is gone! She never came back from her walk. Something is wrong."

Frantically, Walt looked around for pen and paper.

Lily turned off the kitchen light as she headed upstairs to her bedroom, glass of water in hand.

Walt followed Lily up the stairs. "I can't write this in a note!"
Lily yawned and muttered something about being exhausted.
"I need to talk to you, Lily. We need to find Danielle!"

Walt paused a moment and considered what he had just said.
He needed to talk to Lily. The only way he could do that was by
dream hopping.

He watched as Lily passed Danielle's closed bedroom door. He
knew Lily assumed Danielle was inside, safely asleep in her bed. He
started to follow Lily into her bedroom, but when she closed her
door and started to strip off her clothes, he quickly returned to the
hallway.

Sitting alone in the hallway, waiting for Lily to fall asleep, Walt
wondered where Max had gone. If Sadie or Max were in the house,
he could get one of them to rouse Lily and convince her to go check
on Danielle, in the same way they had when Danielle had the nightmare. But Sadie was across the street, and he suspected Max had
slipped outside through the pet door, in search of Danielle.

He considered using his energy to force Lily to go into Danielle's
room, but he was afraid that might frighten her. He needed Lily to
have her wits about her. The most feasible option he could come up
with was a dream hop.

LILY OPENED her eyes and looked around. She sat on Ian's rooftop,
looking over at Marlow House.

"It took you long enough to fall asleep!" Walt snapped.

Lily turned to her right. Walt sat next to her. He looked
annoyed.

"We're sitting on a roof? Seriously, a rooftop? What happened
to Hawaii or the Himalayas? Ian's roof? What a waste for a
dream hop."

"Lily, focus, I need to talk to you."

"Lily, focus? Sheesh, that sounds condescending. Why don't you
just let me sleep? I'm too tired for a dream anyhow. Especially a
lousy one on a rooftop."

"I need to talk to you, and you need to listen. Danielle is
missing!"

Lily frowned. "What do you mean missing?"

"After you left for Astoria, she went for a walk. She told me she

189

was going to visit that new neighbor and then go back to the beach. She never came home."

"Are you saying she isn't sleeping in her bed right now?"

"No. She's not in the house."

Rubbing the heel of her right palm against her temple, Lily narrowed her eyes and stared across the street, focusing on what Walt was telling her. In the dream, the sun was shining. Yet she couldn't see inside Marlow House, all the blinds were drawn.

"I tried calling her today, several times. She never answered her phone."

"She left her cellphone in the downstairs bathroom," Walt explained.

Lily looked at Walt. "She doesn't have her phone with her?"

Walt shook his head. "No. I heard it ringing, thought she had come home, and I went down the hall looking for her. The bathroom door was wide open. The phone was sitting on the counter."

"She must have forgotten it," Lily muttered.

"That's what I'm thinking."

"Where did she say she was going again? I need to get all the information I can, because when I wake up, I'll only be able to ask questions when I go back to sleep—but I hope to find Dani by then!"

"Remember, you can always ask me a question and I can try writing an answer."

"Try? Are you saying you might not be able to?"

"It's not that easy—getting a pen or pencil to move over paper."

"You've done it before."

"It's not something I can always do."

"Then I better get my answers now before I wake up."

"I don't know what more to tell you."

"Do you know what time she left exactly?"

Walt considered the question a moment. "I had just started watching that movie Danielle put on for me, *Harvey*. It had been on for maybe ten, fifteen minutes before she left."

"Okay, I'll check with the television program to see when it started. Anything else?"

"Max watched her leave. She headed down the street toward the new neighbor's house. That's where she said she was going to go."

"Okay, first thing I'll do is talk to Heather, see what time

Danielle left her house. And you say she planned to go to the beach after that?"

"Yes. She said she was going to take a walk on the beach after she left Heather's house. And that she'd be home before you."

"Do you know if she changed her clothes before she left? I remember what she was wearing this morning."

"No, she didn't change her clothes. But I heard her getting something out of the hall closet before she left. I assume it was a jacket."

"You said Max saw her leave. Maybe he'll remember what jacket she had on."

"Max isn't in the house. I don't know where he went, but I suspect he went looking for Danielle. He was worried."

"How long ago did Max leave?"

"I'm not sure exactly. He was sitting with me in the attic when we saw you drive up to Ian's house. I kept wondering what was taking you so long. I didn't notice Max was gone until you returned home."

"I'm sorry about that, Walt. I lay down for just a minute, never intending to go to sleep. But I guess I was more tired than I realized."

"I'm just glad you're back now."

"Unless you have something more to tell me, I suppose I better wake up and find Danielle."

"I can't think of anything else to tell you."

"Okay then." Lily closed her eyes, focused all her energy, and then let out a glass-shattering scream.

THIRTY-ONE

L ily jerked upright into a sitting position. Somewhat dazed, she blinked her eyes and tried to focus. Her heart raced. Sitting in her bed, she looked around the dimly lit room. Morning sunlight filtered in through the curtains. She glanced at the clock on her nightstand. It was almost 8:00 a.m.

"Walt, are you here?" For a brief moment, she didn't know if it had simply been a dream—or a dream hop. *Is Dani really missing?*

In response, across the room from the bed, the lamp lifted several inches above the dresser. It hovered there for just a moment before setting back down again.

Lily swallowed nervously. She felt queasy. She didn't want to ask the question because she knew the answer, yet she hoped she might be wrong. "If it was a dream hop and Danielle is really missing, please lift the lamp again."

Once again, the lamp floated up from the dresser. Lily had her answer.

Tossing her blanket aside, she climbed out of bed. "Walt, I need to get dressed. Let's meet downstairs in the kitchen. Please bring Danielle's phone with you."

In response, the bedroom door opened and closed. Lily knew Walt didn't need to open the doors to move about the house; he could easily walk through the walls. She understood the door opening and closing was simply his way to let her know she was now alone in the bedroom and could dress in private.

After Lily dressed, she took a detour to the parlor before meeting Walt in the kitchen. She wanted to check the television program to see when *Harvey* had played the day before, to give her a better idea when Danielle had left the house.

When she reached the kitchen, she started a pot of coffee and picked up Danielle's cellphone. Walt had left it on the kitchen table. While waiting for the coffee to brew, she checked out the phone. Thankfully, she knew the password.

"It looks like she made a phone call right before she left the house," Lily told Walt as she stared at the phone. "I can't tell who it was, but I can find out." Lily redialed the phone number. A moment later, she disconnected the call and set the phone on the table.

"She called the museum right before she left. I wonder why?" Lily pushed the salt and pepper shakers to the middle of the table. "Walt, if you know why she called the museum, please raise the salt shaker. If you don't know, raise the pepper shaker."

Lily watched as the pepper shaker lifted above the table and then fell back down. "Who would have figured salt and pepper shakers could replace an Ouija board?" she muttered.

Standing up, she walked to the coffee pot. "The first thing I'm going to do is talk to Heather, see what she knows." Lily poured herself a cup of coffee and then headed for the back door.

LILY PERSISTENTLY RANG and re-rang the doorbell. She noticed Heather's car parked in the driveway. Lily was fairly confident the woman was home, yet suspected she was still in bed, considering the drawn blinds, and there didn't seem to be any lights on inside the house.

After pressing the doorbell more than a dozen times, Lily finally heard movement coming from inside. When the door opened, Lily found herself looking into the disgruntled face of Heather Donovan.

Wearing just a nightgown, her hair drawn into two messy pigtails now escaping from their rubber bands, Heather glared at Lily. "Do you have any idea what time it is?"

"Sorry to wake you, but this is important."

"It better be important!" Heather snapped.

Meowing from the direction of Heather's bare feet caught Lily's attention. Glancing down, she saw Bella weaving in and out around Heather's ankles. Without saying a word, Heather used her foot to shove Bella backwards into the entry before stepping out on the front porch with Lily and shutting the door.

Crossing her arms over her chest, she glared at Lily. "What is this about?"

"Danielle is missing."

"What do you mean missing?"

"She didn't come home yesterday."

Heather shrugged. "So? She's an adult. She doesn't need to check in with you."

Inwardly, Lily groaned. She didn't have time to explain things to Heather. "Can you just tell me what time Dani left here yesterday and if she mentioned where she was going."

"I don't know what you're talking about. I didn't see Danielle yesterday. I wasn't even home yesterday."

"You weren't?" Lily's heart sank.

"I went to Vancouver yesterday. Didn't get home until late last night."

"Oh…" Lily glanced around hopelessly.

Heather studied Lily. Her expression softened. "Hey, you really are worried, aren't you?"

Lily nodded. "I borrowed Dani's car yesterday to go to Astoria. So wherever Dani went, she walked. She left her cellphone at the house. She never came home last night. That's not like her."

"What made you think she came over here?"

"Umm…she mentioned she was going to come over and visit you," Lily lied.

"You know, it's always possible someone picked her up."

"That's what I'm afraid of!"

"No…" Heather shook her head. "I don't mean like that. Maybe one of her friends picked her up so they could go some-where. Maybe they had car trouble, and since she didn't have her phone with her, she couldn't call."

"I suppose that's possible," Lily muttered, not really convinced.

"I'm sure it's something like that." Heather smiled.

AFTER LILY LEFT Heather's house, she went to Ian's to pick up Sadie. She considered leaving Sadie at Marlow House while walking along the beach, looking for any sign of Danielle, but changed her mind. She had another idea.

Standing in the entry of Marlow House with Sadie on a leash, Lily called to Walt. In response, the entry table rattled. The next moment she could smell cigar smoke. Sadie wagged her tail.

"Walt, Heather didn't see Dani yesterday because she wasn't home. This means Dani probably went on to the beach after going to Heather's house. I want to take Sadie with me while I walk along the beach. I know that section of the beach doesn't allow dogs, but frankly, I don't care. I was wondering…can you tell Sadie to help me look for her? Maybe…I don't know…sniff her out?"

Walt looked down at Sadie. "You mean like a bloodhound?"

"Obviously, if I tell Sadie to help me look for Dani, she won't really know what I'm saying. She only gets a little of what I say. But I know she understands everything you tell her. What do you think?"

Walt turned to the golden retriever. "Sadie, pay attention."

Sadie immediately sat and stared at Walt.

Lily looked down at Sadie and smiled. She knew Walt was talking to the dog.

Sadie cocked her head.

When Walt finished giving Sadie instructions, he added, "Max is already looking for her."

At the mention of Max, Sadie jumped up and charged for the front door, taking Lily with her.

Walt gave a nod of approval. "I figure a little healthy competition won't hurt."

"HEY, lady, dogs don't belong on this beach! The dog beach is that way!"

Lily ignored the man and continued to walk in the opposite direction from where he pointed. She had been walking up and down the beach for over an hour now, and still there was no sign of her missing friend. She hadn't eaten anything all morning; her stomach was beginning to grumble. Heading back toward the boardwalk, she took Danielle's phone from her pocket.

"Maybe a call to the museum will give me some clues," she muttered. Lily considered making the call from the bench on the boardwalk, yet decided to head back to Marlow House. She didn't want Walt worrying about her, and she figured he was probably waiting anxiously for her return.

"We didn't find anything," Lily announced when she walked through the doorway to Marlow House ten minutes later and unhooked Sadie from the leash. By Sadie's excitable reaction, Lily was fairly confident Walt stood nearby.

"I'm going to make a few phone calls. I struck out at Heather's and the beach. Hopefully I find someone who knows where she is."

The first call Lily made was to the museum. Sitting on the parlor sofa, she waited for someone to answer her call.

"Frederickport Museum," came a male voice.

"Hello, I wanted to find out who would have answered the phone at the museum yesterday, at around—"

"Would have been Millie Samson. She was the only one here yesterday."

"By any chance, is Millie there today?"

"No, sorry. Can I help you with something?"

"No, that's okay. Do you happen to have Millie's number?"

"Sorry, I can't give that information out."

"Okay, no problem. I understand." Lily reluctantly hung up the phone. She glanced over to where Sadie lay by the chair facing the sofa. She figured Walt was probably sitting in the chair, watching her.

Lily stood up, walked to the desk, and picked up the phone book. "They wouldn't give me Millie's phone number. That's who Danielle spoke to yesterday at the museum. But I'm pretty sure her number is in the phone book." Minutes later, she had Millie on the phone.

After Lily hung up, she looked at the empty chair where she assumed Walt sat. "That was odd. According to Millie, all Danielle wanted to know was if the museum hours changed during the off-season. Supposedly, she wanted to know so she could update some flyers. We updated the flyers last week—she knew the answer to that question already; we discussed it."

Lily sat back down on the sofa and stared at the cellphone in her hand. "Even if she wanted to recheck her facts, seems like a random thing to do right before you take a walk."

Shaking her head, Lily made a second call, this one to Adam Nichols.

"I'm calling you because I don't want to upset your grandmother," Lily explained when Adam answered the phone.

"What's wrong?"

"Dani is missing. I need to find out if you or your grandmother happened to see her yesterday afternoon. I don't want to call and upset Marie."

"What do you mean missing?"

"Why do people always ask that? What do you think I mean when I say missing?"

"Obviously I don't know what you mean, or I wouldn't ask."

"I'm sorry, Adam. It's just that I'm so frustrated—so scared—I don't know what to do."

"Why don't you start at the beginning?" Adam suggested.

Lily told Adam about Danielle's disappearance, leaving out the part about Walt jumping into her dream.

"I saw her yesterday; she went with me when I picked up my grandmother."

"I know about that. I saw her when she came back. I was hoping your grandmother might have talked to her again, later in the afternoon."

"I'll ask her. What does Ian say?" Adam asked.

"Ian's in New York on business. He's in meetings this morning; I didn't even try calling him. There's nothing he can do from there, and it would only worry him. Didn't see the point."

"Understandable. But you need to call the police right away."

"Will they even do anything? Danielle's an adult, and don't they usually wait a day or more before they start looking for her?"

"Danielle is also a very wealthy woman, one who might be a target for a kidnapper."

"Oh god! Don't even say that!" Lily moaned.

"I'm just being realistic, Lily. You need to find out if the Missing Thorndike is still sitting in her safe deposit box. If the bank tells you she removed it yesterday, then Danielle might be in serious danger."

"I didn't even think about that damn necklace."

"I tell you what; I'll go over to my grandmother's and see if she talked to Danielle yesterday afternoon. I'll give you a call after I talk to her."

THIRTY-TWO

With trembling fingers, Danielle unbuttoned her blouse and then removed the garment. The room was chilly. She quickly put her jacket back on, covering her bra. She sat on the bottom step of the dimly lit room. Using her molars as a vice, Danielle tugged on the hem of her cotton blouse, tearing it several inches. With her hands, she ripped off a narrow strip of fabric to be used as a makeshift bandage. She repeated the process several times. A memory of her mother flashed in her mind. *Danielle, your teeth are not tools!* She imagined her mother would make an exception this one time.

Her right ankle continued to throb. She had discovered applying pressure with her hands did nothing to soothe the injury. If she wanted to get out of here, she needed to first take care of her ankle. She hoped wrapping it tightly might alleviate some of the searing pain. At the very least, she needed to be able to stand on her own two feet without falling over, something she couldn't yet do.

Harvey had apologized for not warning her about the stairs. It wasn't exactly a room she had entered, as she had originally assumed, but a dark stairwell leading to a second basement. She had hit her head during the fall down the stairs, knocking her unconscious. For how long exactly, she didn't know. Danielle had lost all concept of time.

The urge to close her eyes was overwhelming—if she could just take a quick nap. Yet she knew that was dangerous, especially if the fall had given her a concussion, as she suspected it had. As it was, she felt queasy and nauseous.

Curling up to take a nap on a dusty basement floor—home to all sorts of creepy crawlers—was the last thing Danielle would normally consider. However, the idea appealed to her—she wanted to sleep that much. She had to stay awake.

It had been hours since she had used the bathroom, but wetting herself was simply too humiliating an option to consider. Of course, if she remained locked up in this apparent dungeon, she was going to die anyway, so what did it matter?

There was one plus side of having to pee so desperately, it helped to keep her awake. However, considering the sharp pain she was now experiencing in her side from holding it in, she would rather find some other way to stay awake.

If it weren't for the overhead light fixture that flickered off and on, she would be cloaked in total darkness. Harvey used it as a weapon to control her. Each time she tried to crawl up the stairs toward the door, he plunged the room into total darkness and threatened to push her down the stairs again.

"I really, really need to use the bathroom!" Danielle called out after she finished wrapping her ankle. She sat on the bottom step, one cuff of her jeans rolled up.

The door on the top of the stairwell creaked open. Danielle tried to stand, but instead winced in pain and fell back to the step. She heard something like metal clinking against the wood floor and rolling down the stairs toward her. It was an old coffee can. The door slammed shut again. She heard it lock.

Danielle managed to grab the can before it hit her. She looked at it a moment.

"Is this for what I think it's for?" Danielle asked the empty room.

Ten minutes later, Danielle sat on the step, feeling considerably better. While it was not ideal, going in the can was preferable to wetting her pants.

"Harvey, what do you want with me?" She had already asked the question a dozen times before. However, the only time he had said anything since locking her in the room was when he apologized for not warning her about the stairs and when he had threatened to push her down again if she attempted to climb them.

Glancing around the hidden room, its walls made of stone,

Danielle thought it looked about the size of a single-car garage. *Why did they have a hidden room, I wonder…*

Suddenly the answer came to her. "Moonshine! I bet Presley was a moonshiner! Walt did say he was something of a lush, and it was during prohibition. The man didn't have a job, but he apparently had plenty of money!"

"That was just one of his earlier endeavors," Harvey said as he showed himself. He stood several feet from Danielle. "I was a kid when prohibition ended. Didn't even know Mr. Presley was once a moonshiner. Not until I was older."

Danielle tugged the front of her jacket together and looked up at Harvey. "Why am I here?"

"I need you to help me find it."

"And if we find *it*—whatever it is—will you let me go?" Danielle quickly zipped up the front of her jacket.

"Of course, I don't intend to keep you prisoner. I'm not a monster."

"I'm a prisoner now," Danielle reminded him.

Harvey shrugged. "It can't be helped. I only have a little time left, and then I have to go back."

"Go back where?"

"To the cemetery, of course."

"You haunt the cemetery?" Danielle silently reminded herself that if she ever got out of Presley House, she needed to find out where Harvey was buried and then avoid that section of the cemetery.

"I wouldn't say *haunt* exactly. I'm hoping that once this is resolved, I'll feel comfortable enough to move on."

"Let me see if I understand what you're saying—you have some unresolved issues that are preventing you from moving on. They have something to do with this thing you need to find, which I assume is somewhere in Presley House. And you can only look for this thing around Halloween."

Harvey shrugged. "It's the only time I can leave the cemetery."

"Why is it you can only come to Presley House around Halloween? Is it because you were killed around Halloween, or is it because Halloween is a time spirits can move around more freely—if one is to believe those old stories."

Harvey stared at Danielle for a moment before answering.

THE GHOST OF HALLOWEEN PAST

Finally, his mouth curled into a smile. "You certainly ask a lot of questions."

"If you want me to help you, then I would think you'd be willing to answer my questions."

"And if you want to get out of here alive, I would think you'd be willing to help me."

Renewed fear washed over Danielle. "Does this mean you would leave me here to die if I can't or won't help you?"

Harvey shrugged again. "I'm dead. You'll be dead someday too. Does it really matter if it's now or fifty years from now?"

"Well, yeah, it sorta does matter!"

Harvey cocked his head to one side, a quizzical expression on his face. "Why?"

"Isn't it obvious? I'm young, I'm just thirty. I have a lot I still want to do in this life."

"You've already lived almost twice as long as I did."

Danielle closed her eyes for a moment and told herself to calm down and give Harvey what he wanted so she could get out of this horrid place. She opened her eyes again and looked at Harvey. "Okay, what do you want me to do?"

Harvey smiled. "I need you to help me find two things. And then I need you to take them to…" Harvey's smile faded. "I'm not sure where."

"Umm…what do you mean you aren't sure where? How am I supposed to take them someplace if you don't know where that someplace is?"

"I suppose you'll have to figure that out, won't you?"

Danielle silently cursed herself for forgetting her cellphone. At the very least, she could have text messaged someone for help. But she didn't have her cellphone with her. She was stuck in a hidden basement with an irrational teenage ghost who insisted on getting his own way.

"Why don't you start by telling me what you're looking for. Then I can figure out where I need to take it," Danielle suggested.

"I suppose the most important thing is Bruce's journal." Harvey sat down on the floor and faced Danielle, who remained on the bottom step.

"Bruce? You mean one of the twins?" If Danielle wasn't mistaken, Bruce Presley was the twin who had committed suicide.

"Yes. Bruce wrote it all down. He didn't want to at first. It took me a couple Halloweens to convince him."

"Halloweens…when you say convince him…do you mean after you died?"

"Of course. If I had still been alive, there would have been nothing to write down."

"I understand the family moved when the twins were still in high school. Maybe Bruce took the journal with him. Maybe that's why you can't find it."

Harvey abruptly stood up. He looked down at Danielle and shook his head. "No, he hid it here with the other thing. He owed me that."

"Why are you so certain he hid the journal here?"

"Because I watched him hide it!"

"If you watched him hide it, then you know where it is. Where is it?"

"If I knew that, would I need to be talking to you about this now?" Harvey shouted in frustration. "Would I keep returning to Presley House year after year?"

"You just said you watched him hide it."

"That was a long time ago. Don't you ever forget things?"

"You forgot where he put it?"

"It isn't like it was just yesterday. It has been an awful long time."

"All right…so we're looking for a journal…a book. You mentioned something else you're looking for. What's that?" Danielle asked.

"It will be with the journal. When you find the journal, you'll find it."

"What is this other thing?" Danielle asked.

"It proves what Bruce wrote in the journal."

"Which is?"

"You'll have to find the journal to figure that out."

"At least tell me what this other thing is so I'll know what I'm looking for."

"I told you it will be with the journal; if you find one, you'll find the other."

"What happens if they aren't together? Maybe one got moved over the years."

"I can't imagine that happened, but if it did, you'll know when you find it. It will be obvious."

Danielle groaned. "How am I supposed to know what I'm looking for if I have no idea what it is? If this thing—whatever it is—is not with the journal, how will I know if I find it? For all I know, it's that coffee can you tossed at me."

Harvey frowned and looked over at the coffee can shoved in the corner. "Why would I be looking for a can filled with pee?"

"That wasn't my point!"

"All you really need to know—it's something of value. When you find it, you'll know. It will be obvious."

"What's the point in not telling me?"

Harvey smiled. "I have to have some fun." In the next moment, he vanished.

Danielle surveyed the small room. "Well, if I want to get out of here, I guess I better start looking. And since he has me locked up in this room, I have to assume he wants me to start looking down here."

Danielle glanced up the stairs, expecting some response from Harvey. Nothing.

"If he wants me to look for the missing journal," Danielle said in a loud clear voice, "it would help if he gave me more light." Overhead the lights flickered and went brighter.

"Thanks," Danielle grumbled.

THIRTY-THREE

L ily waited anxiously for Adam's phone call. When it did come, it wasn't what she wanted to hear.

"That was Adam," Lily told Walt after she ended the call. She assumed Walt was still in the room with her. "Marie didn't talk to Dani yesterday afternoon. Adam felt he had to tell his grandmother Dani is missing. Figured once we call the police, they might question her. He wanted her to know what was going on. I suppose that's for the best."

Lily stood up, walked to the window, and looked outside. "I need to go down to the police station and file a missing person's report. Hopefully they'll take one. I'm not sure how much good it will do right now. From what I understand, when an adult goes missing, they wait so many hours before they do anything."

Turning from the window, Lily looked to where she believed Walt sat. "I just realized, wherever Dani is…considering how long she's been gone…there must be some time she's sleeping. Maybe you could dream hop and find out what's going on."

"Wherever she is, she isn't sleeping," Walt responded, even though he knew Lily couldn't hear him. "I've tried off and on since last night. I tried with Isabella too. But Isabella…Isabella could no longer dream."

LESS THAN THIRTY MINUTES LATER, Lily stood in the front office of the Frederickport Police Department. She didn't recognize the young woman behind the counter; she had never seen her before. Lily suspected she was new. Considering the plunging neckline of the blonde's tight sweater, Lily also suspected the woman had skipped over the section on appropriate dress in the *Frederickport Police Department's Employee Handbook.*

"I'm sorry, Chief MacDonald is on vacation," the unsmiling woman told her.

"Crap, I knew that. I forgot," Lily mumbled. "Who's covering for him?"

"I'm sure one of the other officers can help you. Do you really need to speak to the police chief?" the woman asked. "Are you asking for some sort of donation or something?"

"No, I'm not asking for some sort of donation or something!" Lily snapped. "I'd like to see whoever is covering for Chief MacDonald."

"I'm not sure he's available right now. But if you tell me what this is about, then I can direct you to the appropriate officer."

Narrowing her eyes, Lily glared at the woman. "Just get me whoever is covering for MacDonald. I don't have time for this."

"I'm afraid that's impossible. If you can't tell me what this is about, how do you expect me to help you?"

"I expect you to get me whoever is covering for the chief!" Lily shouted.

"And I am going to have you escorted out of my office!" the woman shouted back.

"This is not your office!" Lily shouted even louder. "It is our police department!"

"What is going on out here?" Joe Morelli asked when he stepped out into the front office.

"This woman needs to be escorted out of here!" the blonde said, visibly shaking.

Curious, Joe glanced from the blonde to Lily. "Lily? What's this about?"

The blonde's eyes widened. Nervously, she looked from Lily to Joe.

"I need to speak to whoever is covering for MacDonald," Lily explained.

"That's me. What's the problem?"

Lily flashed a dirty look to the blonde behind the counter and then looked back to Joe. "I should have just asked for you in the first place."

The blonde finally found her voice. "This woman demanded to see Chief MacDonald, and when I explained he was on vacation, she became totally unreasonable!"

"I simply asked to see whoever was covering for the chief."

"But you—" the blonde began, only to be cut off by Joe.

"Marcia, I'm sure this was just some misunderstanding." Joe turned his attention to Lily. "Come with me to my office. You can tell me what this is all about there."

Lily could practically feel the blonde's angry glare on her back as she followed Joe. When they reached Joe's office, he motioned to a chair facing his desk. Just as he sat down behind his desk, Lily blurted out, "Dani is missing."

"Are you saying she took off without telling you where she was going?"

"No. I'm saying she's missing. Yesterday I borrowed her car to go to Astoria. She told me she might visit a neighbor and take a walk on the beach. But she didn't have a car—I had it—so she really couldn't go anywhere. When I came home, she wasn't there. I haven't seen her since I left for Astoria."

"I assume you've tried calling her."

"I tried when I was in Astoria and running late. But she didn't answer. After I got home, I found her phone in the bathroom."

"What about her purse?"

"It's still sitting on her dresser. But Dani doesn't always take her purse with her unless she's driving and needs her license. She usually carries her cellphone in her back pocket."

"Yes, I remember she doesn't always carry a purse. I teased her about it once." Joe pulled out a pad of paper and started jotting down notes. "So what time did you come home yesterday and realize she wasn't there? I'm surprised you didn't call us last night."

"I went to Ian's house when I returned from Astoria. I needed to use his computer. He's in New York on a business trip. The reason I went to Astoria was to pick up a flash drive he forgot at Emma Jackson's. I picked it up, went to his house, and uploaded it to his Dropbox. I lay down for just a few minutes and fell asleep. It was late when I woke up—middle of the night. I figured Dani knew I was at Ian's because I'd parked her car in his driveway, so I didn't think anything about it when she didn't call to ask me where I was."

"So when did you realize she was missing?"

"Not until this morning. Late last night I went back to Marlow House. Figured Dani was asleep in her room. When I got up this morning, she wasn't there."

Joe stopped writing, set his pen on his desk, and looked up at Lily. "So it's possible she was in her room when you got home last night and she got up before you did this morning and went somewhere." Joe glanced at the clock on the wall. "It's not even noon yet. I'd hardly classify that as a missing person."

"No, Joe." Lily shook her head. "Her bed hadn't been slept in."

"How can you be so sure?"

"I just know!" *If the chief was here, he would understand!*

"Lily, go home. Danielle is probably already there, wondering where you are."

"No, Joe, she's missing!" Lily said frantically.

"Lily, unless Danielle has been missing twenty-four hours, there's really nothing I can do. And it sounds to me, she's only been missing for a couple hours. Hardly anything to panic over."

Lily wanted to cry. She stood up. "So you aren't going to do anything?"

"I'm sure Danielle is fine. Go home, you'll see."

Without saying another word, Lily turned and stormed from the office.

"WHY WAS LILY MILLER HERE?" Brian asked a few minutes later when he entered Joe's office. "She about knocked me over in the hallway. Looked like she was crying. I tried talking to her, but she just ran past me. What's up?"

Absently, Joe picked up his pen and repeatedly tapped its end against the pad of paper sitting on his desk. Looking up at Brian, he said, "I think she may have gotten a little too dependent on Danielle."

"What do you mean?" Brian sat down on the chair Lily had occupied just minutes earlier.

"I would imagine she's dealing with some emotional issues over all that happened to her. I know she's relied heavily on both

Danielle and Ian to get her through it. If you remember, Danielle was like a protective mother hen."

"If it wasn't for Danielle, we may never have found Lily," Brian reminded him.

Joe sighed. "Strange to hear you say that, considering your feelings for Danielle."

"I can admit when I'm wrong. But I still don't understand; why was Lily here today?"

"Ian is in New York on a business trip. Apparently, Danielle was gone when Lily got up this morning, and Lily is convinced she's missing. I think Lily irrationally panicked. She just needs someone with her."

"Are you saying Lily came down here just because Danielle left this morning without telling her where she was going?"

"Not exactly..." Joe then told Brian about his conversation with Lily.

OFFICER BRIAN HENDERSON had left the police department to grab some lunch. Instead, he pulled his police car up to the sidewalk in front of Marlow House and parked. Sitting alone in the vehicle, his hands still gripping the steering wheel, he debated going up to the house and ringing the bell.

He owed his freedom to Danielle Boatman. The very least he could do was check and see if she was okay. Joe was convinced Lily was simply overacting out of irrational fear stemming from her recent trauma. Maybe that was true, yet it didn't explain the inexplicable gut feeling Brian had that Danielle was indeed in trouble.

Five minutes later Brian stood on the front porch of Marlow House, facing Lily Miller.

"Oh my god, you found Dani? Something's wrong?" Lily teared up.

"No," Brian said quickly. "I just stopped by to check on you, to see if you've heard from her."

Blinking away unshed tears, her right hand still holding the door's edge, she asked, "Did Joe send you?"

"No. I talked to Joe after you left his office; he told me what was going on. He doesn't think you have anything to worry about."

Lily studied Brian for a moment. "But you don't think that…do you?"

"I've learned recently that maybe you can't be too careful. I hope Joe is right, and Danielle comes walking in here any minute, but if she hasn't…I wanted to see if I could help."

Lily opened the door wide, silently ushering Brian inside. "Would you like some coffee?" she asked.

"I WALKED up and down the beach." Lily sat with Brian at the kitchen table, each drinking a cup of coffee.

"You said she was going to visit a neighbor?"

"Yes, Heather Donovan, couple doors down. She just moved in. But according to Heather, she wasn't home yesterday, so even if Dani had stopped by, she wouldn't know."

"You've checked with all her friends?"

"Dani has a lot of acquaintances in town but no real close friends except for Marie. Nobody she really hangs out with."

"Marie Nichols?"

"Yeah, I think she's become sort of a surrogate mom or grandmother for Dani. Dani doesn't have any family, and Marie was friends with Dani's aunt, the one who left her Marlow House. I called Adam and asked him to check with Marie, see if she'd talked to Dani yesterday afternoon, but she hadn't."

"Danielle's close to Adam too, isn't she?"

"Adam?" Lily chuckled. "I suppose they've become friends. But he hadn't talked to her either. Although he did seem concerned and reminded me that because of Danielle's money, she might be a target for kidnappers."

"I would expect a kidnapper who targeted Danielle would want her free so she could get to her money. Someone like you might be a more likely target if they wanted to extort money from her."

"Adam was thinking more of the Missing Thorndike—if the kidnappers forced her to take the necklace out of the bank. But I called the bank after I got home from the police station. I figured Joe wouldn't do it if I suggested it."

"I assume the necklace is still there?"

"Yes. I made up some story, that I was looking for Dani, that she mentioned she might be taking the necklace out but that I needed to talk to her first before she did. They told me she hadn't been there but promised to call me if she came in."

"Did you call anyone else?"

"I called Joanne, but she hadn't seen her since she was here last, cleaning the house."

"You mentioned she left her cellphone here. Did you check it to see if she'd made any calls before she left?"

"Yes. She made just one; she called the museum and talked to Millie Samson."

"About what?"

Lily shook her head. "Didn't make a lot of sense to me. According to Millie, she just called about the museum hours, but Dani already knew what the hours were."

"Ahh, Millie Samson. I've seen a lot of her this month."

"Millie? Why?"

"She lives down the street from Presley House. This time of year she practically stands guard on the old house."

Lily's eyes widened. "Presley House?"

THIRTY-FOUR

G ripping her ceramic mug with both hands, Lily stared down into her coffee. *Presley House? Was it possible? No...Danielle wouldn't go back over there without the chief. She said so.*

"Fortunately it usually settles down after Halloween, and Millie stops calling us, at least until next October." Brian took a sip of his coffee.

Lily looked up from her cup to Brian. "Because the ghost leaves after Halloween?"

"I suppose that's how the legend goes." Brian shrugged.

If Danielle wanted to talk to Harvey, she couldn't wait for the chief to return from his vacation. According to Max, Harvey leaves every year right after Halloween. Did Danielle forget that when she told me she would wait for the chief before going back—or was she just saying that to make me feel better?

Abruptly, Lily set her mug on the table and looked at Brian. "Would you do me a favor?"

"What?"

"Can you check Presley House?"

"You think Danielle went there? I can't imagine why she would, considering the last time she was there she found Bart Haston."

Licking her lips nervously, Lily wished it were the chief sitting with her instead of Brian. Chief MacDonald would understand. "Danielle was...well, curious about Presley House. She sort of has a thing about...well...old houses."

Brian studied Lily a moment without comment. Finally, he said, "Because of the ghost?"

Lily looked up into Brian's eyes. "Why do you say that?"

"Come on, Lily, I know the stories about Danielle. Cheryl told her attorney; her attorney told us. When Danielle was younger, she claimed she could see ghosts. Her parents sent her to a psychologist."

"Does it really matter why Danielle is curious about Presley House?"

"I don't think it matters as far as the law is concerned. Breaking and entering because you're curious about an old house—or if you think it's haunted—it's still against the law either way."

"I know. So does Danielle." Lily fidgeted with her cup.

After a moment of silence Brian asked, "What do you want me to do?"

Lily took a deep breath and then exhaled, attempting to calm herself. She felt ill inside—helpless—and Brian Henderson, the man who had once been so eager to lock Danielle up, seemed to now be the only one willing to help her. "Go over to Presley House and make sure Danielle isn't there. Old houses can be dangerous. She could have fallen through a broken floorboard—anything. Maybe she's trapped."

"Are you sure you want me to do that? If she's there, I'll have to arrest her, even if she's tripped and broken her leg."

"That's okay." Lily smiled at Brian. "I just want to find Dani and make sure she's okay. And if she broke into Presley House and got herself trapped, then go ahead and arrest her. It will serve her right for making me worry like this. Wouldn't hurt her to spend a couple nights in jail."

Brian laughed. "You're a good friend, Lily."

HARVEY STOOD in the upstairs bedroom, looking out the window. He watched as the cop parked his car and started walking up the stone pathway to the front door. It was the same police officer who had been to the house on numerous occasions since Harvey had returned.

What had the other officer called him? Oh, that's right—Brian. His name is Brian. Brian had carried the lamp out of the house. He had helped carry the trunk out of the house, and while he hadn't actually been the one to carry the body out of the house, he had been the one who had called for the people to remove it. *I don't know why you're here today, but you aren't going to be taking Danielle out of the house!*

Moving from the window to the doorway, Harvey made his way downstairs. He reached the entry just as Brian unlocked the front door and let himself in.

"Aren't you kind of old to be doing this?" Harvey asked. He watched as Brian turned on a flashlight and began searching through the rooms on the first floor. Trailing behind Brian, he followed him down the hallway by the door leading to the kitchen. Harvey smiled when Brian walked past the hidden door.

Harvey didn't follow him down to the basement, where he had originally hidden Bart's body. Nor did he follow him upstairs. Instead, he waited for Brian to finish his little exploration, and then he followed him to the front door and watched him lock up the house and leave.

After Brian drove away in the police car, Harvey went back down to the hidden basement to tell Danielle about their recent visitor and to commend her for being such a quiet and well-behaved prisoner. Had she made a ruckus and attracted Brian's attention, he might have been forced to trap Brian in the room with Danielle, and frankly, he wasn't sure it was within his power to do so. As it was, he could barely keep the lights going for her. He had exhausted his powers by repeatedly opening and closing the secret door—first to trap Danielle and then to give her the coffee can. Of course, he had no intention of telling Danielle *that*.

BRIAN STOPPED at Marlow House to give Lily the bad news. He then picked up a take-out burger and headed back to the police station. Once he entered the front office, Marcia told him Joe wanted to talk to him. Brian went directly to Joe's office, knocking briefly before walking in.

Joe spied the take-out bag in Brian's hand. "I thought you were eating at the diner."

"I had some other things to do. Marcia said you wanted to see me?"

Joe stood up from his desk. "I'll have some coffee with you while you eat, if you don't mind."

A few minutes later, Joe sat alone with Brian in the break room. Joe had yet to take a sip of the coffee sitting before him. Instead, he absently fiddled with the mug, gently pushing it from side to side on the tabletop. Looking up, he watched Brian unwrap his burger.

"So what did you need to talk to me about?" Brian asked just before he took a bite.

"Someone moved Bart's body, and we know it wasn't Chuck."

Brian picked up a napkin and wiped his mouth. "I've been thinking about that."

"I'm thinking it has to be whoever took those movies." Joe pushed his mug aside and looked up at Brian. "I talked to the boys again, and they all insist there wasn't anyone else with them."

"If we would have been more careful when confiscating the cameras from the house, we might have some usable fingerprints."

"That was stupid of us," Joe grumbled.

"What I'm trying to figure out, where did they put that body between the time the boys found it and Danielle did?" Brian set his partially eaten burger down on its wrapper and looked at Joe. "By the way, I went back over there today. That's why I got takeout."

Joe frowned. "Did one of the neighbors call?"

"No. I stopped by Marlow House."

"Marlow House? Did you see Danielle?"

Brian picked his burger back up. "She still hasn't shown up. Lily asked me to check out Presley House to see if Danielle was there. Claimed Danielle was fascinated with the house and was afraid she might have gone back over there and something happened."

"Fascinated why—because they say it's haunted?"

Brian smiled. "I asked Lily that. Originally, she claimed Danielle's fascination had something to do with the fact it's an old house. But whatever the reason, she wasn't there and there wasn't any sign of her."

"She's only been gone for a couple hours. Lily is overreacting."

"Maybe—maybe not..." Brian took a bite of his burger.

"If I seriously thought Danielle was in some trouble, I'd be out looking for her," Joe insisted.

"I know you would."

They were silent for a few moments. Finally, Joe said, "Sometimes I wonder if that place is haunted."

Brian didn't respond. Instead, he finished his burger, wiped his mouth with a napkin, stuffed the trash back into the sack, and tossed it into the trash can. He leaned back in his chair and studied Joe, who stared off blankly.

"It's really bugging you, isn't it, Joe?"

Joe looked Brian in the eyes. "Isn't it bothering you, all these loose ends?"

Brian shrugged. "A little, I suppose. But instead of ghosts, I'm thinking Bart and Chuck may have had a silent partner."

"We've never found anything to indicate anyone else was involved," Joe reminded him.

"Maybe there was someone else. Someone who was afraid Bart and Chuck were going to implicate him."

"The way Bart was singing, I can't believe he wouldn't have done that already if there was someone else."

"Maybe this someone else was a person Bart feared more than Chuck. I'm just saying someone moved that body and we know it wasn't Chuck. According to the coroner, he was already dead when someone was playing hide-and-seek with Bart's body."

Joe sighed. "I suppose if there was a third person, he or she was working with Chuck, considering Chuck's fingerprints were all over that gun, and he was apparently on his way to Canada before the accident, considering what we found in his car."

"And this person—with Bart dead and Chuck heading for Canada—wouldn't have to leave town. But why would he be playing hide-and-seek with the body? What's the point?"

"If there was someone else, what makes you so sure it was a *he*?" Joe asked.

"Just an assumption based on the fact whoever moved that body had to be pretty strong."

"But where did they move it to?" Joe asked. "Why couldn't we find it?"

"I keep thinking about that lightbulb we removed from Presley House. Didn't the chief take it to be tested?"

"That's what he said. I know it's not in the evidence room."

"It has to be some sort of trick bulb—you know, the kind magicians use in magic acts. Maybe that bulb belonged to whoever moved Bart. Magicians know how to make things disappear. I've heard of acts in Vegas where the magician makes an elephant disappear on stage in front of a live audience. Hiding a body would be a piece of cake."

"So you're saying we should be looking for a magician?" Joe asked.

"Either that or a ghost."

THIRTY-FIVE

N̄o one could see Max nestled amongst the overgrown weeds under a dying tree in the center of Presley House's front yard. The police officer hadn't seen him. He had walked right by Max while taking the stone pathway from the street to the front porch. Max was headed for the house when he initially spied the police car pulling up in front of the house. Taking cover, he watched. The police officer had since come and gone, yet Max continued to crouch in the weeds.

When Max had decided to look for Danielle, he had headed in the direction he had last seen her go. While his sense of smell was not as keen as Sadie's, he still managed to pick up Danielle's unique scent. It led him away from the beach, in the direction of Presley House.

According to Walt, she intended to go to the beach after visiting the neighbor—the neighbor with the annoying kitten. He hadn't actually met the kitten—however, he had already decided to loathe the patchy fuzz ball. It was a matter of principle. Max disliked cats. Just because he happened to be one didn't mean he had to associate with other felines.

Danielle's scent had led him back to Presley House—not somewhere he particularly wanted to go. Twitching his whiskers, Max stood up, his black and white ears peeking out over the top of the weeds. He crept stealthily toward the dilapidated house, heading for a boarded-up window where he knew there was a sufficient gap between the window frame and plywood to squeeze inside.

Once Max entered Presley House, his eyes quickly adjusted to the dark interior. Keeping low and out of sight, he stayed close to the furniture, using the upholstery as camouflage to avoid detection. Just as he rounded the sofa, his fur bristled when he heard Harvey.

"I don't think Danielle appreciated my gratitude for her silence when that cop was here."

Without hesitation, Max dived into a worn spot in the back of the sofa where the upholstery had long since torn, providing a snug hidey-hole. Max's golden eyes peeked out from the back of the sofa. He could see Harvey near the doorway leading to the hallway, talking to himself.

"Now she wants water. Acts like she's going to die." Harvey shook his head and started pacing the room. "Doesn't she know if I give her water, she'll just fill up that coffee can? And where does she expect me to get water? I swear, she's demanding!"

YELLOW-ORANGE FLICKERING JACK-O'-LANTERN eyes followed Lily down the street, from their perches atop porches, railings, and windowsills. Their crooked grins and scowls reminded Lily Halloween was just a day away. She and Danielle had looked forward to showing Walt what a twenty-first-century Halloween looked like—an evening of costumed children trick-or-treating for handfuls of candy while adults enjoyed wine and warm cider with friends. In Walt's day, Halloween was nothing more than an excuse for malicious mischief.

Lily was no longer looking forward to Halloween. Her enthusiasm had begun to fizzle when Ian was called away to New York. Now with Danielle missing, Halloween was the last thing on her mind.

She had been driving the streets of Frederickport for hours, stopping at any restaurant and business Danielle had ever frequented. Yet no one had seen Danielle since she had gone missing. As Lily headed home, she glanced down at the gas gauge. It was telling her she needed to fill up. Exhausted, Lily decided to get gas in the morning.

It was dark when Lily finally pulled into the drive at Marlow

House. She was just getting out of the car when she heard someone shouting at her from the street. Turning from the vehicle toward the front of the property, Lily spied Heather Donovan making her way through the side gate, hurrying in Lily's direction.

"Hello!" Heather cried out, walking faster.

Lily pressed the keychain remote, locking the Ford Flex, while waiting for Heather to reach her.

"Evening," Lily greeted her, her voice weary.

"I noticed your car drive by, and I wanted to check and make sure Danielle got home all right."

Lily shook her head. "I'm afraid not. I've been out all afternoon looking for her."

Heather glanced up at the house and smiled. "Maybe she's home!"

"No. I left her cellphone on the kitchen table with a note, telling her to call me the minute she came in, just in case she came back while I was driving around."

"Oh my." Heather looked back to the house again. "Let's go check, just to make sure."

Lily shrugged and then turned to the house, walking to the side door, with Heather trailing behind. Once they got into the kitchen, they heard Sadie charging down the stairs from the attic toward the kitchen. Both women spied the cellphone and note still sitting on the table.

Lily tossed her purse and keys on the counter just as Sadie burst into the room, tail wagging. Kneeling down by the excited golden retriever, Lily gave her a hug and whispered by her floppy ear, "Have you been keeping Walt company? I bet he's worried sick."

"What are the police doing?" Heather asked when Lily stood back up and walked to the table. The two women sat down, facing each other.

"They don't seem overly concerned. I know Danielle didn't come back last night, but Joe's convinced Danielle was here last night and just left this morning."

"Joe?" Heather frowned.

"Sergeant Joe Morelli. He's sort of in charge while Police Chief MacDonald is on vacation."

"Hopefully they'll be more receptive to helping look for her in the morning. From what I understand they normally do nothing for a missing person until after twenty-four hours unless it's a kid."

"Hopefully Danielle will show up before then," Lily countered.

"Of course." Heather smiled and leaned forward, briefly patting Lily's hand. After a moment she asked, "Where is your friend Jon Altar? I would imagine he'd have the clout to get people to take her disappearance seriously."

"You mean Ian—Jon Altar is just his pen name. He's in New York on business right now. I haven't even told him she's missing yet."

"Why not? I was under the impression they're good friends."

"They are. But there really is nothing Ian can do from New York, aside from worry."

"I suppose you're right." Heather sighed and then looked Lily in the eyes. "Now tell me, how can I help?"

"I wish I could think of something. But I'm stumped."

"I keep thinking maybe she just needed to get away; after all, she has had a traumatic week. Her finding that body at Presley house, and then I heard about you two finding that car that had gone over the cliff at Pilgrim's Point."

"Yes, but she would never just take off like that without telling me."

"I heard them talking about her on the radio, how she found the body at Presley House. Speculating what had moved the body."

Lily looked curiously at Heather. "What, not who?"

"Well..." Heather lowered her voice to a whisper. "They do say that house is haunted."

"Do you believe in ghosts?"

Heather shrugged. "I believe in the possibility."

Lily smiled. "Me too. My mother claimed to have seen my grandmother after she died." Lily thought it best not to mention Walt.

"If my mother had ever seen a ghost, she would never have admitted it."

"Why is that?" Lily asked.

"I suppose because my father believed it was a sign of mental illness. That only crazy people believe they can see ghosts."

"My mom can be a little goofy sometimes, but I don't think she's crazy."

"Oh, I'm not saying she is." Heather blushed. "I didn't mean to give that impression."

Lily smiled. "You didn't."

"The thing is—my parents knew someone once who was—well —crazy. Pretty much certifiable, I suppose. Died in a mental institution. He claimed he could see ghosts. Although I'm not sure if it was ghosts exactly—just one ghost."

"Was that why he was in the mental institution? Because he claimed to see a ghost?" Lily couldn't help but think of Danielle and how her parents had sent her to a psychologist after she had claimed to see her grandmother's spirit.

"Partly. Although I suspect had he not been acting erratically— putting himself in danger—he wouldn't have been institutionalized. People are free to enjoy all sorts of delusions as long as they don't become a physical threat to anyone."

"True."

"But unlike my father, who insisted his claim to seeing ghosts was a symptom of his neurosis, I believe the ghost may have been the cause of his insanity."

"Are you saying seeing a ghost made him snap?" Lily asked.

"Yes. At least that's what I hope."

Lily frowned. "Hope? I don't understand."

"I prefer to believe he didn't have some mental illness—that something drove him to his insanity."

"Why is that?"

"Because if something didn't drive him to his insanity, it could mean his mental illness was a hereditary condition…and he was my grandfather."

"Oh…I'm sorry." Lily wasn't quite sure what to say. "Is he still alive?"

"No. He died a while back."

Lily and Heather chatted for another thirty minutes, and while Lily appreciated the distraction, she knew the visit wasn't helping get Danielle home. She wanted to talk to Walt about their next plan of action, and the only way to do that was to go to bed. Whether she would be able to fall asleep was another matter altogether.

By the time Lily finally managed to hustle Heather out the door and home, she could smell cigar smoke. Walt was in the kitchen.

"Walt, I looked everywhere for Danielle; no one has seen her. Has Max come home yet? I haven't seen him." Lily watched as the pepper shaker rose slightly from the table and then fell back down.

In the next moment the doorbell rang. Lily stood up. "Maybe that's news about Danielle."

When Lily opened the front door a minute later, she found Sergeant Joe Morelli standing on her front porch. Dressed in his uniform, he held his baseball cap in hand.

"Joe, any news?" Lily asked anxiously.

"I guess this means she isn't home?" Joe asked.

Lily sighed and shook her head. "No, nothing." Opening the door wider, she silently invited Joe inside. After he entered, she shut the door.

"I really thought she'd show up by now," Joe said. "This isn't like her."

"No, it's not. I'm worried sick."

Joe fiddled with his hat. "I'm sorry I didn't take you more seriously this morning."

"It's just that I know Dani would never take off without leaving a note or something. And considering I had her car...and she left her phone behind...I just figure something has to be wrong. But I do appreciate Brian checking out Presley House for me. I assume he told you."

"Yes, he did. I think it's time you file that missing person report."

I wanted to earlier, Lily thought. "I was under the impression if I file one, you probably won't do anything for twenty-four hours. Does this mean I can't expect you to start looking for her until morning?"

"Didn't you tell me she went missing last night?"

"Yes, but..." Lily didn't finish her sentence. By Joe's thoughtful expression, he was obviously rethinking his original assumption. Or perhaps he was simply willing to accept Lily's contention Danielle had gone missing the day before so that he could place a greater sense of urgency on the investigation.

THIRTY-SIX

R esting her forehead in the palm of her hand, Danielle closed her eyes. She wasn't sure how long she had been locked up in the hidden basement. Hunger pangs sent her stomach growling, and she would kill for a glass of water. No longer worried about staying awake because of a possible concussion, Danielle now believed sleeping was her one hope of being rescued. Once she was asleep, Walt might visit her dreams, and then she could tell him what had happened to her. The only problem would be getting that information to Lily, which would be tricky but not impossible.

"You might as well go to sleep," Harvey announced as he appeared before her a moment later; the lights overhead flickering on.

Danielle looked up at Harvey from where she sat on the bottom step. "Please let me go."

"Not until we find it. Take a nap. You look awful." Harvey disappeared.

Despair washed over Danielle as she curled up on the floor, using her arms as a pillow. She no longer cared about any possible creepy crawlers lurking on the basement floor.

"Save me, Walt…" she whispered as she nodded off to sleep.

HER EYES DID NOT WANT to open; their lids felt heavier than normal. With great effort, she managed to open them despite their reluctance. Glancing around the dingy basement, disappointment swept over her. Danielle was so tired, yet it was impossible to sleep, and she was still trapped in this horrid room.

"I was wondering when you'd join me," Harvey said.

Lifting her head, Danielle turned to the right and found Harvey sitting next to her on the steps.

"Was I sleeping?" Danielle asked. "How long was I asleep?"

"Do I look like I have a clock?"

The basement door rattled and then opened abruptly, flooding the room with a stream of light. Unable to contain herself, Danielle jumped to her feet, failing to notice her ankle no longer throbbed. "Help! I'm down here!"

Harvey chuckled at her outburst. Danielle heard the sound of footsteps clomping down the stairs toward her.

Prepared to rush toward whoever had entered the basement, Danielle froze when three teenage boys neared the bottom steps. Their gazes looked past her—as if she were invisible. Yet that was not what gave her pause—it was the fact that two of the boys appeared to be identical twins and the third—the third was Harvey.

Confused, Danielle looked from the Harvey walking down the stairs toward her to the spirit still sitting on the bottom step.

"They can't see or hear you," Harvey explained.

"Is this a dream?" Danielle asked, her excitement deflated.

"A dream of sorts. Revisiting the past, you might say." Harvey the spirit vanished.

By reflex, Danielle quickly stepped back out of the way of the three boys, who looked as if they were about to walk through her.

"I thought you were just flapping your lips," the Harvey coming down the stairs said.

"We told you there was a secret room!" one of the twins said with a laugh. "But we have to hurry, or Dad will flip his wig if he catches us down here."

Danielle glanced from the boys, who had just reached the bottom of the stairs, to the middle of the basement. It was no longer empty. A desk and chair sat in the middle of the room, along with a file cabinet and a stack of boxes. By its appearance, it looked as if someone had set the secret basement up as an office.

"Ahh, Bruce, Dad won't be back for a couple hours," the other twin said. "He'll never know we were down here."

Danielle looked from one twin to the other. *If that one is Bruce— then the other must be Barney.*

"Pay up, Harvey, we told you our house had a secret room," Barney said.

Harvey dug his hand into his pocket and pulled out some money. He handed it to Barney, who then gave a portion to Bruce.

"What does he do down here?" Harvey asked, glancing around the room.

"Says he uses it to store stuff," Barney said with a shrug.

"You really didn't know it was here?" Harvey asked.

"You're always over here; you never saw it before," Bruce challenged.

"No—you're right. This is swell, a secret room. Too bad we can't use it for a secret club or something." Harvey wandered over to the desk and started opening the drawers.

"I don't think you should be doing that," Barney said nervously.

"Why? I paid my money." Harvey opened another drawer. Whatever was in the drawer gave him pause. "Applesauce! Get a load of this!"

Barney and Bruce rushed to his side and looked in the drawer.

"I don't think we should be going through the desk," Bruce said.

"Are these what I think they are?" Harvey reached into the drawer.

"What are you doing?" a male voice boomed.

Danielle had not noticed a man had come into the basement— and neither had the boys. She turned to face the newcomer. A much older version of the twins stood at the foot of the stairs; she guessed he was their father.

Angry, the man stormed toward the desk and pushed his sons aside. The twins cowered while Harvey stood frozen at the desk, his hand still in the drawer.

"What are you doing in my things?" Mr. Presley growled.

"I know what these are," Harvey said. Unlike his friends, he did not cower.

"Put them down and close the drawer," Mr. Presley ordered.

"Did you steal them?" Harvey asked. "Is that why you have them hidden down here?"

"I said shut the drawer!" Mr. Presley shouted.

Harvey dropped whatever he was holding and looked at Mr. Presley. A small smile flickered on the boy's lips.

"I was so foolish," Harvey the spirit said when he appeared next to Danielle.

Danielle glanced from the spirit to the teenager standing at the desk. Time, it seemed, had frozen. Mr. Presley and Harvey were locked in a silent stare down while Danielle and Harvey the spirit observed.

"How so?" Danielle asked.

"You'll see. He knew what I was thinking."

"What were you thinking?" Danielle asked.

"About getting a share of the action."

Before Danielle could ask another question, Mr. Presley lunged toward Harvey the boy while grabbing a bronze figurine off the desk. Without pause, he slammed the heavy object against Harvey's forehead, sending the teenager crashing to the floor. Danielle let out a startled gasp, horrified at the scene unfolding before her.

Neither twin made an attempt to stop their father as he repeatedly slammed the unconscious boy's head—over and over again.

Breathing heavily, Mr. Presley tossed the bloodied object aside and looked up at his sons. "This is your fault. You're going to help me get rid of his body, and if you say anything, I'll make sure you join him."

The next moment, Danielle was no longer in the basement but sitting on the beach with Harvey. It was night, and overhead a half moon lit the dark sky.

"Where are we?" Danielle asked.

"We're watching them dump my body." Harvey pointed down the beach where three shadowy figures lugged something toward the incoming waves.

"What was in the drawer?" Danielle asked.

"Obviously something Mr. Presley stole. I thought you would have figured that out."

"So your uncle had nothing to do with your death?"

"Hardly. I'm responsible for his death."

Danielle looked at Harvey. "How? You were murdered before your uncle killed himself. You're not responsible."

"I told him I was going over to Bruce and Barney's house. My uncle never cared for old man Presley. He knew him back before Presley was married; they were drinking buddies. They had some sort of falling out. When I disappeared, my uncle didn't believe I had run off. He got drunk, went over to the Presley house…" Harvey let out a sigh and shrugged. He stared off to the ocean. Mr. Presley and his sons were no longer in sight. Harvey and Danielle were alone on the beach.

"They killed your uncle?" Danielle asked.

"Yes. Made it look like a suicide."

"I still don't understand…what are you looking for? Why do you keep coming back to Presley House? And why only on Halloween?"

"I have a vague memory of waking up on the beach… after…after…"

"After they put your body in the ocean?" Danielle finished for him.

Harvey nodded. "And then I was at the cemetery. I don't know how I got there. But there was my headstone. And next to it was my uncle's headstone. He was gone too. But I had no idea why he was there."

"Did you see him after you died?"

Harvey shook his head. "No. I've never seen him, not since before…"

Before you were murdered, Danielle thought.

"I found myself wandering around the cemetery, looking for answers. And then one day…"

Suddenly Danielle was no longer sitting on the beach with Harvey. She now stood with him at the Frederickport Cemetery, looking at his headstone.

Two middle-aged women, each wearing a dress, hat, and gloves, walked up to Harvey's grave and looked down.

"He was a good boy. I still can't believe his uncle would do something like this," one of the women said.

"That's Clara Bennet," Harvey explained. "Her husband owned the local market and I used to stock shelves for him. The other one is her sister, Miss Frances."

"It was the drinking," Miss Frances explained. "Does things to a man. Evil things."

"But to kill a boy he so loved? And I know he loved Harvey."

Miss Frances shook her head. "I imagine he did, which is why he took his own life. Sobered up and realized the evil he perpetrated. I'm just glad there was enough money left over to get them both a decent headstone. Now they're in the good Lord's hands. He'll straighten this all out."

"Miss Frances was always the churchy one," Harvey explained. "When I was younger, she'd drag me off to the Sunday sermon." The women vanished, and once again, Harvey and Danielle were alone.

"Is this how you found out everyone thought your uncle killed you?"

Harvey nodded. "Now that I had my answer, I tried to leave the cemetery. I wanted to find someone who could hear me—so I could tell them what really happened. At the time, I thought my uncle had killed himself because everyone thought he murdered me. But I couldn't leave. I was trapped here."

"When you say you wanted to leave the cemetery, you weren't trying to move on, were you?"

"Move on?" Harvey frowned.

"When we die, we move on to another level."

Harvey looked off into the distance. "I don't know about that, but I couldn't move on. Not until I set things right."

"You say you were stuck at the cemetery, but you obviously managed to go to Presley House."

"A year went by, and all I could think about was going to the Presley house and setting things straight. And then suddenly, without warning, I was there. I saw them all...Barney, Bruce and Mr. Presley. They couldn't see or hear me, but I could hear them. I found out they had murdered my uncle. I figured out how to move things around. That got their attention."

"What happened?"

"I returned to the cemetery as quickly and as unexpectedly as I had gone to Presley House. But then another year went by...and it happened again."

"Always around Halloween?"

"Yes. But this time something extraordinary happened—I was able to make Barney and Bruce see me."

"How did they react?"

"They looked at me with the same fear as they had looked at their father when he killed me. Cowards, both of them. When I returned the next year, they were gone. And so was the journal."

"The journal you're looking for?"

"Yes. I convinced Bruce to write down everything that had

happened in the basement. Unfortunately, after I watched him hide the journal, I was sent back to the cemetery and had to wait another year. But when I returned, they had moved."

"And the journal?"

"It's somewhere in that house. I know it is. I just don't remember exactly where he hid it."

THIRTY-SEVEN

The first quarter moon cast its glow across Marlow House's front landscape. Standing at the attic window, Walt gazed outside, his thoughts on Danielle. Throughout the day and into the night he had tried to find his way into her dreams to no avail. If she were somewhere sleeping—the door was firmly locked.

Lily had been sleeping for over an hour. He knew she was waiting for him, yet he wasn't prepared to talk to her yet—what would he say? What great plan did he have to find Danielle? Closing his eyes, he asked himself the same question he had been asking for the last few hours. Was Danielle now like him? If so, why hadn't she returned to the house—or had she moved on? Would he find her again? Was she lost to him forever, traveling her own cosmic journey?

While deciding what to tell Lily when they met up in her dreams, something caught his eye—a dark shadow moved swiftly down the street and into the yard. Then he heard it. The sound of the pet door swinging back and forth. Sadie, who slept by Walt's feet, lifted her head, her ears perking up.

"I think maybe Max has come home," Walt told her.

Sadie started to jump up, preparing to dash from the room, when Walt stopped her.

"You can't bark, Sadie. You must be quiet. Lily is sleeping, and I need her to sleep so I can talk to her. But first, let's see where Max has been keeping himself."

"DID YOU KNOW YOU SNORE?" Walt asked.

Lily opened her eyes and found Walt staring at her. Clutching her blanket, she sat up in bed and glanced around the room.

"I don't understand. I can see you," Lily whispered in awe.

"You're dreaming," Walt explained.

Lily frowned. "Then why am I still in my bedroom?"

"Is this better?" The next moment Lily sat with Walt on the pier. By the sunrise behind them, it appeared to be early morning.

"I suppose it doesn't matter where we are. For a moment…I forgot about Dani and how she's missing."

"I know where she is," Walt told her.

Lily looked at Walt. "You do?"

"She's at Presley House. Max came home tonight; he found her."

"Is she okay?"

"Max thinks so. He didn't see her exactly, but he knows she's there," Walt explained.

Lily considered Walt's words a moment and then shook her head. "No, she can't be at Presley House. Brian Henderson went over there and checked out the entire house. There wasn't any sign of her."

"She's being kept in a secret room there. I imagine it's the same room where Harvey hid the body."

"Is he keeping her prisoner?"

"According to Max, he has her trapped in the room. Harvey is searching for something, and whatever it is, he wants Danielle to help him."

Lily stood up. "What am I going to do?" She began pacing back and forth in front of Walt.

"You could call Joe and tell him where she is."

Lily stopped pacing and looked at Walt. "How can I convince him to go over there? As far as he's concerned, they've already looked through the house."

"You can tell him about the secret room," Walt suggested.

"Exactly how do I explain I know there's a secret room at Presley House?"

Walt considered the question for a moment. "Perhaps you need to suggest the possibility; after all, they have to be wondering where the body went after the boys found it. I can't believe the idea of a secret room hasn't come up."

"If they do go there, will they be able to get Danielle? If she's being held prisoner, what's to stop Harvey from holding Joe or Brian prisoner? What if he does something worse?"

"Lily, I don't believe Harvey has the power to hold the entire Frederickport Police Department captive—or even a couple of its officers."

"But he is holding Danielle!"

"A spirit only has so much energy to spend."

Frowning, Lily stared at Walt. Cocking her head to one side, she said, "That's pretty much what Dani suggested."

Walt shrugged. "I suppose Danielle knows more than what I sometimes give her credit for."

"So if Joe goes over there...are you saying Harvey wouldn't have the power to keep them both prisoner?"

"I'm saying it would be more difficult for Harvey. I imagine he's already using every ounce of energy he has to keep Danielle there."

"Have you tried talking to her?" Lily asked.

"You mean a dream hop?"

Lily nodded.

"I've been trying since she went missing. I was beginning to worry that something had happened..."

"Like with Isabella?"

"Yes. But now that I know Danielle's alive, I suspect Harvey has in some way invaded her dreams first, preventing me from entering. Which would also be taxing his energy."

"Then what are we waiting for? I need to wake up and get Joe to go over there and rescue Danielle!"

THE PERSISTENT RING of his cellphone refused to stop. Still half asleep, Joe rolled over and snatched the phone off his nightstand. Sitting up in bed, rubbing his eyes, he looked down at the annoying device.

Had the caller been anyone other than Lily, he might have answered the phone by telling the caller he or she better have a good reason for waking him at 3:55 a.m.

"Lily, is Danielle home?" Joe asked when he answered the call.

"No, Joe. But I know where she is! She's at Presley House."

Joe sat up in bed and put his feet on the floor. "Presley House?"

"Yes, she's trapped there. You have to go get her!"

Joe reached over to the lamp on the nightstand and turned it on. "Lily, I'm afraid I'm not following you. Brian was already over there. There was no sign of Danielle."

"I know, but she's trapped in a secret room."

"Secret room?"

"Yes. I bet it's the same room where the body was hidden after the boys found it."

"Are you saying whoever hid the body has Danielle? Do you have some idea who that is?"

"Umm...no...I'm just saying if you couldn't find the body when the boys told you about it, then it had to have been somewhere like a secret room. After all, a body can't just vanish in thin air."

Rubbing his forehead, Joe shook his head wearily. "Lily, what made you think of a secret room—in the middle of the night." He glanced up at the clock on the nightstand. "It's 4:00 a.m."

"That's not exactly the middle of the night, Joe. It's morning. Sure, it's early, but it's still morning and not the middle of the night."

"Okay, Lily, I'm going to ask you again. What makes you think Danielle is in a secret room at Presley House?"

After a few moments of silence Lily said, "I had a dream."

"A dream?"

"Yes, but it's not that far-fetched, considering the body that disappeared and reappeared."

"Lily, I understand you're worried about Danielle. We're all worried about her, but..."

"Does this mean you aren't going to look?"

Joe took a deep breath. "We'll look, Lily. If it makes you feel better."

"You'll find the door to the secret room in the hallway off the kitchen."

"A secret door in the hallway? How exactly do you know where the door is?" When Lily didn't respond, Joe said, "You dreamt about it, didn't you?"

"Just go look, Joe. You'll see I'm right."

"Okay, Lily."

When the call ended, Joe stared at the cellphone in his hand for a few moments. Finally, he let out a sigh, tossed the phone back onto the nightstand, turned off the light, and went back to sleep.

"A SECRET ROOM?" Brian asked. He sat with Joe at the lunch counter at the Pier Café, having breakfast.

"That's what she said." Joe took a sip of his coffee. "I know she's just worried about Danielle; we all are."

"What did you tell her you were going to do?" Brian set his coffee cup on the counter.

"You mean about the secret room?"

Brian nodded.

Joe shrugged. "I told her we would check it out. It's not a lie exactly. Someone will be going over there anyway since it's Halloween."

"And she said she knew this because of a dream?"

Joe nodded.

"She really expected you to take her seriously?" Brian asked.

"Like I said, she's just worried about her friend. Grasping at straws."

"Well, according to the neighbors, no one remembers seeing Danielle since she went missing. Hopefully that little radio blitz on her disappearance might help. There will be a lot of people walking around town tonight—and if we can get them aware that a woman is missing, someone might find something we can use."

When Joe's phone began to ring, he picked it up and looked at it. "It's Lily again. She's called me three times already since she woke me up this morning."

"What have you told her?"

"I haven't answered her call."

"Seriously? You can't just ignore her call."

"I know." Joe sighed. "When I told her we would check the house, I didn't expect her to start calling me every hour."

"I imagine she'll call the station."

"She has. Marcia told her I was out."

"Maybe we should just go over to Presley House and check it out again."

"Come on, Brian, you don't honestly believe the answer to Danielle's disappearance will be found in Lily's dream?"

"You're the one who said you would go check Presley House again, not me!"

"I know." Joe combed his fingers through his hair. "But it was four in the morning, I was half asleep, and I just wanted to get her off the phone so I could get back to sleep because I knew we were going to have a big day today. I'll just run over to Presley House, check it out again, and then call her up so she'll stop calling me."

Joe's phone rang again. This time when he looked at it, he answered it.

"I think we may have our first lead," Joe said when he got off the phone.

"What is it?"

"We finally have some activity on one of Danielle's credit cards. Last night someone used it to check into a motel in Portland."

"I thought Lily said Danielle left her purse at home."

"She did, but it looks like Danielle may have taken one of her credit cards with her."

"Are you still going to go over to Presley House?"

Joe shook his head. "My first priority is finding Danielle, not placating Lily. I'd say a lead on a missing person's credit card takes precedence over Lily's dream. Someone will be going over to Presley House later tonight anyway."

Joe's phone began ringing again. He picked it up and looked at it. "I will say one thing for Lily, she is persistent."

"Are you going to answer that?" Brian asked.

Joe sighed again. "I suppose I should."

THIRTY-EIGHT

W alt hadn't left Lily's side since she had woken up that morning. He watched as she angrily paced the kitchen while cursing Joe Morelli under her breath.

She paused a moment and faced Walt, who sat at the kitchen table. "And just what does Joe mean there's a more critical lead that takes precedence that he needs to first check out? He tells me his first priority is bringing Danielle home, yet he can't take ten minutes to check out Presley House like he promised he would do?"

Grabbing a mug from the overhead cabinet, Lily angrily poured herself a cup of coffee and then sat down at the table, facing Walt. "If I knew where the chief was staying, I would call him, and he'd have Danielle home within the hour!"

Walt watched Lily. While he felt helpless being trapped at Marlow House, he was relieved to know Danielle's location. After a long chat with Max, he didn't believe she was in real danger, but he imagined she was probably hungry and thirsty. He had a friend once who survived a week without water, so Walt wasn't ready to start panicking yet. Why panic? Lily was already doing that for him.

"And to top it off, when I was talking to Joe on the phone, I missed a call from Ian! And now he's in a meeting, and I can't reach him." Lily took a quick swig of coffee, burning her mouth. Cursing, she set the mug on the table and licked her lip. "But maybe that's for the best. I don't know what to tell him anyhow."

Lily sat quietly for a moment, staring at her coffee mug. Finally, she looked in Walt's direction. "I suppose the only thing I can do—I need to go over there myself."

The pepper shaker rose up several inches and then fell back down on the tabletop. "If you go over there, you could get trapped with Danielle, and then you'll both be missing."

"I have to do this, Walt."

The pepper shaker rose up again, this time almost reaching the ceiling before crashing back down and shattering on the tabletop.

Lily looked down at the splintered glass scattered across the tablecloth. She shook her head. "Dani isn't going to be happy you broke her pepper shaker."

"I don't really care about the pepper shaker," Walt said angrily. "You can't just barge over there without a plan!"

Lily stood up and looked at the chair where she assumed Walt sat. "Maybe I need a plan."

Taken aback briefly by the fact Lily virtually parroted his words, Walt cocked his head slightly and said, "Someone needs to know you're going over there so they'll look for you if you get trapped with Danielle."

Tapping her finger against her chin while trying to formulate a plan, Lily was silent a moment before she burst into a smile and announced, "I know! I'll make sure someone knows where I'm going so if I do get trapped, they'll know to come looking for me!"

Walt smiled. "Interesting…"

Lily snatched her cellphone from the counter. "I'll call Marie!"

Walt frowned. "Marie? She's ninety. How will she be able to help you?"

Holding the phone to her ear, she waited for Marie to answer her call.

Walt stood up. "Lily, call someone else. Not Marie. She's ninety. At ninety she might forget in ten minutes you ever called!"

"Hello, Marie? This is Lily…no, Dani isn't home yet, but I think I know where she may be…"

"Lily, please call someone else!" Walt looked over to the table and the broken pepper shaker. He raised its lid.

Phone in hand, Lily wandered back to the table and sat down. The pepper shaker lid hovering over the table caught her eye. She dismissed it with a wave and focused on her phone conversation.

"I can't really explain it now, not enough time, but I know

Danielle went over to Presley House, and I have reason to believe she may be trapped there...A secret room...How do I know?...I was thinking about how that body went missing...I did call the police...Joe says they're working on another lead and can't be bothered...I just want you to know I'm going over there, and if you don't hear from me in two hours, please let someone know where I went...Yes, I am going alone...Ian is out of town...No, I don't think anyone is holding her...Okay...Thank you!"

When Lily got off the phone, she shoved it in her pocket. "Okay, Marie knows where I'm going, so if I don't call her in two hours, she'll send someone looking for me."

"I think this is a bad idea." Walt shook his head.

"Although...now that I think about it, it wasn't really necessary to call Marie. After all, I'll be driving Dani's car over there. If I get trapped with Dani, someone is bound to notice the car parked in front of the house." Lily snatched the car keys from the counter and then opened the junk drawer, looking for something to use to pick the lock.

"I suppose that makes me feel slightly better." Walt looked down at Sadie. "Go with Lily, Sadie, she might need your help."

Sadie jumped up, tail wagging, and ran to Lily, who was now heading for the back door.

"No, girl, you need to stay here," Lily told her.

"Take her!" Walt shouted.

Lily paused a moment. "Well, I suppose it wouldn't hurt if you came along. Might actually be helpful."

LILY WAS two streets away from Presley House when the Flex ran out of gas. Cursing, Lily got out of the car with Sadie and began walking toward Presley House.

Pulling her phone from her pocket, she looked at the battery level and let out a sigh of relief. Glancing down at Sadie, she tucked the phone back in her pocket. "I got a little afraid for a moment there, Sadie. Figured it would be just my luck to have a dead battery on top of an empty gas tank. But it's over eighty percent, so we're fine."

When Sadie and Lily reached Presley House, Lily knelt by the front door with the small screwdriver she had brought with her.

Fiddling with the lock, she glanced down at Sadie. "I saw how to do this in a YouTube video once."

After ten minutes of frustration, Lily tossed the tool aside. "It sure looked a heck of a lot easier in the video!" Standing up, Lily headed for the back of the house, looking for some other form of entry.

HARVEY HEARD the rattling at the front door. Under other circumstances, he would be tempted to simply open the door and have a little fun with whoever was trying to break in. But it was Halloween, and as history proved, when this night ended, he would be whisked back to the cemetery for another year. He needed to find the journal and then make Danielle promise to make it public so the world would know what had really happened to himself and his uncle. The fact the world believed the loving uncle—the man who cared for Harvey when everyone else abandoned him—had been his murderer was unbearable.

Harvey then heard something in the kitchen. Someone was trying to remove the plywood covering the broken kitchen window.

LILY MANAGED to squeeze through the small opening between the plywood and window frame. By the missing nails and angles of the plywood, it was obvious someone else had been messing with the makeshift covering. It looked as if it had already been removed and then reattached, yet whoever reattached it didn't do a very good job, which was fortunate for Lily.

"I'll go open the front door and let you in, and then we'll find Dani," Lily called to Sadie in a hushed voice. Sadie sat outside the house, looking up at the partially boarded-up window, her tail wagging.

The minute Lily was inside the kitchen, she cursed herself for not bringing a flashlight. "I guess I didn't think this out very well."

Once her eyes adjusted to the dim lighting, she made her way through the kitchen into the hallway. Just as she was about to turn in the direction of the front door to let Sadie in, she heard a knocking on the wall coming from the opposite direction.

239

"Danielle?" Lily whispered, looking in the direction of the knock.

Lured by the steady knocking, Lily continued in the direction of the sound when suddenly a door swung open.

"Is someone there?" came Danielle's voice from below.

"Dani!" Lily called out, heading for the open doorway.

"Lily, is that you? Be careful! There's stairs, and watch the door, it will—"

Just as Lily stepped through the doorway, the door slammed close behind her and locked. Fortunately, she managed to grab onto a handrail and steady herself, avoiding a tumble down the stairs. Turning back to the door, Lily tried opening it.

"It's locked!" Lily called out.

"I was afraid of that," came Danielle's reply.

"Are you okay?" Lily looked down the stairs. Overhead, a light flickered on. She could see Danielle sitting on the bottom step. Without thought, she hurried down the stairs to her friend.

"I sprained my ankle," Danielle explained as Lily gave her an enthusiastic hug.

"Who is this?" Harvey asked when he appeared a moment later.

"Harvey is here," Danielle explained.

"Where?" Lily asked.

Danielle pointed to Harvey, who stood in the middle of the room. Although Lily could not see him, she glared in his direction.

"Do you have any idea how worried we've been?" Lily shouted at Harvey.

Startled at Lily's outburst, he took a step back away from the women, his eyes wide.

"And she has hurt her ankle! What kind of monster are you?" Lily charged forward toward Harvey.

"Can she see me?" Harvey asked in a quivering voice.

"No. But she knows you're there," Danielle explained.

Harvey disappeared.

Lily launched into a fresh verbal attack when Danielle interrupted her. "He's gone, Lily. I think you scared him away."

"We have to get you out of here," Lily whispered. "Aside from your ankle, how are you?"

"I don't think I've ever been as thirsty in my life before. Which helps me not think about being hungry."

"We'll take care of that." Lily pulled her phone from her pocket.

"What are you doing?"

"Calling for help."

"You came alone?"

Instead of answering, Lily frowned at her phone. "I don't understand."

"What's wrong?"

Lily rubbed her temple as she stared at her cellphone. "I had over eighty percent charge on this phone fifteen minutes ago. Now it's dead."

Danielle glanced up to the ceiling. "It's probably Harvey. I was cursing myself for forgetting my cellphone, but I guess it wouldn't have helped me."

"Harvey? You saying he's messing with my phone?"

"Angela did it to me that time she forced me to stop at the cemetery. Remember, she did something to my car and phone. Neither of them would work. Most spirits seem to be able to mess with phones or anything electric." Danielle glanced to the ceiling light. "Presley House doesn't have an electric meter."

Lily glanced up to the lit ceiling light. "Then I suppose all we can do is wait. Wish I had brought something for you to drink."

"Wait?"

"Reinforcements should be here in a couple hours. And poor Sadie is outside; I hope she's okay. But first, let me see if that door is really locked."

Danielle watched as Lily walked back up the stairs and rattled the doorknob. She then repeatedly slammed her shoulder against the door.

"Crap, it's locked all right. Anything down here we can use as tools?" Lily walked back down the stairs and glanced around.

"I'm afraid not. This room's empty."

Lily nodded to the coffee can sitting in the far corner. "What's that?"

"Umm...nothing..."

"Hey, maybe there are some tools in it!"

"Lily, trust me. You do not want to be looking in that coffee can."

THIRTY-NINE

M arcia wedged the tip of the letter opener under her thumbnail, digging out a piece of pumpkin. The night before she had helped her son carve a jack-o'-lantern, yet the removal of the pumpkin seeds and pulp had fallen on her and had destroyed her manicure. Frowning, she tossed the letter opener onto the desk and glanced up at the wall clock. It was almost time for her lunch break. She would miss lunch today because she would be spending that time at the grocery store, picking up Halloween candy.

The phone rang and she answered it. "Frederickport Police Department."

"I need to speak to Joe Morelli," came an elderly woman's voice.

"I'm afraid Sergeant Morelli is out of the office right now. Would you like to leave a message for him?"

"This is very important; I need to speak to Officer Morelli, now!"

"I'm sorry, but he's not here right now. Is there someone else who can help you?"

"No. Do you know when he's going to be back?"

"He should be back any minute now. Would you like me to leave him a message to call you?"

"No. He doesn't need to call me. Just give him a message from me. Can you do that?"

"Certainly." Marcia grabbed a pen and pad of paper.

"Who am I talking to?" Marie asked.

"This is Marcia, Marcia Hoffman."

"Tell Joe Marie Nichols called. He needs to know Lily went over to Presley House to find Danielle, and now she's stuck there."

"Stuck there?" Marcia frowned.

"She must be. She didn't call me."

"Call you?"

"Are you listening to me?" Marie snapped. "Why do you keep repeating everything I'm saying?"

Marcia rolled her eyes and tapped the end of the pen against the pad of paper. "I'm just trying to understand, ma'am."

"Lily Miller told me to have Joe go over to Presley House and look for her if she didn't call me. And she hasn't called me. Danielle is there. Do you understand?"

"Yes, I think so." Marcia jotted down notes on the pad of paper. "You want Sergeant Morelli to go to Presley House because Lily Miller didn't call you."

"Yes. And he needs to do it right away."

"Okay, I'll make sure he gets this note as soon as he gets into the office."

When Marcia got off the phone, she looked at the note she had just written and wrinkled her nose. Crumpling up the paper, she tossed it in the trash and grabbed a fresh piece of paper. Starting to rewrite the note in a more legible handwriting, she paused a moment, trying to remember the name of the caller. Shaking her head, she figured it really didn't matter considering the woman didn't want Joe to call her back.

After Marcia finished writing the note, she stood up and took it to Joe's office, tossing it on his desk before taking off for lunch.

When Joe returned to his office that afternoon, he found a note on his desk. Picking it up, he read it: *Lily Miller wants you to go to Presley House to get Danielle.*

"I DON'T UNDERSTAND." Lily paced the basement. "I was sure someone would have been here a couple of hours ago."

"I've lost all track of time. I can't believe it's Halloween."

Danielle stood up, attempting to walk on her still-sore ankle, but the pain was too great, so she sat down again.

"Halloween morning, at least it was when I got here. I figure it must be close to evening by now."

"I just hope Harvey has the good sense to unlock that door before the night is over."

"If he wants you to find the missing journal, I don't see how he expects you to do it locked up in the basement."

"I've begun to think it's not so much me finding the journal—it's about me taking the journal with me after it's found and making it public. He wants to keep me safely tucked away until he finds it. Although, I did try looking for it down here."

"That couldn't have taken long. Can't imagine where someone would hide something down here."

Danielle glanced up to the ceiling and then back to Lily. "Quite honestly, I suspect the journal is long gone. Probably went with the Presleys when they moved. Or maybe one of the tenants found it; this place was a rental for a number of years. Who knows?"

"On the plus side, this is Halloween, and if Marie can't get the police over here, I don't expect we'll be alone for long."

Danielle smiled. "I assume you're talking about the teenagers who can't resist breaking into a haunted house on Halloween?"

"Exactly. And we need to be prepared to make a lot of noise."

SEAN KELLEY WANTED to be a member of the Hell Raisers. What freshman wouldn't want to be a member of the secret club? Unfortunately, being asked was just the beginning. He had to pass the initiation. Silently, he watched as three of his classmates—all seniors—climbed through the window at Presley House. They wedged their bodies between the window frame and the piece of plywood. He was next. Glancing behind him, he looked at Steve Potts, a junior.

Steve gave Sean a little shove. "What are you waiting for? Go in."

Reluctantly, Sean climbed into Presley House, with Steve right behind him. Once in the house, the four boys led Sean upstairs to the second floor and into a bedroom, its window completely covered on the outside with plywood. Without the flashlights the other boys carried, Sean would not be able to see anything.

"Are you going to leave me a flashlight?" Sean asked nervously.

"You don't need a flashlight," one of the boys said with a laugh. He then reached into his pocket and pulled out two short candles and a book of matches. He handed them to Sean.

"Remember, you have to spend the entire night upstairs. We'll come back in the morning and get you," Steve explained.

Sean looked at the candles in his hand. "I don't think they'll last all night."

The other boys laughed. "That's sort of the idea," one of them said.

"You also have an entire book of matches," another one reminded him.

"Hey, you don't have to do this. You can leave with us right now. But if you want to be a member of the Hell Raisers, you have to prove you have the right stuff," Steve told him. "We don't take chickens."

Sean clutched the candles in his hand and glared up at the boys. "I can do this. You'll see. No big deal. This will be easy!"

"Remember, there will probably be some other kids who come here tonight, trying to be cool. Don't let them know you're here. Scare them away."

Sean nodded. "This will be fun." He didn't quite believe that.

SEAN STOOD at the top of the staircase, watching the members of the Hell Raisers make their way to the entry. Instead of exiting the way they had come in, they left through the front door, leaving it unlocked. With the flashlights gone, darkness engulfed the interior of Presley House.

Instead of lighting a candle, Sean went into the one bedroom that still had a windowpane. He looked outside. He watched as the boys who had brought him to Presley House walked down the street. They weren't the only ones on the streets; costume-clad trick-or-treaters made their way to the other houses in the neighborhood.

Sean had been standing at the window for over an hour when he heard what sounded like pounding noise coming from downstairs. He walked into the hallway, but it was pitch black and he couldn't see anything. Retreating into the first bedroom the boys had taken him to, he lit one of the candles and looked around for someplace to set it. He noticed a broken beer bottle lying in the corner. Picking it up, he used it as a makeshift candleholder and set it on the dresser. He then lit the second candle and took it with him to investigate the noise.

HARVEY WATCHED as the teenage boy slunk down the stairs, candle in hand. He wished Danielle and her friend would stop making all that racket. He needed to concentrate on finding the journal before the night ended. He didn't have time to deal with the teenager and whatever prank he was attempting to perpetrate.

The boy approached the hallway, walking in the direction of the pounding sound, the candle held high over his head.

"This will not do at all. I will not have three of you locked in the basement! You must leave!" Focusing his energy on a footstool in the living room, he made it lift up into the air and float in the direction of the intruder. Harvey couldn't help but laugh at the wide-eyed horrified expression of the teenager when he spied the small piece of furniture floating his way. The boy let out a scream and then raced for the door his friends had left through earlier that evening.

Upstairs, the candle shifted and slipped, falling from the makeshift holder. Still lit, it rolled off the dresser, fell onto the floor, and rolled toward the bed. Its flame flickered and flared, teasing the hem of the tattered bedspread.

"DON'T you ever answer your cellphone?" Adam Nichols asked Joe Morelli when he found him sitting in the diner, drinking a cup of coffee with Brian Henderson.

Joe looked up from his coffee. "Sorry, Adam, it has been a crazy night. Unless the call comes from the station, I'm not answering it."

"Not so busy you couldn't stop for a donut break," Adam snapped.

Unamused, Brian glared up from his coffee. "Cool it with the donut jokes. We're entitled to a cup of coffee. Like Joe said, it's been a hell of an evening."

Hands on hips, Adam looked down at the officers. "Well, my grandmother is about to have a stroke, worrying about Danielle."

Joe set his mug on the table and looked up at Adam. "We're worried about her too, and we're doing everything we can to find her."

"And what about Lily?" Adam asked.

"I told Lily we were checking out some leads. Like I said, we're doing everything we can."

"That's not what I'm talking about." Adam looked from Joe to Brian and back to Joe. "Did you get my grandmother's message?"

"Your grandmother's message? I don't know what you're talking about."

"She spoke to that new girl you have working in the front office," Adam explained. "A Marcia somebody. It was around lunchtime. She promised my grandmother she'd give you her message."

Joe shrugged. "Marcia left a note on my desk around that time, but I was under the impression it was from Lily, not your grandmother."

"What did it say?"

"Lily has it in her head Danielle is at Presley House, but we've already been over there. It was just another message asking me to check the house again."

"That note was from my grandmother. Lily is missing."

Brian set his mug on the table and looked up at Adam. "What do you mean missing?"

"Lily called my grandmother this morning and told her she was going over to Presley House. She was convinced Danielle was trapped there in some secret room. Told Grandma if she didn't call her by noon, that she was to call you and have you go over to Presley House to help her. When Lily didn't call my grandmother back, Grandma called the police station and talked to Marcia. Grandma has been waiting all afternoon to hear something; she finally called me. I just went over to Marlow House, no one is there, but I found Ian's golden retriever sitting on the front porch. The back gate was shut but not locked. I went ahead and put the dog in the side yard. I then drove over to Presley House, but didn't see Danielle's car. But I did find it about two blocks away, parked. No Lily in sight."

Brian slammed his fist on the table. "What the hell is going on around here? Women just up and disappearing?"

FORTY

A quarter moon lit Halloween's night sky. Trick-or-treaters raced by Heather, their focus on the prize of more candy. They paid little attention to the woman dressed in black walking alone down the street towards Presley House. Those who did look assumed she wore a witch's costume, considering the long skirt and cape. Yet there was no witch's hat, just her dark hair pulled into two low ponytails.

Heather clutched a flashlight in one hand and a key in the other. She had heard the police had called a locksmith, yet she didn't know if that meant her key would no longer work. *Had they changed the locks?* If the key didn't work, she would need to find some other way into the house.

When she reached the sidewalk in front of Presley House, she paused a moment and looked up at the dilapidated Victorian. She told herself if one looked up *haunted house* in the dictionary, they would probably see a picture of Presley House. Making her way past the gate, she walked up the stone pathway leading to the entry.

Stepping up onto the front porch, she directed the beam of her flashlight at the front door. It was ajar. There would be no need for the key. She wondered if someone was inside. Tucking the key into the pocket of her skirt, she approached the front door and peeked inside.

Hesitantly, she entered the dark house while directing the beam of her flashlight over its walls. Walking to the center of the living room, she looked around.

"Harvey?" she called out. "If you are here, please make yourself known!"

A knocking came from the direction of the hallway.

"Is that you, Harvey?"

The knocking continued.

"I am the granddaughter of Barney Presley. He was my mother's father. I know what they did to you—to your uncle. I know what my great-grandfather did. I know why you haunt this place. I've come to tell the truth."

The overhead lights flickered on and the knocking continued.

"I've read the journal written by my grandfather's brother. I have it."

The overhead lights flickered off, and in the next instant, Harvey showed himself to Heather. He stood just six feet from her in the living room, standing in the beam of her flashlight.

Heather let out a gasp of surprise yet did not waver. She continued to stand in the center of the living room, her light on Harvey.

"It's really you," she said in a whisper.

"Where is the journal?" he asked.

"I have it at my house. I plan to make it public, to tell the world about the injustice that was done to you. To your uncle."

"Why would you do that?" he asked.

"Because that's what my grandfather wanted. That's what he needs for his soul to be at peace."

It sounded like an explosion coming from upstairs. Both Heather and Harvey looked up to the second-floor landing. Erratic flames danced and flickered, making their way down the hallway, touching the ceiling and clinging to the walls.

"The house is on fire!" Heather shouted, quickly turning from Harvey, preparing to run outside.

"Wait!" Harvey shouted.

Heather looked back at the spirit. "I promise I'll do what I say. I just wanted you to know. But I have to get out of here!"

"It's not that! They're trapped in the basement! I can't open the door—I've used all my power showing myself to you!"

"What are you talking about?" Heather looked up nervously to the growing fire.

"Danielle and her friend Lily, I have them locked in the secret room. You need to get them out! Follow me, quick!" Harvey turned and headed for the hallway.

———

MILLIE HAD CALLED the fire department, and Joe and Brian could hear the sirens as they turned up the street. By the time they reached Presley House, the entire roof was ablaze, and sections of the house were beginning to fall in on themselves. Trick-or-treaters and their parents gathered across the street, watching the fire. Joe parked the car a safe distance from Presley House, and he and Brian quickly got out of the car and directed the growing crowd back, away from the fire.

Just as the firetruck came roaring down the street in their direction, Joe and Brian turned to Presley House and were horrified to see three figures emerging from the blaze. They weren't running to safety but slowly and methodically struggling toward the street—Danielle on her injured ankle while Lily held her right arm and Heather her left.

Without hesitation, Joe and Brian raced toward the fire. Timbers from the front porch roof crashed behind the three women, flying embers just missing them. When Joe reached the threesome, he quickly scooped Danielle up in his arms, carrying her to safety, while Brian hurriedly ushered Heather and Lily away from the blaze.

———

EXHAUSTED AND EMOTIONALLY DRAINED, Danielle lay back in the hospital bed and stared at her IV. Taking a deep breath, she smiled. While she would rather be home in her own bed, she was happy to be anywhere other than Presley House.

"How you feeling?" Lily asked when she entered the hospital room with Heather at her side. The two women approached the bed.

"Much better. They say they want to keep me for observation for a couple days."

"Yeah, I heard." Lily reached out and gave Danielle's hand a quick, reassuring squeeze.

Danielle looked from Lily to Heather. "Thanks again, both of you, for getting me out of there."

"I'm just really sorry I didn't come sooner," Heather apologized. "I never even considered you might be trapped in the secret room."

"Hello," came a male voice from the doorway.

The three women looked in the direction of the greeting. They watched as Joe and Brian entered the room.

"I understand they're keeping you for observation," Joe said as he approached the bed with Brian.

"That's what they tell me." Danielle forced a smile.

"We were hoping you would be up to a few questions," Joe said.

"Sure. Now that I have something to drink, I feel pretty terrific," Danielle lied. "I suppose you want to know why I was there."

Joe nodded. "For starters."

"I kept wondering where someone might have hidden Bart's body. Before the chief left for vacation, we discussed the possibility of a secret room."

Joe frowned. "You and the chief talked about that?"

"Yes. You can ask him about it when he comes home. Anyway, I went over there to snoop around, found the secret room, fell down the stairs, and got myself trapped. Lily came looking for me, and unfortunately, the door to the secret room locked on her. If it wasn't for Heather, we wouldn't be here now."

Lily looked from Danielle to the officers. "I'd like to know how that fire started."

"I think we have the answer to that," Brian said. "Some local teenagers showed up after you left. They were frantic that their friend was inside. Seems they had left him there to spend the night."

"Oh my god, is he okay?" Heather gasped.

Brian nodded his head. "Yes, we found him safe and sound at his house. He claims he saw some furniture floating around and ran out in a panic. Admitted to leaving a candle burning upstairs."

"At least no one was hurt," Lily said.

"While I don't foresee charges being brought against any of you for breaking into the house, I don't know how the owners of Presley House are going to feel—and what pressure they might apply to the DA. Considering Danielle's financial situation, they might decide to bring civil charges," Joe explained.

Heather spoke up. "I don't think that's going to happen."

Joe and Brian turned to Heather.

Putting out her hand to Joe, she said, "We haven't been formally introduced. I'm Heather Donovan and the owner of Presley House. My grandfather was Barney Presley; his father was the original owner."

Taken aback by the announcement, Joe silently shook Heather's hand. When Brian took his turn, he said, "I hate to be the one to tell you this, Ms. Donovan, but the house is gone. They weren't able to save anything."

"I'm not surprised. When we left in the police car, I didn't see how they could possibly save it," Heather said.

Lily silently watched Danielle, noticing the dark circles under her eyes and her forced smile.

"I think we need to let Dani get some rest." Lily spoke up. "Joe, you and Brian can ask the rest of your questions tomorrow."

After Joe and Brian left five minutes later, Danielle looked up at Heather, her eyes weary. "You really saw Harvey?"

"Yes. Until I actually saw him standing there in Presley House, I wasn't sure he was real—or if my poor grandfather had simply been delusional all these years."

"I wonder what Harvey is going to do now?" Danielle asked. "If the journal he was looking for was in the house, it's gone now."

"I have the journal," Heather said.

"You do?" Lily and Danielle chorused.

Heather nodded. "Seeing their father brutally kill their best friend—being forced to get rid of the body and then to kill Harvey's uncle—was too much for my grandfather and his brother. My grandfather's brother ended up killing himself. After that, my grandfather would have nothing to do with his parents. He had the journal his brother had written. They both had seen Harvey."

"Did he ever consider going to the police?" Lily asked.

"I don't think so. But the guilt weighed on him. After his parents died and he inherited their estate, he seemed to snap. He started telling everyone about the ghost. Of course, no one would listen to him. He threatened to kill himself, which was why he was committed. It was right after I was born."

"Why did your family keep Presley House all these years?" Danielle asked.

"It belonged to my grandfather; he was adamant about not selling it. I remember once my father convinced him to rent it out as a vacation property, and at the last minute, my grandfather changed his mind. Mother had her father's power of attorney and could have gone ahead and rented it out anyway, but she felt guilty enough about having him institutionalized, she wouldn't force him to rent out the house."

"Did you visit your grandfather?" Danielle asked.

"Not until after my father died. He was adamant about keeping me away from him. Dad was convinced his father-in-law was simply a nutcase. But my mother, she loved her father in spite of everything."

"Where did you find the journal?" Danielle asked. "Harvey has been looking for it for decades."

"I found it in a trunk in my mother's attic after she died. My grandfather had told me about the journal, about how he needed to make it public and set things straight with Harvey or he would go to hell. I doubt my mother ever looked in that trunk after they moved it from her father's house."

"Harvey wasn't just looking for a journal. There was something else he was also looking for," Danielle said.

"What do you mean?" Heather asked.

"According to Harvey, he wasn't just looking for your great-uncle's journal. He was looking for something that would support his claim. He wouldn't say what that was, just that it was something of value and that when I found it, I would know."

"I'm sure it's lost in the fire now," Lily said.

"No, it wasn't." Heather opened her purse and pulled out a leather pouch. "When the police dropped me off at my house, I had something else I needed to get besides my car...this." Heather handed the pouch to Danielle.

"What is it?" Danielle opened the small leather pouch and peeked inside.

"It belongs to you now," Heather explained.

Danielle reached into the pouch and pulled out an emerald—its cut and size was identical to the emeralds in the Missing Thorndike. She looked up to Heather and frowned. "I don't understand."

"My great-grandfather worked for the Thorndikes. He conspired with Eva Thorndike's husband to steal the necklace. Apparently, they removed the stones and replaced them with fakes. Harvey discovered my grandfather's share of the stones in the secret room. By this time Eva had died and the necklace had disappeared."

"Harvey recognized the stones," Danielle murmured.

"Yes, that's what it says in the journal. My grandfather and his brother stole this emerald from their father before they moved from Frederickport. They were going to use it against him. Of course, they never came forward. I found the emerald with the journal, which is why I'm pretty sure my parents never looked through that trunk."

"Why do you say it's mine now?" Danielle tucked the stone back in the pouch and handed it back to Heather.

"The Missing Thorndike legally belongs to you. I would assume any gems stolen from the necklace would also belong to you. If I'm to set this thing right, the emerald must go back to its rightful owner."

FORTY-ONE

S he heard waves crashing along the shore and felt their spray's mist tickling her bare feet. Opening her eyes, Danielle found herself lying on a blanket spread over the warm sand. Overhead the sun was shining—much warmer than normal for October along the Oregon coast. She sat up and stretched lazily. It was then she noticed Walt sitting on his half of the blanket, silently watching her. He wore white linen slacks and a pale blue, button-down shirt, the first three buttons undone. His feet, like hers, were bare.

Curious as to her own attire, she glanced down and saw that she wore a long pale blue cotton dress—its shade matched Walt's shirt. Running her hand over the fabric, it felt soft and gently wrinkled. Smiling, she thought how feminine she felt when Walt dressed her for a dream.

"What made you smile?" Walt asked softly.

"Just how you dress me." Danielle grinned.

"Dress you?"

"You chose this dress, didn't you?"

Walt smiled. "No, Danielle. This time your subconscious did. I rather like how you picked the same color as my shirt."

Without thought, Danielle reached up and touched the ends of her hair. She wore it free flowing; it fell in dark curls over her shoulders. She wondered if that too had been her subconscious choice.

"I was worried about you," Walt said.

"I was worried about me too." Danielle glanced around. She and Walt were the only ones on the beach.

"Lily told me what happened."

"Hopefully now Harvey has moved on."

"If I could get my hands on Harvey, I'd give him a good thrashing."

"He was really just a scared kid." Danielle sighed wearily.

"I don't care. What he put you through was inexcusable!"

Danielle looked down and fiddled with the seam of her dress. "I really don't want to talk about it all now."

"All right. I understand. You've been through a lot. We can talk about what happened later."

"Thank you."

"But I do think it would be a good idea if I helped you learn how to give a good shout out."

Danielle looked up at Walt. "What do you mean?"

"So you can wake yourself up when needed, in case some other unwelcome spirit hops in your dream. Lily suggested it. She's actually very good at it. Can wake herself right up."

"You mean now?"

"Unless you'd rather do it another time."

Danielle absently toyed with a lock of her hair. "Maybe another time. I don't want to wake up right now."

Walt silently studied Danielle. Finally, he said, "I understand. I'll go and let you sleep; you need your rest. We can talk later. I just wanted to make sure you were okay."

"Wait!" Danielle looked up into Walt's eyes.

"What?"

"Don't go yet."

"Okay. We can just sit here quietly if you want."

"Do you think…" Danielle looked down.

"Do I think what?" Walt asked, his voice gentle.

Danielle looked back up at Walt. "Would it be possible…could you just hold me? I need someone to hold me…" *I need you to hold me.*

Without another word, Walt gathered Danielle up in his arms. He held her as he looked out to the ocean and watched the sea make its way toward them and then retreat in a steady and constant rhythm.

THE GHOST WHO CAME FOR CHRISTMAS

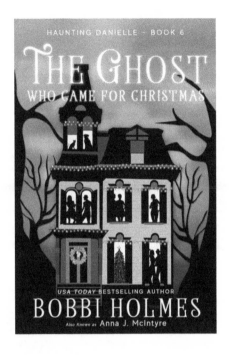

RETURN TO MARLOW HOUSE IN

THE GHOST WHO CAME FOR CHRISTMAS

HAUNTING DANIELLE, BOOK 6

It's Christmastime at Marlow House Bed and Breakfast, and Danielle has a full house.

When a woman, stranded far from home, shows up on the doorstep and begs for a room for the night, how can Danielle tell her the inn is full and turn her away? After all, it's almost Christmas.

The woman makes quite an impression on the other guests, especially when she mysteriously disappears. Is it foul play—or something supernatural?

NON-FICTION BY

BOBBI ANN JOHNSON HOLMES

HAVASU PALMS, A HOSTILE TAKEOVER

WHERE THE ROAD ENDS, RECIPES & REMEMBRANCES

MOTHERHOOD, A BOOK OF POETRY

THE STORY OF THE CHRISTMAS VILLAGE

BOOKS BY ANNA J. MCINTYRE

CPSIA information can be obtained
at www.ICGtesting.com
Printed in the USA
LVHW031638170220
647192LV00005B/1143